Compulsion

The Toni Barston Series

TERRI BRENEMAN

Bella
BOOKS

2008

Bella Books, Inc.
P.O. Box 10543
Tallahassee, FL 32302

Printed in the United States of America on acid-free paper
First Edition

Editor: Christi Cassidy
Cover designer: Stephanie Solomon-Lopez

ISBN-10: 1-59493-126-7
ISBN-13: 978-1-59493-126-0

Acknowledgments

This book was a labor of love and would not have been possible without the help and support of many people. As always, my editor, Christi Cassidy, helped me produce a wonderful finished product. I'd like to thank both her and Linda Hill for believing in Toni Barston. A special thanks to my friend Robin Schultz, RN, who continues to amaze me with her medical knowledge. Reference books by D.P. Lyle, MD, were also incredibly helpful for this book. A special thanks to John who helped me understand the frightening possibilities of a webcam. I'd also like to thank my mother, Dorth, for her belief in me and her light in this world. And of course I am most grateful for the love and support of my partner, Cat. She makes me laugh and inspires me on so many levels. She definitely makes the sky bluer in my world. Lastly, I'd like to thank all of those people who believed in me enough to buy my books. I am very grateful. Thank you.

About the Author

Terri Breneman was born and raised in a suburb of Kansas City. She received a Bachelor of Arts degree in psychology and sociology from Pittsburg State University in Pittsburg, Kansas. While living in Germany she earned a master's degree in counseling. As a psychotherapist specializing in borderline personality disorders, she worked with high-risk adolescents, juvenile sex offenders and their victims. She also worked with patients with multiple personality disorders. She decided to change careers and attended St. Louis University School of Law. After graduating, she opened her own practice. One year of that was quite enough and she was fortunate to find her current job as a research and writing attorney, working in federal criminal law. She also supervises students earning their master's degrees in social work.

Terri lives with her partner, Cat, in St. Louis, where they share their home with three cats—Dexter, Sam and Felix. The cat featured in this series, Mr. Rupert, was a longtime companion. Rupert Eugene died in 2003 at the age of 17 and weighing 22 pounds. He is still loved and missed terribly. Dexter (Little Stuffy) has moved up as the number one cat in Terri's life and makes his debut in *Compulsion*.

Compulsion:

1) behavior or mental acts aimed at reducing distress or preventing some dreaded event, however these behaviors have no realistic connection to the event.

Diagnostic and Statistical Manual of Mental Disorders, 4th Ed., Text Revision, Washington, D.C., American Psychiatric Association, 2000.

2) an irresistible impulse to perform an act.

Collegiate Dictionary, 11th Ed., Springfield, Massachusetts: Merriam-Webster, 2003.

Chapter 1

The woman sat in her study looking at the screen on her laptop. She made a few more entries and stared once again. She was nothing if not meticulous in her recordkeeping. Everything balanced to the penny. Satisfied, she turned her attention to the yellow legal pad on her desk and picked up her mechanical pencil. It was the same one she'd bought herself when she was sixteen years old. It had been a part of her for over thirty years. She carefully wrote the heading *To Do* on the top of the page and underlined it twice. She had repeated this exact routine almost every afternoon of her life.

Before entering the first item on her list, she picked up the lead crystal tumbler that held a generous amount of Famous Grouse. There were three ice cubes in the dark amber liquid. She placed her left index finger in the mixture and stirred in a circular motion exactly three times. After tapping her finger twice on the rim, she licked off the remaining Scotch. She slowly lifted the glass to her lips and took a healthy swallow. She breathed deeply and smiled before setting the tumbler back on its heavy square coaster. She didn't even need to look when she put it exactly in the center. Some things just came naturally.

The woman returned her attention to her list. She wrote *Balance checkbook* even though she had just completed that task. She added *Set up meeting with Karl, Get birthday card for Susan, Organize bedroom closet* and *Go to grocery store.* She crossed off the first item and took another drink, again placing the glass on the center of its coaster. What she really needed to do was to find two replacements for the two who'd been killed a couple months ago. But that wasn't something she would put on her to-do list. She took another sip and leaned back in her tall, dark leather chair. Only a few minutes passed before she heard the front door open.

A few months ago she would have assumed it was her girl-friend coming in, but things had changed. Her girlfriend of two years had packed her bags and moved to San Francisco with little warning. Her only explanation had been that she needed to find herself. She wasn't the kind to chase after anyone, so she let her girlfriend go without an argument, but she'd kept her anger inside. The only thing she'd made sure of was that her girlfriend took nothing more than what she had arrived with. At least that memory usually made her happy. She was still smiling when her assistant came into the study.

"Hey, boss," Jan said, her voice deep and husky as usual. A voice, she knew, that earned its tone from many years of heavy drinking and smoking. "Can I get you anything?"

The woman shook her head and gestured to one of the leather club chairs across from her desk. "Make yourself a drink, Jan. We've got a lot of ground to cover tonight." She ran her fingers through her hair on the right side, three times.

Jan mixed herself a rum and Coke, carefully replacing the bottles on the bar. She picked up the ashtray from the shelf below the bar. Even though her boss didn't smoke, she didn't mind if Jan did as long as she emptied the ashtray when she left. There was a metal can with a lid for just that purpose. Before sitting down she made sure there was a coaster on the end table, another one of her boss's quirks. Satisfied, she sat down, crossed her legs and lit a cigarette.

Jan had worked for the woman for over ten years now. She did a little bit of everything, and her best qualities were that she was smart, worked hard and kept her mouth shut. She wasn't afraid to either break the law or someone's jaw and for that she was paid handsomely. She also knew enough not to ever mention the somewhat obsessive traits her boss often displayed, like insisting on checking her bank balance at least ten times a day. She waited patiently for her boss to begin.

"We need to find another judge," the woman said, "and we need to figure out which lawyer can take over Butch's job."

Jan nodded and took a sip of her drink. She knew no response was needed at this time. Her boss was just thinking out loud. The judge would be a tough call. They'd had Judge Smith on their payroll for years and things had been going smoothly until some crazed woman had killed both the judge and an attorney, Butch Henley. This had put a real crimp in their organization.

"Judge Smith was an asshole, but we had him by the balls," the woman said. "We still have Judge Carmen, but he's only good for the small stuff. His appetite for young Asian girls is embarrassing for him, but not enough to push him. What about Judge Wilson? Did you get the video on him yet?"

Jan smiled and set her drink on its coaster. She put out her cigarette and produced a DVD and a few photos from her old gray backpack and handed them to her boss. "We've got about two hours total on the DVD. I made a couple still photos from it." He'd been using their services for about six months now. "He's done a few things for us in court and there's been no problem so far. He's married and has two young boys of his own. In fact, they're about the same age as the ones he asks for from us. He's also active in his church and has the backing of the local Republican Party. I think he's perfect."

The woman looked at the photos, frowned in disgust, then quickly pushed them back across her desk. Jan smiled, tucking them back inside her bag.

"Okay. What about a replacement for Butch? Do you think Bill Hogan can handle things?"

"I talked to Mike this morning and he thinks that Bill's the best choice. He can handle the additional cases. Mike says we can pay him a little less if we give him a supply of ecstasy and GHB." That was the popular date rape drug.

Mike Johnson was a senior detective on the Fairfield Police Department in Missouri. Jan had worked with him off and on for almost twenty years and his take on people was rarely wrong. He was also the only one with the exception of her who knew who actually ran this organization. Jan knew her boss had always been very careful about that.

The woman nodded. "Tell Mike to go ahead, but he needs to take things slowly. I want to be sure these guys are on board. And make sure you've got enough on both these guys to make them squirm if we need them to."

The woman turned to her laptop and typed in a few things. She was frowning as she emptied her glass. Jan quickly rose to refill the drink. She placed the fresh one back on its coaster and made sure it was centered. The woman nodded and looked at her glass. Jan had made sure it was filled exactly right. Out of habit the woman put her left index finger in the liquid and stirred three times. She tapped her finger twice on the rim and licked up the last drop. After a long swallow she replaced the glass on the coaster.

"It's going to take at least another couple months for us to get back up to speed," she hissed. "All because of that psycho bitch."

Jan nodded but said nothing. She pulled out another cigarette, lit it and slowly exhaled the smoke. She'd seen her boss upset before, but this seemed more extreme than usual. Jan supposed it was because her girlfriend had left at about the same time as the murders. She tried to soothe her. "It shouldn't be a problem, boss. Mike will get these guys up to speed in no time and we'll be back as strong as ever. And if Davey can make us this new designer drug, we may have an even larger market."

The woman was adjusting items on her desk, apparently making sure each one was in its exact right place. "I know," she responded with a sigh.

Davey was the boss's younger brother and at thirty-nine years old, he would rather play video games than work. He'd had a few jobs when he was younger, but his inability to work with others always resulted in him getting fired. The man was brilliant, Jan thought, and wrote his own computer games. He was also an excellent chemist and supplied the organization with all the drugs they needed. Even though he cooked, he never used. But as long as he could cook enough to meet the supply, his sister let him play as often as he liked. She paid him well and he always seemed content when Jan saw him.

"Davey told me yesterday he's just about got the formula right," the boss said. "We should have some samples by the weekend. But that doesn't help this situation. If that bitch hadn't killed Judge Smith and Butch, we'd be ahead of the game. Where is she now? I want her dead."

The "psycho bitch" was actually a woman who'd been infatuated with Toni Barston, an assistant prosecuting attorney, several months ago. She'd killed Judge Smith and Butch, a lawyer, out of a distorted love for Toni. The two dead men had worked for the woman and their demise created a slump in her business.

"She's in a locked psych ward with twenty-four-hour guards.

The cops are all over this. Mike told me that she also injured two women, one of them an assistant prosecuting attorney and the other an investigator. Apparently the psycho woman was in love with the attorney and was killing anyone who she thought this attorney didn't like."

"So this psychotic bitch killed our guys because she wanted to get in the attorney's pants? Who is this dyke lawyer?"

"Her name is Toni Barston and she's given us some trouble before."

"Find out everything you can about her. I don't want her to give us any more shit." The woman logged onto her bank account and dismissed Jan with a wave of her hand.

Jan left, shaking her head. She assumed that the loss of the judge and attorney had finally affected the bottom line and that's why her boss was concerned. Disgusted, she slammed her car door shut. *I saw this coming the day they were killed.*

Chapter 2

Toni Barston sat at her desk in the Fairfield Metropolitan Prosecuting Attorney's Office and looked at her pile of cases. She was glad to be back to work full time. She'd received a concussion and two broken fingers on her right hand from a crazed woman about two months ago. Her hand was basically healed, but it still gave her trouble every once in a while and her typing was dreadfully slow. She felt glad to just be alive. She was studying a preliminary file on a murder charge when she heard a knock on her door.

"Hey, gorgeous," Boggs said, poking her head inside. "Got a minute?"

Toni grinned and motioned her inside. Victoria "Boggs" Boggsworth was one of the investigators at the prosecuting attorney's office and there was no doubt she was the best. She was also Toni's lover of almost eight months. Boggs was five-feet six-inches tall with an incredibly athletic body. Her hair was short and stylish, light brown with a few gray strands scattered about. At thirty-nine years old she could still turn heads, and her green eyes were the kind that made you look twice. Her voice was deep and a little gravelly. She could make Toni's knees weak with just a few words.

"Stop saying things like that. You know our rule—work is work. Okay?"

Boggs grinned. "I know, but it's true. You are gorgeous. But okay, I'll try to contain myself. Unless, of course, you want me to close your door and then you can discipline me."

Toni rolled her eyes, but she was smiling. "Maybe later. What's up?"

"You got the Martin case, right?"

"Yeah. I was just looking at it. The police report is pretty straightforward. Martin shot the victim, let's see . . . Kevin Tucker, kicked him a few times while calling him a fag and then shot him again. He was sitting next to the body when the police arrived. The officer called it a 'hate crime' in his report." Toni was slowly shaking her head. Sometimes she just couldn't understand the stupidity of people.

"Right," Boggs said. "But I talked to a couple people this morning and something doesn't sound right to me."

"You don't think Martin is our guy?" Toni asked.

"No, he's our guy for sure." Boggs stretched her legs out and leaned back in the chair. "But I don't think it's a hate crime. I talked to the neighbors and Martin's sister. Martin's son was gay and Martin was involved with PFLAG. And his son died two weeks ago from a drug overdose."

"Do we know anything about the victim?"

"I'm looking into that. He's got a few priors, mostly misdemeanor possession charges, but I'm going to ask around. Are you going to talk to Martin?"

"He's got a public defender," Toni said as she looked at the file. "Jill Barger. I know her from law school. I'll give her a call and see if I can set something up. If this isn't a hate crime, it'll take a lot of years off his sentence."

Boggs stood up to leave. "I'll let you know what I find out, okay? And how about if I bring dinner over tonight? We can have a quick bite to eat, but then I've got to do some laundry. *Someone* kept me so busy over the weekend I never had a chance to wash clothes. I'm down to my 'emergency' underwear, for God's sake."

Toni laughed. "That sounds wonderful, but why don't you just bring your laundry over to my place? We can do it while we eat and then maybe watch a movie or something."

"Are you sure?"

"Hell, yes. Now go away so I can get some work done. And let me know if you find out anything new, okay?"

Boggs crossed the tiny office, heading not for the door but straight toward Toni. She leaned down and kissed her passionately. Toni reacted immediately, putting her arms up around Boggs's strong shoulders. She felt her entire body pulse. Boggs pulled away and winked at her before leaving. It took Toni several minutes to regain her focus. She sometimes had a difficult time after seeing Boggs because the thought of making love with her still drove her crazy. Working in the same office with someone you were in love with wasn't easy. She shook off her thoughts of lust and put in a call to Jill, scheduling a meeting for later in the day.

By the time Jill arrived, Toni had learned from Boggs that Kevin Tucker, the victim, might have had ties to a drug organization. Although he'd never been specifically linked, he'd been a person of interest. She also knew that Harold Martin had no criminal record and had been employed as a mechanic for thirty years.

"Thanks for coming over, Jill," Toni said as she ushered her into her office. "How've you been?"

"Great." Jill took a seat. "Hard to believe that we've been out of school for almost a year. Seems like I've been doing this forever. How about you?"

"Swamped, just like you, I'm sure. But I love it. Did you get a chance to talk to Mr. Martin?"

"Yes. I talked to him right after you called this morning. He's pretty devastated by what he did and wants to get this resolved as soon as possible."

"Do you think he'll talk to me? He may have some information."

"Yes," Jill said. "In fact he *wants* to talk to you. I don't know what information he may or may not have, but let's set it up. Maybe we can work out some kind of plea agreement."

"Okay." Toni looked at her calendar. "Are you free in the morning?"

"Nine o'clock would be good for me," Jill said after checking in her day planner.

"Perfect. I'll have Mr. Martin brought over here at nine."

After chatting a few more minutes about classmates they both knew, Jill left. Toni finished up some last-minute work and headed home.

She kicked off her shoes the moment she walked inside her townhouse. She absolutely detested wearing high heels. She got away with wearing flats most days, but when she had a scheduled motion hearing or trial, she almost always wore a skirt and heels. Today she was definitely rethinking that mindset. Her feet were killing her. She was leaning against the wall, rubbing her foot, when Mr. Rupert appeared. He pushed his twenty pounds of fur against her leg and meowed loudly.

"Hiya, buddy. Are you starving to death?" She scratched his head before he darted off to the kitchen. She left her shoes and briefcase by the front door and followed him. He was already sitting on the countertop, waiting for her to get his food. She put half a can of wet food on a plate in front of him. "Yummy, salmon

10

with garden greens. Your favorite."

She laughed as he basically inhaled the food. She refilled his dry food bowl and got him fresh water. By the time she finished, he was washing his face. She put the plate in the dishwasher.

"You know you really shouldn't eat that fast, Mr. Rupert."

He burped in response and Toni laughed out loud. She loved that cat. He'd been with her longer than any human and was her confidant. He comforted her when she was down and cuddled her when she was happy. He seemed to love her unconditionally and she felt the same way about him. She rubbed his huge head, retrieved her shoes and headed upstairs to change. She carefully hung up her gray skirt and blazer and tossed her white silk blouse in the pile to go to the cleaners. As she peeled off her pantyhose, she wondered for the hundredth time who in the hell had invented those torture devices. She pulled on a pair of old baggy shorts and a T-shirt and went to the bathroom to wash her face. Mr. Rupert was sitting on the counter. She leaned closer to the mirror.

"See? Another gray hair," she said as she plucked it from her head and showed it to Mr. Rupert. "I swear if I keep this up I'm going to be bald."

She ran her fingers through her short, light brown hair. She'd gotten it cut a few months ago, and although it had taken some getting used to, she now loved the look. It still looked professional for work, but with a little gel it could look downright sexy. She pulled up her shirt and looked at herself in the mirror. At thirty-five years old, she didn't look too bad. She could probably stand to lose a few pounds and tone up, but it wasn't awful. She smiled at her reflection, gave Mr. Rupert a kiss and went to her desk in the corner of her bedroom.

She sat down and pulled her laptop computer closer. She checked her e-mail and responded to a few of them. One was from her favorite aunt, Aunt Doozie, who lived in San Diego. She'd married Toni's uncle when Toni was three years old, and she'd adored her from that moment on. She'd always treated Toni as a real person and not just another kid. Doozie wasn't her real name, just a nickname Toni had given her thirty years ago and it'd stuck. Toni didn't get to see her very often, so every month or so they talked online, using their webcams. It wasn't as good as being together, but it was much better than the phone.

While she was reading another e-mail, she heard the familiar *ding* of her webcam, which was built into her laptop. A message appeared on her screen announcing that Aunt Doozie was calling. She clicked on the "accept" button and her aunt's face filled the screen.

"Hiya, Aunt Doozie!" Toni said, grinning broadly.

"Hi, sweetie."

Toni noticed that she was wearing an old T-shirt and had a blue bandana on her head. "What are you doing?"

"I'm taking a break from cleaning the house." Aunt Doozie was laughing and pointing to her head. "Can't you tell? I'm a mess. I've just been thinking about you all day and I wanted to say hi."

"Well, it's a wonderful surprise," Toni said. "When are you coming out for a visit?"

"We've decided to come in for the Fourth of July. I just made the reservations. We'll come in the Saturday before and leave a week later. Make sure you block out some time, okay? And I want to meet that girlfriend of yours."

"That would be great, Aunt Doozie." She smiled, realizing how lucky she was to have family who were so open to her being gay. Her parents had accepted her lifestyle almost immediately. They had treated she and her ex as a couple. Her aunt was also very accepting and would ask questions about stereotypes and the daily struggles. *Yes, I'm lucky*, she thought, *all the way around.*

"Perfect, sweetie," her aunt continued. "Is there anything I can bring you from here?"

"Nope, just you."

"Okay, gotta run. Love you." With that the screen went black.

Just then, the doorbell rang. She ran downstairs, looked out the peephole and saw a distorted view of Boggs holding a large brown bag of take-out, a duffle bag slung over her shoulder. She let her in, put the bags on the table and then wrapped her arms around her. Even after eight months of dating, she still felt the thrill and excitement of just holding her close. Mr. Rupert joined in by rubbing against Boggs's leg.

"This is a great welcome," Boggs said after she kissed Toni and scratched Mr. Rupert's head. "I'll never get tired of this."

"I hope not." Toni took the food into the kitchen. "I've kinda got a crush on you, in case you hadn't noticed."

Boggs joined her and they effortlessly moved about gathering plates, forks and napkins and opening the containers of Chinese food. Toni gathered the extra packs of soy sauce and sweet and sour and tossed them in a drawer.

Boggs was shaking her head. "Why do you save those? We never use them."

Toni shrugged. "You never know. Anyway, Vicky always uses a ton of soy sauce. I don't know how she eats her food with that much."

She got wine while Boggs took their plates to the living room and set them on the coffee table.

"Oh, Aunt Doozie is coming in for the Fourth," Toni said from the kitchen. "She's anxious to meet you."

Boggs grinned. "Well, since I survived meeting your parents, I guess I'll be okay. You've talked about her so much, I'm even kind of excited to meet her."

"She's wonderful." Toni took a sip of her wine, an excellent Riesling.

"Hey, is it okay if I throw in a load of clothes before we eat?" Boggs asked as she picked up her duffle bag. "I've got a load of lights and one of darks."

13

"Absolutely," Toni said as she brought in the wine. "In fact, I think I have a few things upstairs in the hamper. If you don't mind, I'll put them in with your stuff."

"Great," Boggs said. "And I think we need to talk after dinner, okay?" She took her duffle to the small laundry room off the kitchen.

"Sure. We'll talk after dinner." Toni felt her heart beat faster as she climbed the stairs. *Oh, my God. Talk?* She willed herself to be calm. Boggs had broken off their relationship a few months ago because she was afraid to commit. It was devastating and the thought of losing her now made it hard to even breathe. She loved Boggs more than she had loved anyone in her life. Her hands were shaking as she gathered the few items from the hamper. She took a deep breath. *It's okay. It's okay.* She went back downstairs and tried to smile.

Boggs had separated her laundry and put the lights in the washer. Toni handed her a few T-shirts and a pair of socks. She apparently wasn't able to hide the look of doom on her face.

"Babe? Are you okay?" Boggs gently touched her arm.

"Um, sure." Toni could hear her voice squeak and felt her arms shake. "You wanted to talk?" Tears began to well up in her eyes, even though she was pleading with herself to remain calm.

"Oh, babe, I love you." Boggs wrapped her arms around her. "It's nothing like that. Come on, let's go sit down." She led Toni back to the living room and they sat side by side on the old green sectional couch that curved around two sides of the room. Toni pulled her legs up and wrapped her arms around them. She was ready for the blow to come. *We need to talk?* That was never good, she thought.

"I love you, babe," Boggs repeated as she reached out to touch Toni's arm. "It's just that I want, um, to . . ."

Toni could feel her insides tremble. *Shit. See other people?* She couldn't handle seeing her with someone else. She took a deep breath and smiled weakly. "Go ahead, hon. Just say what you want."

Boggs took a healthy swallow of wine and cleared her throat. "I, um, I want us to live together."

"What?" Toni blinked several times. She wasn't sure she heard that right.

"I want us to live together," Boggs repeated. "If, well, if you want to. I mean you don't have to. I just thought, well, I—I don't know." Boggs looked down at her glass of wine and took another gulp.

"You want to live together?" Toni asked. It wasn't quite sinking in.

"Well, um, yes. But that's okay if you don't want to. I understand, I mean . . . it's not like I'm the best catch out there." Boggs was stammering now and wouldn't look at her.

Suddenly she got it. She took the glass from Boggs's hand and set it on the coffee table. She cupped Boggs's face in her hands and kissed her gently, pulling away with a huge smile on her face.

"I'd *love* to live with you, honey. Oh, my God! I'd love to." Toni grabbed her again and hugged her fiercely. "And you're the best catch for me. I love you."

Boggs hugged her, then pulled away. "Are you sure? I mean this is a big step, you know."

"I'm positive," Toni said as she lifted her glass of wine. "A toast, to us."

Boggs returned the gesture. "I guess I could have started the conversation a little better." She shrugged. "I've been wanting to ask you for a couple months now, but I was, well, nervous, I guess." She took another gulp of wine.

"I was a little nervous myself," Toni admitted. "I thought maybe you were going to break up with me."

"Hell, no." Boggs kissed her on the cheek. "Not on your life."

"So, what do we do now? Do you want to move in here?"

"What if we got our own place?" Boggs said as she picked up her plate of food. "Not yours and not mine, but ours." She took a bite of beef with broccoli.

"Okay, that sounds good. I've been here almost two years and my lease will be up on June thirtieth. That's only three and a half weeks away. Do you think we could find another apartment that quick? Of course I might be able to do an extra month without signing a new lease." Toni was tapping her finger against her wineglass, calculating.

"I'm on a month-to-month right now, so that won't be a problem," Boggs said, between bites. "But I wasn't thinking of an apartment."

"A house?" Toni laughed. "Well, I hate to disappoint you, but all lawyers aren't rich. And I still have my student loans. I don't think I could afford a house."

"I was actually thinking about a loft. Down in the warehouse district. They're rehabbing old places into three-level homes. Big and open."

Toni finished off her egg roll. "Wow. I'd love to live in a place down there, but I don't think I have enough money to even go there. There's the down payment and everything else." Her heart sank at the realization.

"I looked at some of the properties a few months ago." Boggs stole a piece of chicken off Toni's plate and grinned. "There are some really good deals. A few need work, but they're still affordable."

"I remember you mentioning that when we were looking for that crazy woman. I didn't know you were serious. Well, I'd love to do it, really. But I'm not sure I could afford much more than I pay now for rent. And my savings account is pathetic. How much money are we talking here?"

Toni got another bottle of wine from the kitchen. She returned with Mr. Rupert following her and refilled their glasses. He sat on the coffee table, staring at Boggs's plate.

"I'm done, buddy. Go ahead." He helped himself to some rice. Boggs took a sip of her wine. "Before we get into specifics," she said, still grinning, "how do you feel about doing some renovations?"

"I don't know how good I'd be," Toni said, suddenly excited at the prospect, "but I'm willing to give it a try. I can paint and I know how to tile. And I know a little about electric."

"Perfect." Boggs chuckled. "This is going to be great. I've done some drywalling before and I've installed a garbage disposal. The rest we'll figure out as we go. Let's do it."

Toni was tingling with excitement. Even though she had lived with her ex for several years, it never felt like this before. She could hardly contain herself. But the logical side of her quickly returned. "Oh, Boggs. How in the hell are we going to afford a loft? Like I said, I've got virtually no savings to speak of. I want to make this work, but it may take a little time. It doesn't matter to me where we live, as long as we're together."

Boggs leaned back on the couch. The look on her face seemed very serious. Toni wondered what she was thinking, but before she could ask, Boggs spoke. "So it wouldn't matter to you what the place looked like as long as we're together?"

"Of course not." Toni said, a little puzzled. "We could live here until we saved enough money. Or maybe even find a cheaper place. As long as I'm with you, and I have indoor plumbing, I'm fine."

Boggs laughed. "So indoor plumbing is your only condition?"

"That and you. Mr. Rupert and I aren't fussy."

Again Boggs took on a serious look. "So, you're willing to spend your life with me? Even if I told you that I'm pretty much capped off, salarywise? Even if I never made a ton of money?"

Toni looked at Boggs in disbelief. The thought of having tons of money had never occurred to her. "Money's not important, hon. I mean, don't get me wrong. I wouldn't turn it down, but as long as we have enough to pay our bills, I'm fine. It's not like I'm going to become a millionaire working as an assistant prosecuting attorney. It's far more important to me to be happy and enjoy life, and that doesn't take money. It takes love."

"That's exactly how I feel." Boggs appeared to relax. "I love what I'm doing and I love you. That's all that matters."

"I agree." Toni chuckled. "So I guess we've determined we're not in this for each other's money, 'cause you're sure as hell not looking at a rich woman here."

"Now that that's settled, do you want to look at some lofts this weekend? I know a realtor and I'm sure if I call her tomorrow, she can set something up for Saturday."

"I'd love to, but we still don't have enough for a down payment."

"Maybe it won't be as much as we think." Boggs shrugged. "And we can at least get an idea of what's available. It'll be fun. What do you think?"

"I guess so. What the heck. Let's do it." Toni felt the tingle of excitement again. It might take a while to save the down payment, but it would be fun to look. And as long as she was with Boggs, it didn't matter how long it took.

"And we'll need to talk about furniture, babe." Boggs was shaking her head. "Do you think you could part with your waterbed?"

"Hey, I thought you loved my waterbed." Toni couldn't help but laugh. She knew the bed was old and she was probably the only one left in the state who still had one.

"I love *you* in your waterbed." Boggs said, "but, if you really love it, I guess we could bring it with us."

"I think I'm ready for a change," Toni confessed. "I think a new home for us deserves a new bed."

They spent the rest of the evening discussing what furniture they would keep from each household and what new things they might need. By the time they went to bed that night, Toni was feeling more content and in love than she had ever felt before.

Chapter 3

Toni arrived at work Friday morning still feeling excited at the prospect of living with Boggs. It took some effort to focus on her work. She had several things to do before she met with Jill and Mr. Martin.

By eleven o'clock she was back in her office, calling Boggs. "Do you think you could call Vicky and the three of us could meet? I think there's more than meets the eye on the Martin case."

"Sure," Boggs said. "I'll give her a call and get back to you."

Vicky Carter was a senior detective on the Fairfield Police Department. She was also a good friend who had helped in both the serial killer case last fall and the crazed stalker woman a couple months ago. Two hours later the three women were sitting at a back table in Phil's Deli.

After they had gotten their food, Toni filled them in. "There's no question that Martin killed Kevin Tucker last week, but it wasn't a hate crime. Martin told me that Tucker had given his son the drugs that killed him. They met at a gay club. From what Martin was able to figure out from his son's e-mails, Tucker gave him some free samples. He said he didn't think his son usually used drugs, but he apparently trusted this Tucker guy. Then he died. I asked for the tox reports and Martin gave his consent."

"That fits the MO I've heard on the street," Vicky said, taking a bite of her sandwich. "Free samples at some of the clubs to get people hooked. But we've never been able to finger anyone. Are you thinking this could get us close to the head honcho?"

"It's a place to start," Toni said with a shrug. "And I want to get as much info as I can from Martin. He's going to give us his son's computer."

"What are you recommending for him?" Boggs asked. "I've talked to some of his family and friends. The guy is devastated by what he did."

"I know." Toni snatched a chip from Boggs's plate. "I have to run it by Anne, but I'm thinking voluntary manslaughter." Anne Mulhoney was the prosecuting attorney and would have the final say on any plea offer.

"Under the circumstances, I think Anne would go for that." Vicky pushed her plate away. "I'll start looking into it as soon as I get back to the office. I need something solid to sink my teeth into. I've hit dead ends on Butch and the judge."

"Are you still working on that?" Toni knew that Anne Mulhoney had asked Vicky to look into the dealings of both Judge Smith and the defense lawyer, Butch Henley. When they'd been killed two months ago, Anne felt they had both been involved in bribery or something more, but there wasn't any hard evidence.

"I've found a few things, but nothing concrete," Vicky said. "Maybe if I work on something else for a while, I can get back to it with a fresh eye." She drained her glass of iced tea. "But now to more important things, ladies. Tomorrow is Patty's birthday, as you know, and I reserved a room at Gertrude's Garage. I would appreciate your help in decorating. I'm counting on your hot air, Boggs, to help fill a crapload of balloons."

Boggs rolled her eyes and Toni laughed. Gertrude's Garage was one of the gay bars in town and was perfect for a party. It had lots of room, pool tables, darts, a dance floor and a small kitchen for food. The four of them had spent many fun evenings there.

"We can help, but not until about five o'clock." Boggs was smiling at Vicky.

"What are you grinning about? What are you two up to?"

"We're going house hunting, or rather loft hunting," Boggs said matter-of-factly.

"Are you kidding?" Vicky seemed almost beside herself. "That's fabulous." She punched Boggs in the arm. "Why the hell didn't you tell me? You're such a shit."

"We just decided last night," Toni said, trying to defend Boggs. "And you're the first to know, so there."

Vicky reached over and hugged Toni, then punched Boggs in the arm again. "I'm so happy for you both. When's the loft-warming party?"

"Wait until we find a place. Jeez, Vic." Boggs was shaking her head and rubbing her arm, but she was grinning. "But you're top on the list of invitees."

"This is so exciting. Where are you looking?" Vicky asked.

"There's some really cool places in the warehouse district," Boggs explained. "But some need a lot of work."

"Well, sign me up as a helper. I've done some plumbing and I can always paint. I'm just so happy for you guys."

Boggs reached across the table and squeezed Toni's hand. "We're so happy, too."

"Ugh. You guys are sickening." Vicky smirked at both of them. "And I love that."

"So how about if we come by the club at around five?" Toni asked. "Is there anything we can bring? And what about ideas for a gift?"

"No, I've got that all under control. As for gifts, I've got an idea." Vicky snickered. She had that look that said she knew a secret.

"What do you know?" Boggs poked her in the side. "Give it up."

"Well, I got the list for the detective's test," she whispered. "It won't be made public until Monday, but Captain Billings said I could tell Patty."

"She made it?" Toni asked. An officer for the Fairfield P.D., Patty had taken the detective's test over a month ago.

"She sure did. Patty Green's top in the group."

"That's great," Boggs said, winking at Toni. "I think some gag gifts are in order."

"That's what I was thinking," Vicky said. "We can give them to her privately, so nobody else knows until Monday. I think a Sherlock Holmes-type pipe would be perfect."

Toni was giggling. "I'm going to get her a Charlie Chan video. I'm so proud of her. Does she have any idea?"

"Not a clue. It'll be perfect."

"She won't be assigned to you as a partner, will she?" Toni asked.

"No. I've already talked to Captain Billings about that. He knows we're friends. He'll hook her up with one of the other senior detectives, maybe Frank Parker or Mike Johnson."

"Yuck," Toni said, disgusted. "Frank is such an arrogant son of a bitch."

"True," Vicky said, nodding. "But he's one of the best. Patty could learn a lot from him, if he'll give her a chance. But I'm thinking the captain will go for Mike."

"I don't think I've ever met him," Toni said, trying to remember. "Is he an okay guy?"

Vicky shrugged. "I used to hear that he was on the take when he was a beat cop, but I haven't heard anything like that for a number of years. He's mostly in narcotics now, and organized crime. Patty will be okay. She's a good kid." She then gave them a few more details on the party and then left to go back to work.

Toni finished her iced tea. "I guess we better get back to work ourselves."

"Or we could have a little afternoon delight," Boggs suggested with a wink.

"I would *love* that, but unfortunately I've got a hearing in a half-hour." Toni pushed her chair back to leave. "Rain check?"

"Try and stop me," Boggs whispered.

Chapter 4

The woman sat in her study on Friday afternoon. She'd just checked her bank balance again, and was satisfied that it was correct. She was grateful that when she reached the age of fifty, she was able to work at her "normal" job only part-time. She kept working because her job allowed her to keep a hand in things. Money was not an issue. She'd made enough money providing "escorts" and drugs to idiots to keep her living handsomely for the rest of her life.

She put three ice cubes in a lead crystal tumbler and added a healthy amount of Famous Grouse. She put her left index finger in the mixture and circled the glass three times. She tapped her finger twice on the rim and licked the amber liquid. She placed the tumbler on the square coaster. It wasn't exactly centered. She stared at it.

It's okay. It doesn't matter. She continued to stare at the tumbler and then willed herself to look away. She took out her mechanical pencil and held it poised above her yellow legal pad. Just write the words, she told herself. *To Do. Just write it.* She held the pencil so tightly that the tips of her fingers turned white. She forced herself to put the tip of the pencil to the paper. Her hand was shaking and the lead tip broke. She clicked until the lead reappeared and looked back at her drink. She *knew* if she didn't center that tumbler that the rest of the day would go wrong. Very wrong. The urge was so strong that she finally reached over and moved the glass. She took a deep breath and let it out slowly. Now everything would be fine. *Better than fine.* She ran her fingers through her hair on the right side three times and felt better. She quickly wrote *To Do* on the top of her pad and underlined it twice. She added several items to her list and then crossed off the ones she'd already completed earlier. Accidentally, she crossed off an item she hadn't completed.

She stared at the pad of paper as though she'd never seen it before. Disbelief filled her and she felt her heart beat faster. *Fuck.* Her eyes darted back and forth and her hands began to shake. *How did that happen?* She stared at the pad again. It was completely ruined now. She pushed back her tall, dark leather chair, feeling the need to get away. Her fists were clenched tightly and she began slowly rocking back and forth. Her breathing was fast and shallow. *Fuck. Fuck. Fuck. The list is ruined. The list is ruined. The list is ruined.* True panic was setting in. The yellow pad was taunting her. She ran her fingers through her hair three times. That helped, but not much.

After several minutes she was able to gain a little more control. She gingerly tore off the top page of the pad, barely letting her fingers touch the paper, as though it might burn her. She held it on the very corner and carried it to the trash can and let it go. As it fluttered down, it almost missed and she felt her heart skip a beat. When she finally saw it land on the bottom of the trash can, she breathed a little easier. She returned to her desk and again picked up her pencil, repeating the process of writing the heading, underlining it twice and listing all the items. This time she was careful in crossing off what she'd already accomplished. *Perfect. I won't make that mistake again.*

She took a healthy swallow of her drink and smiled as she set it down exactly in the center of the coaster without looking. She glanced at her watch. It would be at least twenty minutes until Jan arrived. She emptied the glass and made herself another. Again she stirred it three times with her left index finger and tapped it twice on the rim. As she put her finger in her mouth, she realized this was always the best taste. After another sip, she replaced the heavy tumbler and leaned back in her chair.

She reviewed the events of the last few months in her mind. Things hadn't been going as well as she'd hoped. First Judge Smith was killed, then Butch Henley. This had affected her bottom line. Her clients paid big bucks to have their lawsuits decided in their favor, or to keep them from doing any jail time. It would take a while to find reliable replacements. Then her girlfriend had left her. It wasn't as though she'd been madly in love with her, but it was comfortable. In fact, she'd never let her girlfriend in on her real business, but still, it was a loss nonetheless. It had caused her to be distracted from her business. And finally, one of her best dealers, Kevin Tucker, had been killed. She'd met Kevin only one time, but she liked him and he'd been doing a great job of getting new clients. He'd operated in most of the gay bars and now he was gone.

She took another sip of her drink just as she heard Jan come in the front door. She appeared in her study a moment later and the woman gestured toward the bar. Jan fixed herself a rum and Coke, grabbed the ashtray and sat down in one of the leather club chairs.

"What did you find out?" the woman said without any preliminary niceties.

"Doug Bradley is going to take over Kevin's turf," Jan said as she lit a cigarette. "He helped Kevin a few times and should have no trouble fitting into the bar scene. Our other dealers are doing okay with their own clientele."

"And Judge Wilson?"

"I was in his courtroom this morning. Our client got straight probation. No problems. And I talked to Mike this morning. He's got everything set up with Bill Hogan, so that should take care of the attorney problem. Mike wants to go a little slow at first, just to make sure."

The woman nodded. "Tell Mike to do what he thinks is best."

"Mike said he'd need to be a little careful for about a month. He's going to have a new partner for a while. Some newly crowned detective. It shouldn't be a problem, though."

The woman nodded again and finished off her drink. Jan immediately rose to get her another one. After carefully setting it down in the center of the coaster, she returned to her chair.

"Thanks. Now what about that dyke lawyer?" She almost spit out the question.

"I don't have a lot yet."

The woman glared at Jan. She didn't like sloppy work.

"She's been at Metro for almost a year," Jan said quickly, opening her notebook. "She was a therapist or social worker or something like that before she went to law school. Oh, and she's prosecuting the guy who killed Kevin."

"At least that's something." She took a sip of her drink after completing her routine. "What about her personal life? Is she living with anyone? Where does she socialize? Does she have any hobbies? I want to know more about the bitch who screwed up my organization."

"As far as I know, she's single. She lives alone." Jan put her notebook away. "Do you want her hurt?"

She thought for a moment. "No, not yet. Maybe we'll set her up. Ruin her career. Or maybe just kill her. I'll have to think about that."

Jan nodded her understanding. "I picked up some samples from Davey on my way here. They look good. If it's okay with you, I'll drop them off to Doug."

"That's fine." She dismissed Jan with a wave of her hand. She needed to think about what she wanted to do. It seemed like all of her troubles began and ended with Toni Barston, and she didn't like that at all.

Chapter 5

On Saturday morning Toni and Boggs sat at the dining room table, drinking coffee and looking at several property information sheets that the realtor had printed for them. Their realtor, Francine Winburn, was going to show them five different lofts in the warehouse district. The cheapest one would definitely need quite a bit of work, but it was in a good area. The middle three all needed some work. The priciest one was not only in a great area, it had been completely renovated.

"I think this one is really out of our league," Toni said, pointing to the last sheet. "But it'll be fun to look at, and maybe it'll give us some ideas on how we can fix our place." She grinned.

"What?" Boggs asked, apparently noticing her smile.

"It just sounds so good to say that. 'Our place.' I like the sound of that."

"Me, too," Boggs said as she kissed Toni's cheek. "Need a

refill or should I just fill our go cups."

Toni glanced at her watch. "Francine said she'd pick us up at nine, right?"

Before Boggs could respond, the doorbell rang and she let Francine inside. "Thanks for coming to get us." She pointed to Toni. "I'd like you to meet Toni."

Toni got up and shook Francine's outstretched hand. It was soft and warm. Francine was about five feet two inches tall and rather round. She had short, bushy white hair and wore bright red-framed glasses. Like Sally Jesse Raphael's.

"It's nice to meet you, Francine," Toni said, smiling. "Can I get you a cup of coffee?"

"Got some in the car," she answered in a deep voice that seemed full of life. "Are you girls ready? I've got some great places to show you."

Toni had never seen someone so full of energy, especially at her age of sixty or so. "Just need to fill our coffee cups and we're ready." She went into the kitchen while Boggs gathered up the sheets from the table and a notebook. They were out the door in minutes and Francine ushered them into her bright yellow PT Cruiser.

Francine showed them the three medium-priced lofts first. After the last one they stopped at Izzy's coffeehouse. Boggs went inside for the drinks and Toni and Francine sat outside at one of the tables.

"What do you think so far?"

"I just can't get over the amount of space they have," Toni said as she looked at the information sheets. "I've never had a place that big. It seems almost overwhelming."

"I showed you those three because even though they're about the same size, the layouts are completely different." Francine took her iced coffee from Boggs. "Is there a style you prefer?"

"I like the last one the best," Boggs said as she sat down next to Toni. She picked up an information sheet. "This one. The kitchen area was big and it had that wonderful island in the middle."

"That was my favorite, too. I liked the kitchen and that room on the second floor. It would be a perfect study."

"And what about the rooftop area?" Boggs smiled at Francine. "That could be gorgeous with a little work, don't you think?"

"I agree." Francine winked at Boggs. "I'm glad you both liked the layout of the last place. It is basically the same in the next two I've got lined up. I'll show you the fixer-upper first, then the one that's all decked out."

"I'm glad you're showing us some places that have been redone." Toni sipped her latté. "It gives us some great ideas, because I think we're only going to be able to afford the fixer-upper." She glanced at Boggs. "But that's okay with me. Just being able to work on our own place will be fabulous."

Boggs reached out and squeezed Toni's hand. "This is great, isn't it, babe? I can't wait to get moved in."

Francine excused herself to visit the restroom. As soon as she'd left, Toni scooted closer to Boggs and hugged her. "I can't believe we're actually looking at lofts. I'm so excited, and, well— I love you."

Boggs kissed her lightly. "This is our new beginning. We just need to find the perfect place for us and the kids."

"Kids?" Toni's eyes widened. Boggs had never mentioned wanting children and the idea terrified her. "Am I missing something?"

Boggs laughed. "You, me, Mr. Rupert and the fish. And who knows, maybe we'll add someone new."

Relieved, Toni couldn't help but smile. "The kids. I think Mr. Rupert will be fine with whatever we chose, but do you think the fish will be okay?"

"I think so." Boggs laughed again. "Hey, do you think Mr. Rupert will be okay with the fish? I hadn't even thought about that."

"He would love to have his own fish again." Toni finished her latté. "He had his own fish when he was little. Sadie had a small fishtank, only twenty gallons."

"Well, now he can have his very own fifty-five gallon tank."

"Perfect." Toni was in heaven. She had never been so ready to make a change in her life. She knew the new place would take a lot of work, but she was more than ready and she could just picture them sanding the floors and painting the walls. "I think I can come up with about five thousand dollars for our down payment and expenses. I rolled over my retirement fund from when I was a therapist. It's in an IRA. I can borrow a percentage from it and pay myself back."

Boggs was shaking her head. "No way. We're not going to dip into your retirement fund."

"But I'd be paying myself back with interest," Toni explained. "And I want to do this. It's our home, hon."

"I can't believe you'd be willing to do that, for us." Boggs seemed to get a little teary. "I love you more than you know. But let's just see what we need before we go and rob your retirement, okay? I've got some money in my savings that's just sitting there."

"Okay." Toni kissed her cheek. "But we'll figure out a way to make this work, okay?"

Boggs simply nodded.

Francine appeared at their table. "Are you girls ready? We've got two more to go."

Within five minutes they were parked outside another loft. "This is the fixer-upper," Francine said, smiling. "Think potential." She ushered them inside. The layout was like that of the last loft, but that was where the similarities ended. The place had been gutted. There were no appliances in the kitchen, and the floor in that area had been ripped out, leaving only the subfloor. They stepped over trash in the living area to get to the stairs.

The second floor was in worse shape than the first, and the third floor looked like it had been hit by a tornado. After the tour was complete, they returned to the main floor. Toni sat on a five-gallon bucket and Boggs joined her, sitting on the floor. Francine leaned against the wall.

"This place needs some work," Toni said quietly, "but it's got good bones." She was picturing how it *could* be and determined they could make it so. "The layout is perfect and the location is the best we've seen." She looked at Boggs. "It's going to take some time, and a lot of elbow grease, but we can do it, don't you think?"

"You'd be willing?" Boggs asked.

Toni looked into Boggs's eyes and saw an almost unbelievable amount of emotion, a mixture of hope, love and tenderness. She loved this woman so deeply and she could feel how much Boggs loved her. No matter how hard the work was, she was absolutely willing to put in the time to make this their home. "I'll do whatever needs to be done, hon." She saw a tear roll down Boggs's cheek and she got up to hug her. "Whatever needs to be done," she whispered.

Boggs brushed the tear from her face. "I love you." She kissed Toni, then looked at Francine and nodded slightly. "Let's go see the last one."

Francine drove them three blocks over and stopped in front of a beautiful huge brick building. There were several steps that led up to a double door, which was painted a dark red with brushed nickel hardware. A brushed nickel light hung above the door.

"This is breathtaking," Toni said. "I can't wait to see the inside, but I'm afraid we're a bit out of our league."

"A girl can always dream," Boggs said, grinning.

"There's a two-car garage with this one," Francine said as she opened the front door. "You can access that from the alley. This place has all the bells and whistles, not to mention a pretty complicated security system. There are cameras outside and monitors in almost every room. Let me give you girls the tour."

Off the foyer was a small bathroom and there were stairs leading up to the second floor. The kitchen was to the left and as Francine led them from room to room, Toni was speechless. It was the most beautiful place she'd ever seen. The kitchen featured stainless steel appliances, including a double oven, gas range, dishwasher, microwave, side-by-side refrigerator, wine cooler and sink. The floor was tiled with gray slate. The walls, painted a deep red, contrasted with the white cabinets. Some of the upper cabinets had glass insets. There was a huge center island with a matching sparkling black granite countertop. A wrought-iron pot rack hung above the island on one side with three pendant lights hanging on the other side. Five counter-height stools sat on one side.

"This looks like a picture out of a magazine." Toni was finally able to speak. She just kept shaking her head and caressing the countertop, which was cool to the touch. "Unbelievable."

The kitchen opened up to a large living area. Polished hardwood floors gleamed throughout, a light maple with a dark inlay around the edges. The walls were painted a soft sage accented by white crown molding in every room. On one side of the living room, an exposed brick wall surrounded a large fireplace. The far side had sliding glass doors that opened up to a spacious deck. Toni poked her head outside and noticed a gas grill the size of her car at the end of the deck. Stairs led down to a manicured yard that was bordered by a tall privacy fence.

"This is fabulous. I feel like I'm on some kind of house tour." She closed the sliding glass doors and followed Francine upstairs.

Boggs was right behind her. "Do you like it?" she whispered.

Toni turned around and rolled her eyes in response. Francine showed them the master suite and a second bedroom and bath on that floor. The third floor had a study, complete with built-in bookcases and yet a third bedroom and bath. Off the hall were stairs that led to a rooftop deck. A Jacuzzi was in the corner with bench seating all around.

Back in the kitchen, Francine pointed to her left. "Out this doorway is the garage and basement."

Going down a few stairs to a landing, Francine unlocked a heavy steel door that opened out to the garage. Toni had never seen a garage so clean. Back at the landing, they took the stairs that led down to the basement. Not far from the steps was a laundry room with top-of-the-line washer and dryer, with room for an ironing board.

"Wow." Toni was impressed. "This beats my twenty-year-old washer by a mile."

"Wait until you see this." Francine guided her around a corner. "This is the game room."

"Holy shit." Toni's jaw dropped once again. There was a stone fireplace in one corner and a beautiful mahogany bar adjacent to it. An oak pool table with red felt was placed across the room and a pinball machine stood nearby. Even though this was a basement, plenty of light streamed in from upper windows and the room felt warm and cozy.

"So, ladies. What do you think? Pretty nice place, huh?"

Toni could only nod as Francine led them back up to the kitchen and slid onto one of the stools. She sat next to Francine. "It's beautiful, Francine. I don't think I'd change a thing. It's just, wow."

Francine smiled. "I thought you might like it. It comes with everything you see, even the pool table and the stools we're sitting on. And I know she loves it." She nodded toward Boggs.

Toni looked from Francine to Boggs, both of them grinning like kids on Christmas morning. "What am I missing?"

"So you really like it?" Boggs's grin widened into a smile.

"Of course," Toni said, not sure what was going on. She adored the place, but it was way out of their price range. Boggs was acting peculiar. Something wasn't right.

"What about the kitchen? Do you like the appliances?" Boggs was pointing to the range top. "Is gas okay?"

Suspicious, Toni turned her gaze from Boggs to Francine. They both looked almost giddy.

"Have you been here before?" she asked Boggs, who shrugged. Toni eyed Francine.

"I showed it to her last week," Francine finally admitted. "She thought you'd like it."

Toni went over to Boggs. "What's going on?" she whispered. "Are you nuts? We can't afford a place like this. I'm not sure we can afford the last one."

"But if we could afford it," Boggs whispered back, "would you want to live here?"

"Not if it meant we couldn't afford to eat. Honey, listen, I'm fine with doing the work ourselves. This place probably costs a million dollars."

"A million two," Francine said. Both Toni and Boggs turned to look at her. "I'm sixty-two years old, but I'm not deaf."

They joined Francine at the island. She had her portfolio open and her pen in hand. She had a look of expectation.

"A million two hundred thousand, huh?" Boggs put her arm around Toni, who felt uncomfortable and confused about Boggs's nonchalance regarding the price. "Do you think they'll take nine hundred, cash?"

Toni's mouth opened on its own accord. Did she just hear what she thought she heard? Did Boggs actually say nine hundred thousands *dollars*? In cash? *What the hell?*

"I don't know," Francine said as she began to fill out an offer, "but we can give it a shot."

Boggs did say she had money in savings, but nine hundred thousand? No way. This had to be a joke, but Francine was scribbling away. Her head was spinning. She tried to focus.

"Are you serious?" She looked at Boggs, who was still grinning.

Boggs nodded. "If it's okay with you, I'd like us to live here. It's everything we want and we wouldn't have to do all the work."

"I, um, it's beautiful, but, we don't have the money. I mean, *I* don't have the money." She still couldn't fathom that Boggs had nine hundred thousand dollars. *Did she win the frickin' Powerball or something?* "Boggs, I can't let you spend all your money. We can get the fixer-upper and split the costs." She kissed Boggs gently. "I love that you would empty your savings for a home for us, but you don't have to do that. Honest."

Boggs jumped up and grabbed Toni, pulling her from the stool. She held her close, lifting her off the floor and twirled her around several times. When she set Toni down, she kissed her firmly on the lips. "I love you *so* much. It means the world to me that you'd rather we get the less expensive loft so that I wouldn't spend all my savings. I think that's amazing and fantastic." She looked at Francine. "I picked a winner, didn't I, Aunt Francie."

"You sure did, sweetie. And it's about time." Francine got up and gave Toni a big hug. "Welcome to the family, sweetie."

"What?" Toni gaped at her with disbelief. "You're her aunt? Really?"

"Yes, sweetie. I'm Victoria's aunt."

Boggs lowered her eyes and shook her head.

"Sorry." Francine reached out and touched Boggs's cheek. "I mean Boggs."

Toni felt relieved. "So you guys were putting me on, huh? Very funny."

"I am a realtor, though." Francine went back to her paperwork. "Both names?" she asked Boggs, who nodded.

Toni was feeling dazed and confused. How did an investigator in the prosecuting attorney's office save that much money? Lord knows they weren't paid that well. Did she really win the lottery? Or maybe an inheritance? Why hadn't Boggs told her this before? Of course she'd always been rather private about her finances. Maybe that was why.

"You better tell her the rest," Francine said to Boggs. "Take her out on the deck while I finish this offer. I want to get it in before noon."

Boggs did as she was told and gently led her outside on the deck. Toni was shaking and Boggs sat her down on the built-in bench along the side. "Are you okay?"

Toni nodded and blinked several times. She wasn't sure what "the rest" was.

"I guess I should have told you sooner, but I was afraid." Boggs sat down beside her. "Anytime in my past, when I would tell anyone, well, they always acted differently toward me. It's like they didn't like me for me, but liked me only for the money."

"Oh, honey. I don't care if you have money." Toni sensed that Boggs had really been hurt in the past. Her heart went out to her and she held her hand. "And you don't need to spend all your money." She pulled her hand to her lips and kissed it lightly. "Why don't you just keep that money in the bank, save it for some other time."

Boggs laughed and Toni felt puzzled.

"What's so funny? I'm serious."

"I know you're serious and that makes me love you even more." Boggs held both of Toni's hands. "It's not like that's all I have, babe."

Toni's eyebrows shot up. "You mean you've got more than *nine hundred thousand*? I mean, well, I don't want to pry or anything, but there's more?"

Boggs grinned broadly. "Yeah, babe. Quite a bit more."

"Quite a bit more?" Toni echoed, her voice barely more than a squeak.

Boggs nodded. "Oh, yeah. Many millions more. So, what do you think? How about we call this home?"

"If you're sure, then yes. I'd love to live with you in your new house. It's beautiful and I absolutely love it." Toni kissed her, then looked down at her shoes. "Um, I don't mean to pry or anything, but where in the hell did you get all that money?"

Boggs touched Toni's face, lifting it so their eyes met. "I didn't want to keep this from you, but I wanted to be sure. Vicky is the only other person that knows, aside from my family of course." She kissed Toni lightly. "My great aunt left me a little over five hundred thousand dollars when I was eighteen. I guess I have a knack for investing. This is the first time I've ever used any of the money. It's mostly in mutual funds right now and some real estate. This was the first time I ever *wanted* to spend any of it. I love you and I love this house."

Toni wrapped her arms around Boggs.

"Our house." Boggs squeezed her tightly. "Our house. It will belong to both of us and the kids. Of course their names won't be on the deed, but I'm sure they'll get over that."

"I can't let you do that," Toni said seriously, pulling away. No one had ever done so much for her. "It's your money, Boggs."

"And we're a team now," Boggs countered. "So this will be ours, not mine or yours, okay? Is it a deal?"

Toni nodded, still dumbfounded. Boggs led her back into the kitchen.

"Are you girls ready? I need to drop you off and get to the office." Francine gathered her things and headed to the door. "I'll put this in as a twelve-hour offer. I know the selling agent and I'll give her a call, just to see what her gut feeling is."

An hour later Toni and Boggs were sitting in her living room with Mr. Rupert. Toni was still shaking her head. "I still can't believe this. So you saw this place last week?"

"Yeah. Aunt Francie showed it to me and I fell in love with the place." Boggs opened a bottle of water. "But after you said you'd move in with me, I wanted to see a couple others, just to make sure."

"I can't believe you never told me you had a few dollars tucked away." Toni shook her head again and laughed. "Is there anything else I should know about you?"

Boggs thought for a moment. "Well, I don't like onions. Or sushi."

Toni laughed again. "I think I can handle that." She hugged Boggs. "You know, it still doesn't matter to me whether or not you have money, but I'm thrilled at just the possibility that we could get that loft. It doesn't even seem real."

"I know," Boggs said. "It seems perfect for us, don't you think?"

Before Toni could respond, Boggs's cell phone rang.

Boggs looked at the display. "It's Aunt Francie." She listened for several minutes. "I agree. Right. We'd like to close on June twenty-ninth so we can move our stuff on the thirtieth. Yeah, so we can be out of our places by the first. No sense in paying rent for July if we don't have to. Okay, thanks, Aunt Francie. Call me when it's a go." She closed her phone. "They countered with nine hundred and fifty. We're a go."

"What?" Toni's jaw dropped for the third time that day. "That quick? You mean it's ours?"

"Just a couple details and the paperwork, and yup, it's ours." Boggs was beaming.

"Don't we need to get it inspected or something?"

"Aunt Francie told me it was inspected last month and passed with flying colors. The buyer's financing fell through. I doubt if anything has changed in four weeks. Aunt Francie showed me the inspection report."

Toni got up and began to pace. "What do we do now? We have to pack. I need to give notice here. Oh, wait. My year's lease is up anyway. Okay." She looked around the room. "I need to find some boxes."

Boggs stretched out on the couch, just smiling and watching her pace around the room. "Slow down, babe. We've got some time here. Well, we've got about three weeks. Let's make a list of what we need to do."

"Okay." Toni grabbed a pad of paper from the bookcase and sat back down. She couldn't believe this had all happened so fast. She was still on a high from the thought of living with Boggs and now they just bought a loft. One that cost close to a million dollars, for God's sake. She didn't know what to do. She sat with her pencil poised above the pad.

"I don't know about you," Boggs said, putting her feet on the coffee table, "but I for one don't want to move shit myself. I say we have movers do the heavy work."

"That would probably cost us a few hundred dollars." Toni put the tip of the pencil in her mouth and began to mentally check off pieces of furniture. "We don't have a whole lot of stuff so we could probably do it ourselves." She looked at Boggs, who was shaking her head.

"Oh, I don't know," she said. "A lot of the things we have are pretty heavy, or at least bulky to carry. Why don't we throw caution to the wind and splurge. Let's hire someone to do the heavy stuff."

"You're right. It's worth it. Just the thought of having to carry this giant sectional couch is enough to convince me. A couple hundred apiece for not having a sore back is a small price to pay."

Boggs turned serious. "We're partners, right?"

"Absolutely." Toni wasn't sure where Boggs was going with this.

"Okay. Then let me ask you this. If you won twenty million dollars in the lottery tonight, how would you feel about that? Would you consider it your money or our money?"

"It would be ours. No question. What are you getting at?" Toni believed that wholeheartedly. "We're partners," she continued. "If you have a problem, that means we have a problem. If I won money, that means we won money. We're in this together."

Boggs let out a deep sigh and smiled. "That's exactly how I

feel. I've never felt that way before with anyone, but I feel that way now. My money is your money and vice versa. This is our life."

Toni felt the tears begin to well in her eyes. She noticed that Boggs was starting to cry too. She put down her pad and crawled into Boggs's arms. They held each other silently for a long time. Toni never felt happier or more content than she did at that moment.

After almost a half-hour, Boggs finally spoke. "Now let's think about getting some new furniture, beginning with a new bed."

Toni giggled. She knew she was the luckiest person in the whole world.

Chapter 6

On Saturday afternoon Jan came in to find her boss pacing the study. Not unusual, she thought, given the circumstances.

"Hi, boss." Jan put her backpack down and made herself a rum and Coke at the bar. She picked up the ashtray and sat down in one of the leather club chairs. She watched her boss continue to pace while she lit a cigarette. "I just dropped off some more samples for Doug. He's going to hit the gay bars tonight and then go to the strip clubs after midnight. I think he'll do okay. He knows that Kevin usually went on Fridays and Sundays, but he wants to get started."

The woman sat at her desk. "Good, good. We need to get that going again. It may take some time for Doug to get up to Kevin's level, and there's no one else to do the bars right now. Fix me a drink, will you?"

Jan did as she was instructed, careful to put in three ice cubes and fill the tumbler to the exact level. She set the drink down on the coaster, centering it. The woman stirred the liquid three times with her left index finger, tapped it twice on the rim and brought her finger to her lips. She nodded her thanks to Jan, who returned to her own chair.

"I talked to Mike earlier today," she informed Jan. "He said that one of the detectives was digging into Kevin's business. He pulled rank and took over the investigation and he suggested we remove anything we could from his apartment before he executed a search warrant for the place on Monday. Can you take care of that?"

"Sure. I'll go over there tonight."

"Can you get in?"

"I can always get in." Jan smiled. She always made sure she could access whatever she needed to access. And since Mike was going to be the one who executed the search, she didn't have to be as careful as she normally would be. This would be a piece of cake.

"And I'd like to go to the club tonight." She took a healthy swallow of her Famous Grouse. "I want to see Doug in action and just scope out some things. How about you come by and pick me up at nine. Will that give you enough time to do what you need to do?"

"Nine would be fine." It wasn't unusual for Jan to be asked to accompany her to a bar. Even when she had a girlfriend, her boss would request Jan's presence. She figured it was mostly so she wouldn't have to go alone, but she also knew that her boss valued her opinions. And she was also pretty good at finding a woman for her boss to spend the night with. That wasn't too hard. It was fairly well known that her boss had a lot of money and didn't bat an eye at spending it on someone.

Jan hadn't been to Gertrude's Garage in a while and she was hoping she could find herself a date there. It was a good dance bar and always crowded on a Saturday night.

"Maybe we could get a bite to eat there."

"That sounds good," her boss said. "I love Trish's chicken wings."

Jan finished her drink in one big gulp and picked up the ashtray. She emptied it in the can and washed it, then grabbed her backpack. "I'll see you at nine."

As she left the house she pulled out her cell phone. She had two cell phones. One was registered to her and only used to talk to her boss. The other was registered to her grandmother, who had passed away a few years ago. This was the one she used for business, and now she dialed Mike's number. She needed to know what detective had been snooping around. They couldn't afford to attract any attention. Now that Judge Smith and Butch were dead, their connections were a bit shaky. They still had a good income from the escort service, and the drug business should be picking up soon. Still, she didn't like to take any unnecessary chances. And if her boss was still obsessing over Toni Barston, that would be another mess she'd have to clean up, as usual.

Jan thought that Mike's phone was about to go to voice mail when he picked up.

"Detective Johnson."

"Hi, Mike. It's Jan. I just left the boss."

"Are you going to take care of that?"

"Yeah. Tonight. What detective is snooping around?"

"Carter." Mike sighed loudly. "Barston put her up to it. She's got Kevin's murder case and I heard that she talked to the doer. Apparently his son got the stuff from Kevin and then OD'd. They're looking for some kind of connection."

"Shit." Jan was racking her brain trying to think if there was anything that would tie Kevin to the boss. Nothing came to mind immediately.

"Just get the basics and I'll take care of the rest." Mike disconnected without saying anything else.

45

She drove to her house, stopping first at the Hardee's drive-through for dinner. By the time she finished her burger and fries, she was fairly confident that the only tie might be his cell phone. It would surely show contact with her phone, but not the one registered to her. If it was on him when he died, the police would have that and Mike could take care of it. She would check Kevin's computer and do a quick search of his drawers, but she really couldn't think of anything that would be incriminating. They always paid him in cash and he had no idea who the boss was. Still, she wouldn't rest easy until she was sure.

Two hours later Jan pulled on a pair of latex gloves and let herself into Kevin's small apartment with her duplicate key. It was on the top floor of a four-family flat located in one of the depressed areas of Fairfield. There was a car on blocks parked out front and a discarded toilet in the side yard. She could hear loud punk rock music from one of the bottom apartments and a man screaming profanities from the other. No one seemed to notice her or, if they did, they apparently didn't care.

The smell hit her as soon as she opened the front door. Although Kevin had been dead for just over a week, he obviously hadn't cleaned in at least a month. She stepped over several pizza boxes and spotted the source of the smell. There was a half-eaten container of Chinese food on the counter that seemed to have a life of its own.

Thoroughly disgusted, she backed out of the kitchen and headed to the living room where she picked through the mounds of trash and dirty clothes. *What the hell am I thinking? There's nothing here.* She made her way back to the only bedroom and pushed open the door with her foot. This room was in the same condition as the living room, with pizza boxes littering the floor and fast-food wrappers on the bed. *This is so gross.* She opened the drawer of the nightstand and found a pile of condoms and some lube. She rolled her eyes and shut the drawer. Kevin's computer was hidden under a pair of smelly, somewhat stiff sweat-

46

pants on the desk in the corner. Carefully she removed them with just two fingers and turned on the computer. She wasn't even tempted to sit in the chair and instead leaned over, waiting for the screen to come up.

After about ten minutes she was convinced that there was nothing on the computer that could be tied to the organization. The only document in Word was a half-written letter to some guy, professing his love. He had an AOL account and there was no way to know if he had e-mails without a password. His collection of gay porn seemed quite extensive. After opening a file called "fun," she was treated to several photos of naked men in suggestive poses. She quickly closed that file and moved on. As far as she could tell, he had no ledgers or information about his drug clients on the computer, but she wasn't exactly computer savvy.

Jan shut down the computer and returned the sweatpants to their rightful position. She looked in several drawers, under the bed and in the closet. There was no sign of any type of ledger or list. She stood in his bathroom, thinking. Usually she took Kevin the drugs on a Friday morning, telling him how much money she expected in a week. She would return the following week and he would give her that amount of money. She didn't care if he charged a higher price, as long as she got what she expected. Kevin would get the money from a can in the kitchen and count out what he owed her. Was it possible he never kept track of anything and just used what was left for himself? He wasn't the smartest guy in the world, so that was possible. She returned to the kitchen and found the can in one of the cabinets. Inside she found four thousand dollars. That was about half of what he owed her.

He probably only had time to sell half the drugs. That sounded right because he was killed on a Monday. She figured the rest of the drugs were either hidden inside the apartment or in his car. She thought about searching for them but reconsidered after looking at the kitchen again. It didn't matter. At least she got half the money. She stuffed it in her jeans and left. She'd done all she could do. She glanced at her watch as she returned to her car and realized she had just enough time to go home, shower and then pick up her boss.

Chapter 7

Toni and Boggs arrived at Gertrude's Garage a little before five. They had stopped at the mall and had several gifts in tow. Toni insisted that they get regular birthday gifts as well as gag gifts and she'd found the perfect thing, a silver candleholder. There were silver silhouettes of six people, holding hands and standing in a circle. The center held a votive candle. It represented a circle of friends. Toni had one herself and Patty had commented on it several times. It was gift-wrapped in a beautiful red box with a white bow. Boggs had found a thin black leather case that would hold Patty's new detective badge. For gag gifts they bought two Charlie Chan videos and a child's notepad with a pencil attached. The gag gifts were wrapped in a newspaper from Boggs's car.

They wound their way through the pool tables and dance floor and found Vicky in one of the backrooms. She'd already put up a huge sign for Patty and was sitting on the floor, digging into a large paper bag.

"Hey, sweetie," Toni called out.

Vicky turned and grinned. "Well, it's about time." She got up and hugged her. "I'm much better at supervising than actually doing the work myself." She sat at one of the tables and motioned for Toni to join her. "Ooh. Presents! What did you get?"

Toni explained the two sets of gifts and Vicky pointed to a large box on the floor in the corner. "I'm putting the gag gifts in there. We'll have her open those after things settle down. The real presents go on the table in the corner."

Boggs put the gifts in the proper locations and began digging in the paper bag. "Hey, cool stuff in here." She pulled out several streamers and some inflatable pink flamingos. From the bottom she pulled out at least fifty balloons in need of air. "Jeez, Vic, did you get enough frickin' balloons?"

Vicky rolled her eyes. "Let's get moving on this. It shouldn't take us too long. I told people to come around six."

Boggs and Vicky started hanging the streamers. Toni noticed a long table on one side and a small box with purple wristbands. "Hey, what are these?"

Vicky, standing on one of the chairs, turned. "Those are for food. Anyone who has one on can eat the food. You've got to buy your own drinks, but I ordered a bunch of munchies. Go ahead and put one on and give one to Boggs." She held up her arm. "I've already got one."

Toni did as instructed, then began putting the colorful table-cloths on the tables. Just as she finished, Johnnie Layton came into the room. She was tall with an athletic build, her light brown hair cut short, above her collar. Her eyes were an icy blue and her voice like butter. Toni and the gang had become friends with Johnnie a few months ago when Toni was suspected of killing a judge. Johnnie, an FBI agent, had been involved in the federal investigation. Even though Johnnie initially had feelings for Toni, she had hopefully resigned herself to just being friends. In the last couple months Johnnie had become one of the gang.

"Hey, Johnnie." Toni hugged her and took the gifts she was carrying.

"The one in the paper bag is the gag gift," Johnnie explained.

Toni nodded and put it in the box on the floor and the other one on the table. She handed Johnnie a wristband.

Vicky and Boggs had finished with the streamers and had just started on the balloons. "Give us a hand, will ya?" Vicky pointed to the pile of balloons.

Johnnie sat down and picked one up. "I guess I should have gotten here twenty minutes later. I didn't know I had to work." She laughed and blew up her first balloon.

As the four women worked on the balloons, they chatted in between puffs. They were on the last few when Trish came in carrying a bucket that held six bottles of beer. She was the cook at Gertrude's.

"This is on the house, ladies," she said as she set the bucket on the table. "And here's some tape for the balloons." She looked around the room. "You guys have done a great job. I'll start bringing out the food at about six. Is that okay?"

"That would be great, Trish," Vicky said as she grabbed one of the bottles of beer. "I can't wait to have some of your wings. You make the best in town."

Trish seemed to blush slightly and quickly left the room.

"I think you embarrassed the girl," Boggs said as she opened her own beer. "And isn't she a little young for you?"

"Shut up and start hanging up these balloons." Vicky sat down next to Toni. "I've done enough for one night." She grinned at Toni and watched Boggs and Johnnie finish the work. By the time they were done, Vicky was swallowing the last of her beer. She opened another and glanced at her watch. "People should be showing up any minute now."

"How many people did you invite?" Toni asked.

"I think we'll have about twenty." Vicky retrieved a cake box from under the food table. She placed the cake in the center of the table.

Toni went over to inspect the cake. "It looks great. I take it Patty likes pink flamingos?"

"I have no idea," Vicky said, chuckling. "They just crack me up, so I went with it."

"And here's our birthday girl," Boggs said as Patty entered the room. She took the last beer from the bucket and opened it for Patty. "Happy birthday." She hugged her quickly and Vicky snapped a picture.

Patty stood about five foot five and was by no means slender. She considered herself fluffy and often described herself as such. Her blond hair was curly and unruly and she wore it about collar length. Her brown eyes were warm and inviting and her smile was infectious.

"I can't believe you guys," Patty said as she hugged everyone else. "You shouldn't have gone to so much trouble, but I'm glad you did." She grinned broadly.

"This was all Vicky's doing," Toni said as she hugged Patty. "And Johnnie's here," she whispered. "Go get a birthday kiss." She knew that Patty had a bad case of lust for Johnnie and she enjoyed teasing her about it.

Patty hugged Toni harder and giggled. "Maybe after a few more beers," she murmured.

Vicky appeared and handed a giant button to Patty. "Here. This is your first birthday gift." The button was about four inches in diameter and said, "Kiss Me, It's My Birthday" in bright orange letters. She pinned it on Patty's shirt and then kissed her. Patty smiled, then looked down at her button and frowned.

"Don't worry," Toni said. "If you don't like who's coming toward you, just turn your head and point to your cheek."

Patty looked relieved. "Good idea. I mean, I don't want to be rude, but there are some women that I just wouldn't want to kiss."

"I know exactly what you mean." Toni smiled and then noticed Johnnie coming toward them. "But then again, there are some that you would." She moved away and let Johnnie get closer.

"Happy birthday, Patty." She looked down at the button and smiled. "May I?"

Patty blinked several times and then just nodded. Toni thought the kiss was just a fraction of a second longer than friendly. She saw Johnnie wink at Patty and then walk away. Toni went back over to Patty, whose face was now red.

"So?"

"Wow." Patty took a deep breath. "I've been wishing she'd do that since the first time I saw her. I think this is the best birthday I've ever had."

Toni laughed and gently shook her. "Back to earth, girl. The party's just started."

Chapter 8

Jan and her boss pulled up to Gertrude's Garage a little after nine o'clock. Jan stopped outside the front door and let her out.

"Get us a table in the back," she ordered Jan. "And tell Trish we want a couple orders of wings. I'm going to make the circuit first." She slammed the car door shut and went inside.

It wasn't very crowded yet and she stopped in the game room and watched two women shooting pool. One was very good and she was impressed with the speed in which she sunk the balls. Her opponent was clearly a novice. She looked to be about thirty years old with a trim body and long blond hair. She was intrigued, so she stopped one of the waitresses and told her to get the woman a drink, on her. Before leaving the room, she winked at the blonde and was rewarded with a smile.

The dance floor had at least twenty women on it and she stopped to admire a redhead. She was tempted to ask her to dance when a slow song came on, so she decided to wait until later. Even though she was probably twenty years older than the redhead, she knew her reputation for being very generous preceded her, and most women did not turn her down. Smiling at that thought, she headed back toward the private rooms. One had obviously been reserved for a birthday party. Trish entered carrying a huge pan of chicken wings, and toward the back of the room a familiar face was parked near the food table. Ah-ha, she thought. One of the Fairfield police detectives, Vicky Carter. She'd met her once before and never passed up an opportunity to be kind to the police.

It never hurt to be friendly to the enemy. Vicky Carter was an excellent detective and wasn't on the take. But one never knew what the future could hold, and of course everyone had a price. She entered the room, nodded to Trish, and walked straight up to Vicky, her hand outstretched.

Chapter 9

Toni and Boggs were sitting at one of the tables in the private room, drinking beer. They'd just finished dancing to about four songs. Johnnie and Patty joined them, having just come from the dance floor themselves. Patty was beaming.

"Are you having a good time?" Toni asked.

"I swear, this is the best birthday I've ever had." Patty reached for a beer from the bucket on the table. Johnnie opened it for her and smiled.

There might be something between these two, Toni thought. She hoped that Patty wouldn't get hurt. Johnnie had a reputation of being very smooth and Toni had found that assessment to be accurate a few months ago. While Boggs, Patty and Johnnie continued to talk, Toni scanned the room. There were quite a few people milling about. Vicky was standing next to the food table chatting with a redhead who looked barely old enough to drive, let alone old enough to get into a bar. Toni chuckled to herself. Vicky had the type of personality that drew people. She was funny and confident. Even the long scar on her neck didn't seem to faze her. She'd gotten it last fall in a near brush with death and she never bothered to cover it with makeup or high collars.

A few minutes later Toni looked over again and saw Nancy Manford talking to Vicky. Toni had known Nancy for several years. She worked part-time as an activist and they were both on the Community Awareness committee that met monthly. She excused herself from the table and went over to say hi. Even though she wasn't necessarily close to Nancy, she did consider her a friend.

"Hey, Nancy. How've you been?"

"Oh, hi, Toni." She hugged her and kissed her on the cheek. "I saw Vicky and thought I'd crash the party. Is that the birthday girl?" She pointed to their table.

"Yup, that's her. You know Boggs—she's sitting next to Patty—so go over and say hello."

"I think I will." Nancy winked. "Is she available?"

"I don't think so, but go over and say hello anyway." Toni chuckled and hugged her again.

Vicky pulled Toni closer. "I only met Nancy once and that was ages ago. I can't believe she knew who I was. I mean, I think she's nice and all, but after what we found out about her a few months ago, I think I'll keep my distance."

Toni nodded and giggled. They'd run a background check on her a few months ago and found a stalking charge. "Me, too. That's why I told her Patty wasn't available."

Before Vicky could respond, a woman approached them.

"Detective, nice to see you again."

Vicky shook her hand. "Nice to see you, Your Honor."

"So Officer Green is another year older. Where is the birthday girl?"

"She's right over there." Vicky gestured to the table.

57

Toni raised her eyebrows at Vicky.

"Oh, I'm sorry," Vicky said immediately. "Judge Crayton, this is Toni Barston. She's one of our assistant prosecuting attorneys."

Toni reached out her hand and smiled. "Very nice to meet you, judge."

Judge Crayton shook her hand. "So you're Toni Barston." She smiled. "I've heard a lot about you. I'm moving over from civil to criminal next week, so I may see you in my courtroom."

"I look forward to that, Your Honor." Toni remembered hearing the judge's name but had never seen her before. She was racking her brain, trying to remember anything about the judge. She came up with nothing.

"Well, great seeing you again, detective. And nice meeting you, Ms. Barston. I must go over and wish Officer Green a happy birthday."

"Good to meet you, judge." Toni watched the woman walk over to her table. She turned back to Vicky. "Well, that was interesting. What's she like?"

"I don't really know her," Vicky admitted. "She's been around forever, though. She used to work criminal exclusively but moved over to civil a couple years ago. She's semi-retired now. Mostly she fills in for other judges. I had no idea she was coming back to criminal. I testified in her courtroom once and she seemed fair."

"Pretty cool that she's open," Toni commented. "I mean, coming into a gay bar and all." She felt good about that. Even though she knew that law was still a good ol' boys' network, it was nice to know that an openly gay woman could be a judge. Maybe Fairfield wasn't as backward as she'd thought.

Another woman approached Vicky and broke Toni's train of thought.

"Detective Carter, right?" the woman said. "I'm Karen Young. I think we met about two years ago."

Vicky shook her hand. "That's right. I remember. I was investigating a bank embezzlement case and you were one of the bank vice presidents there, right?"

"I used to be, yes. Over in the advertising department. Now I work for the main bank part-time, mostly just board meetings. I also freelance. Good to see you again."

Vicky turned to Toni. "This is Toni Barston. Toni, this is Karen Young."

Toni greeted her. "Nice to meet you, Karen."

Karen smiled. "So, you're Toni Barston. I've heard of you, on the news if I'm not mistaken. Pleased to meet you." She said to Vicky, "I didn't mean to crash a birthday party, but I saw you and thought I'd say hello." She turned to leave. "And nice to meet you, Toni. See you both around."

After she left, Toni laughed. "Jeez, Vicky. Do you know every woman in town or what?"

"Hey, I can't help it if I'm so memorable, can I?" She was still laughing when yet another woman approached her.

"Hi. It's Detective Carter, isn't it?" The woman held out her hand. "I'm Doris Jackson."

Vicky responded in kind. "Yes, of course. I think we met a few years ago." She nodded toward Toni. "Toni, this is Doris Jackson. She's the owner of Gertrude's Garage."

Toni shook her hand. "Great to meet you. I really love this place. You've done an excellent job. I was here for your grand opening last year."

Doris smiled. "Well, thank you. I'm glad you're enjoying yourselves. Let me know if there's anything I can do for you." With that, she turned and left.

"Is it me, or did that seem rather odd and abrupt?" Toni looked at Vicky, wondering if she felt the same thing.

"It felt weird to me too." Vicky laughed. "Of course, maybe it's because I'm standing here in full view of the rest of the bar, next to the food table. Maybe this looks like a pathetic receiving line and people just feel obligated to talk to me. Let's go sit down."

Toni chuckled at Vicky's description. She always had a way of saying things that made you laugh. She followed her back to the table where a fresh bucket of beer had just been delivered. Boggs was just sitting down after filling a plate with fresh wings. Even though the bar was loud, it was tolerable in their little corner and she could actually hear the conversation. Gathered at the table with her were Vicky, Johnnie, Patty and Boggs. Nancy Manford had apparently moved on.

"I just want to thank all of you for making this so special for me." Patty smiled at each of them. "It means a lot. And thank you all for the wonderful gifts."

"There's more," Vicky said with that famous smirk of hers. "We have a couple special gifts. We're going to let you open them now, but you can't tell anyone else about them. At least not until next week. Agreed?"

Patty looked confused. "I guess so." She looked to Johnnie for help, but she only shrugged.

Vicky pulled the box from underneath the table and presented Patty with the first gift. It was the pad of paper with a pencil attached from Boggs, who grinned like an idiot. Patty thanked her and opened the next one. It was the videos from Toni. Again she looked confused but thanked Toni. The next was a book from Johnnie. It was titled *How to Eat Doughnuts Without Being Obvious*. Boggs burst out laughing and Vicky punched her in the arm.

"Um, thank you, Johnnie."

Johnnie kept her face serious. "You're very welcome."

Patty opened the last gift from Vicky. It was a plastic pipe and Sherlock Holmes hat.

Clearly very confused, she said, "Um, thank you everyone. They're very nice." Her smile looked frozen and plastic.

"And remember, you can't tell anyone about these gifts,"

Vicky reminded her.

Patty nodded. Toni couldn't take it anymore. "Oh, for God's sake, Vicky. Tell her. This is killing me."

Uncertainty and expectation played in Patty's eyes.

Vicky pulled out a small brown leather business card holder from her pocket and presented it. Patty held it in her hands, still looking confused. "Go ahead," Vicky said, grinning. "Open it."

Patty slowly opened the holder and took out one of the cards. Her eyes opened wide and her jaw dropped.

"As of Monday," Vicky said seriously, "you are officially a detective with the Fairfield Police Department." She leaned over and kissed Patty on the cheek. "Congratulations."

Toni jumped up and ran over to hug Patty. "I'm so happy for you and so proud. Congratulations!"

Patty seemed stunned. "Are you serious? I really made it?" She shot a dubious glance at Vicky, then looked back at the business card. The word *Detective* was in front of her name and the emblem of the Fairfield P.D. was in the upper left-hand corner.

"Yes. In fact, you made the highest score on the exam." Vicky was smiling. "But you can't tell anyone until Monday. Captain Billings made me promise, okay? But I'm sure your sister and Cathy already know."

Everyone laughed. Patty's sister, Lori, was a medium and her friend Cathy was a psychic. Cathy had helped them figure out who was stalking Toni a few months ago.

Patty was just beaming. "I can't believe this. Now this really is the best birthday I've ever had." She picked up the plastic pipe. "And I swear, these are the best gifts *ever*."

As Patty started asking Vicky a hundred questions, Boggs leaned over and whispered to Toni, "Do you want to tell them about us?"

Toni squeezed her hand. She'd never been so excited about anything in her life, but she didn't want to tell everyone yet. Maybe it was because she didn't want to pull the focus away from

Patty, or maybe she just couldn't believe it was really true. It almost seemed magical at the moment and she was afraid to break the spell. "Let's wait until everything is finalized," she whispered back to Boggs, who nodded. Toni curled her arm through Boggs's and scooted a little closer.

The feeling of Boggs's strong arm comforted her and she almost had to pinch herself to make sure this was real. Boggs winked at her before turning her attention back to the group. Toni felt her entire body react immediately. *How can even a wink still make me weak in the knees after this long?* She kissed Boggs on the cheek. Could things get any better? she wondered.

Chapter 10

The woman sat at a table in the back of the bar with Jan.
They'd just started on their second order of wings. They'd
watched Doug mingle with quite a few people and he seemed to
be doing fine and wasn't being obvious about his transactions.
She smiled. A waitress appeared with another round of drinks.
The woman looked at her glass. It was centered on the small
cardboard coaster and contained exactly three ice cubes, floating
in Scotch.

Carefully she stirred the liquid three times with her left index
finger, then tapped it twice on the rim. As she licked the Scotch
from her finger, anger surged inside her. Her eyes narrowed and
she pushed her chair a few inches from the table. Her breathing
quickened and her heart pounded. She looked at Jan then back at
her drink. "This is *not* my Scotch," she snarled through clenched
teeth.

Jan nodded and stood up. She quickly caught the attention of the bartender, who appeared at the table in less than a minute. "Oh, my God," she said, stricken, as she took the drink from Jan's hand. "I didn't realize." Her hands were shaking as she whisked the drink away. She reappeared moments later with another drink and set it on the empty coaster. "I'm very sorry." Her voice was trembling as she spoke. "Is there anything I can do?"

"Just don't ever let it happen again." Jan's husky voice and angry glare was enough to scare even the most self-assured barkeep.

The woman repeated her routine and relaxed after tasting the Scotch. She nodded to Jan, who leaned back in her chair and lit another cigarette.

The woman took a healthy swallow, then a deep breath. "I met Toni Barston when I came in," she said quietly. "Now, I remember seeing her on the news last fall." She took another drink. "She looks stunning in person. I wouldn't mind having her on the payroll. It would be helpful if we had someone from the prosecuting attorney's office."

Jan simply nodded.

"Did you get the job done tonight?" She looked at Jan, who'd worked for her for many years. She trusted no one as much as Jan. But there were some things that she wouldn't tell even her. She wondered why so many things had gone wrong in the last few months. Could it be because of Jan? Or was it because of Toni Barston? She didn't think it was anything she'd done herself. Or was it? No, she'd been very careful. But earlier she'd made the mistake on her list. *Fuck*. She was getting worried and began tapping her fingers nervously on the table. Then she ran her fingers through her hair three times. It didn't work. She did it two more times and felt better.

"I got half the money he owed us." Jan took a sip of her rum and Coke. "There was nothing on his computer and I didn't find any ledger or list."

"What about the rest of the merchandise?" She didn't feel right about this. She needed all this to just go away. She was losing control, and her anxiety was growing. Things used to be so simple.

"I didn't find anything," Jan said. "But it could've been on Kevin when he was killed, so the cops would have it. Mike can take care of that."

She nodded. "Fine." She could feel her heart pounding. She excused herself and went to the bathroom. She detested public restrooms, but at least this one she knew was cleaner than most. She balanced herself above the toilet, careful not to make contact. Afterward she flushed the toilet with her foot. At the sink she scrubbed her hands furiously with soap while she counted to thirty, rinsed thoroughly and dried her hands. She repeated the sequence and was on twenty-two when two women came barging into the bathroom. They were giggling and kissing and went into one of the stalls together.

Damn it. Now, I've got to start over. She added more soap to her hands, concentrating as she counted to thirty again, trying to ignore the sounds of passion coming from the last stall. She rinsed again and pulled out the paper towels. After drying her hands she took another paper towel and used it to open the door. Using her foot to keep the door open, she tossed the paper towel in the trash.

Back at the table she finished her drink with one large gulp, feeling her world was crashing down around her. Nothing was right.

"Can I get you another?"

"No. I want to go home." She was overwhelmed.

Jan got up immediately. "I'll get the car." She swallowed the last of her drink. "I'll be out front in five minutes."

The woman didn't respond. She watched Jan leave, then scanned the rest of the bar. She needed to do something, but she didn't know what. *Maybe get laid?* Things were spiraling out of control and that meant something very bad was going to happen. She ran her fingers through her hair five times. That helped. Maybe Toni Barston was the problem. She'd try and get her on her payroll. She was a beautiful woman and having her close would be nice. And if that didn't work, she'd set her up and ruin her life. Or kill her. It didn't matter. One way or another she'd make things right again.

She got up and headed to the door. She'd ask Jan to dig a little deeper into Toni's life. She felt good about that decision and walked outside feeling a little more in charge of her life.

Chapter 11

Sunday morning Toni and Boggs were sitting at Toni's dining room table drinking coffee after they'd finished breakfast. Toni had made their favorite, scrambled eggs with Gouda cheese. The Sunday paper was lying on floor and Mr. Rupert was chewing on it. Toni had a pad of paper in front of her.

"We need to make of list of things to do," she told Boggs.

"And finish our list of things we need to buy," Boggs reminded her. "Like a new bed and couch."

Toni laughed. "I still can't believe you don't like my ancient waterbed or the hand-me-down couch."

Boggs shook her head. "Well, your couch is in better shape than mine, but I think we'll need something different for the living room, don't you?"

"Yeah, I think so. There's no place to put a wraparound couch there." Toni thought for a moment, picturing the space. "But it could go in the basement. I can't remember how big that one side is, can you?"

"I think it'd fit, but let's see if Aunt Francie can let us take another look so we can measure things."

She pulled out her cell phone and made the call while Toni refilled their cups.

"She said she could meet us there at one o'clock today," Boggs explained. "My softball game is at eleven, so we could make it. We'd still have time for me to shower and change. Then maybe we could do a little shopping afterward. What do you think?"

"Perfect." Toni glanced at her watch. "Time for you to put on your uniform. I'll get my measuring tape and measure the couch while you get ready. We can stop at your apartment for you to shower after the game and I'll measure some of your stuff while we're there."

While Boggs got ready, Toni measured and took notes. With two extra bedrooms, they could use her waterbed for one and Boggs's full-size bed for the other. On the other hand, her waterbed was really old and moving it and filling it was a pain in the ass. Maybe she'd better scrap that idea and just donate the damn thing. She wasn't sure about the study. They'd definitely need a good-sized desk and maybe the one Boggs had would work. As for the living room, they would need a new couch and a couple chairs at least. And some lighting. She looked at her old square coffee table. That would probably have to go in the basement with her couch, if it'd fit.

This was all so new and exciting for Toni. She still wasn't super comfortable buying furniture with Boggs's money, but she had to admit that what they currently had really wouldn't work too well. But still . . .

"Hey, hon," she called out to Boggs. "Why don't we just work with what furniture we have and buy new things a little at a time?" Toni thought this way she'd be able to contribute more.

"Nah," Boggs said as she came down the stairs with her softball uniform on. "I want us to have a Fourth of July party. So we'll have to have something for people to sit on by then."

"What?" Toni was stunned. Even if they were able to move all their things on the thirtieth, it would take a while to get settled in. "Are you kidding? We can't be ready by then."

"Sure we can." Boggs hugged her. "We'll have movers do all the work and we just have to unpack stuff. And we can have the new furniture delivered on the thirtieth." Boggs was obviously jazzed about the idea.

Toni pondered that for a moment. She didn't really have that much, so unpacking wouldn't be too hard. And the new place was already spotless, so they wouldn't have to spend much time cleaning. She was still trying to wrap her brain around the idea when Boggs spoke.

"We can do it, babe. It'll be great." She kissed Toni. "After we take another look at the loft, we'll go shopping."

"I guess so." Toni was still hesitant. "Are you sure you want to buy all these things now?"

"Absolutely," Boggs said as she grabbed her equipment bag. "As long as we can find things we both like."

Toni joined her by the front door. "Okay." Toni hugged her tightly. "This is going to be great, shopping together."

"It will be. I've always wanted to get nice things, but it never seemed worth it for just me. And now I just want to splurge a little. Is that okay?"

Toni was so touched that she felt tears well up. No one had ever made her feel so special and so loved. She kissed her passionately.

After a few minutes of kissing, Boggs pulled away. "Um, we're either going to have to stop right now or I'm going to miss my game. And at this moment I'm thinking they can do without me." She started to pull Toni toward the couch.

Toni stopped her and laughed. "Let's save that for later, okay?

You can't miss a game and we've got plenty of time."

Boggs sighed. "I suppose so, but let's celebrate when we get home tonight?"

Toni agreed and patted Mr. Rupert on the head before they left.

Chapter 12

Sunday afternoon the woman was again sitting in her study. She couldn't stop thinking of Toni Barston. She'd been fantasizing about having sex with her since she'd gotten home last night. It'd been the best night she'd had in months.

She's absolutely stunning, the woman thought. *She'd be perfect for me, she's beautiful, and her eyes are the bluest I've ever seen.* She replayed their meeting the night before and recalled how soft Toni's hand was when they touched. She knew that having Toni, both personally and professionally, would be the key to her success. She wasn't sure whether she should ask her out first or buy her services first. It would probably be better if she got her on the payroll first. Then she was sure that Toni would jump at the chance of dating "the boss." She smiled at the thought.

She fixed herself a drink, the first of the day. After sitting in her tall, dark leather chair for several minutes she pulled out her cell phone. Before dialing, she swirled the Scotch three times with her left index finger, then tapped it twice on the rim. She was licking the Famous Grouse from her finger as she called Mike Johnson.

"Detective Johnson," he said tersely.

"Hi, Mike. It's me. How are you?"

"Oh, hi, boss." Mike's voice warmed. "Doing good. What can I do for you?"

"I met Toni Barston last night," she said quickly. Just at the mention of her name she felt her heart beat faster. She recalled one of her fantasies and took a sip of her Scotch. "I was thinking of adding her to the payroll," she continued. "Can you arrange that?"

"Barston?" Mike laughed. "Sorry, boss, but from everything I've heard she's as straight as an arrow. And she's friends with Captain Billings."

She felt dizzy. She reached for her lead glass tumbler and noticed it wasn't centered on the coaster. Her hand was shaking. She centered the glass, then picked it up and took a healthy swallow. How could this be? She'd made all the plans. Carefully, she recentered her drink on the coaster. Everything would have been perfect but she ruined it all. *That bitch.*

"Boss? Are you there?"

"What?" She had to regain some control. "Yes, I'm here. Okay, never mind. Are you executing the search warrant for Kevin's apartment tomorrow?" She needed to change the subject. She couldn't let him hear how upset she was.

"Yeah. I have to take a newbie along with me, but there shouldn't be a problem."

"What was found on his body?" She noticed her hands were still shaking. She ran her fingers through her hair five times.

"Some drugs, but not much."

"What about his cell phone?"

"I don't know," Mike admitted. "I'll check on that. But don't

72

worry, I'll take care of anything that comes up. You can trust me, boss."

She didn't trust him. She didn't trust anyone. Too many bad things were happening to her. And all of it began and ended with Toni Barston. She ran her fingers through her hair five more times. That helped some. She needed to think.

"Okay, Mike." She had to end this call. "Just let me know what you get tomorrow, okay?"

"Sure. Anything else I can do?"

"No. I'll talk to you tomorrow." She closed her phone.

She took another drink and ran her fingers through her hair five more times. Her best judge and best attorney had been killed. Her girlfriend suddenly left her. Her best drug dealer had been killed. Everything pointed to Toni as the root of her problems. Now that she knew the bitch thought she was too good to be on the payroll, she must resort to another plan.

Her fantasy from last night beckoned and her anger turned into lust. She wanted Toni to pay, but she was torn as to how. She wanted her. Wanted her bad, but she was trouble. She could have Jan shoot her and it would be over, but she wasn't quite there yet. Toni was too pretty to kill right now. Maybe she'd just take something that was important to Toni, just like she'd done to her. *A little tit for tat.* That would be perfect. She'd have Jan do some more research. All she knew now was that Toni lived alone. Well, if nothing else, she could always have her car torched. That would make a statement. She called Jan.

"Hi, boss."

"I need more background on Toni Barston," she said without any preliminaries. "I want to make her pay."

"Okay, no problem."

"I'm thinking we should torch her car to start. Can you handle that?"

"Sure." Jan chuckled. "Do you want her in it?"

"No. Not yet. I just want her scared." She smiled at the

thought.

"When?"

"Can you do it tonight?"

"Not a problem. Anything else?"

"No, that's all. Call me when it's done. I'll still be up." She hung up without saying anything else.

This would be good. Maybe she'd wait a week or so and then torch the new car that she'd have to buy. Then if Jan found anything worthwhile in her digging, maybe she'd step it up a notch. She drained the last of her Famous Grouse and made herself another.

Even though she was happy that Jan was going to torch the car, she wanted more. She wanted to be near Toni, to see her, to touch her. But she didn't know how that was possible. She wanted to learn all she could about her.

While sipping her drink, she had an idea. Maybe Davey could find a way to hack into Toni's computer. Maybe if she could read some of her e-mails, she'd get to know more about her. Hopeful, she called Davey. He answered on the third ring and she quickly explained what she wanted.

"Sure. I can do that, no problem," Davey said. "All I need is an e-mail address."

"Okay. I'm sure Jan can get that for me."

"Do you know if she's got a webcam?" he asked.

"I have no idea. Why?"

Davey laughed. "I figured out how to access someone's webcam," he explained. "I was playing this online game against this dude in Texas. He was always beating me and I just *knew* he was cheating somehow."

He laughed again and she could tell he was really excited.

"So I programmed this Trojan and sent it to him in an e-mail. His antivirus software didn't catch it. All he had to do was open the attachment once. I was in and could activate his webcam without him knowing it. I watched him for a couple days until I caught him. He was using this new device that would double his score."

"Couldn't he tell you were using his webcam? Wasn't there one of those picture icon things on his screen?"

"Nope. That icon only shows up when you use the standard webcam software. My program goes around that. He had no idea."

Her hands were shaking. Could this be possible? Could she actually *see* Toni in her home? Watch her? She fantasized about watching Toni walking around, maybe not even dressed. *Mmm.*

"Sis? You still there?"

She shook the image from her mind and licked her lips. Her hand was shaking as she brought her drink to her mouth. She took a healthy swallow before answering. "I'm here. That would be wonderful. I'll get you the e-mail address as soon as I can." As an afterthought she asked, "So, did you beat the guy?"

"Oh, yeah." He laughed again. "And he can't figure out how, because I wrote a program to disable his device. You should see him sitting at his computer, cussing me out."

They talked for only a few more minutes. Now that she knew about this possibility, she felt a little better. She desperately hoped that Toni had a webcam. She turned on her own laptop and checked her bank balance and her stocks.

Chapter 13

Toni and Boggs were drinking beer and sitting on the patio of an outdoor café. "I can't believe we just bought an entire room of furniture." Toni had her pad of paper with all the measurements in front of her and the bill of sale for the furniture. They'd purchased a cream-colored microfiber couch. It had classic clean lines and down-filled cushions. Since the living area was so large, they'd also gotten a loveseat in the same style. To complement the couch, they picked out two club chairs covered in a worn-looking brown leather. Boggs had been thrilled when she'd found out they were also recliners. They'd also found a couple of oversized ottomans that could be used for extra seating or to just put your feet up. A coffee table, two end tables and a few lamps rounded out their haul.

"That was so fun." Boggs took a sip of her beer. "And I think we got some really good deals, especially with that sale. I love bargains."

"Me, too. I think we did great." Toni looked at their list. "Next on our list is a bed and, of course, bedding. All your stuff is for a full-size bed and mine is for a queen-size waterbed. Are you sure you want to get a king-size?"

"Hell, yes." Boggs laughed. "The master suite is huge and anyway, Mr. Rupert hogs half the bed now."

"That's true," Toni agreed. "Okay, king-size it is. I've never shopped for a mattress before. Do you have something in mind?"

"I want a Tempur-Pedic."

"Are you serious? Aren't those, well, a little pricey?"

"But they're so worth every penny. Aunt Francie has one and I've slept on it before. And they've got like a twenty-five-year warranty or something." Boggs took another drink. "Just wait till you try it. I know you're going to love it."

Toni was a little hesitant. She'd heard those mattresses cost close to five thousand dollars. But if that was what Boggs wanted, it was okay with her.

"Okay, I'll give it a try." She finished her beer and glanced at her watch. "It's still early. Do you want to do some more shopping?"

Boggs had already finished her beer. "There's a great furniture store right down the street and the mattress place is next door." She took Toni's hand. "Let's go."

A little over two hours later they were back at Toni's townhouse with a frozen pizza in the oven. Boggs was stretched out on one side of the couch with a beer in her hand. Toni was curled up next to her with a bottle of lemon water. She was rubbing Mr. Rupert's tummy.

"I can't believe all we bought today," Toni said, sipping her water. "I've never done that in my entire life. And I've never had a real bedroom set."

"Me either. And I can hardly believe the deal we got on the

furniture. Just because there was a scratch on the back of one of the dressers. I mean, who'd ever see that anyway?"

"I know." Toni giggled. "I feel like we almost stole the thing." She looked at the list on the coffee table. "The only thing left is bedding. Not bad for a day of shopping."

"I'll line up the movers." Boggs sat up and took a sip of her beer. "And I'll get a bunch of boxes for us tomorrow. We can pack a little every night. That way it won't seem so overwhelming."

The timer on the oven went off and Toni went to get the pizza. She placed it on a rack to cool a few minutes before cutting it. She felt a little strange, but she couldn't put her finger on it. Several minutes passed and Boggs appeared by her side.

"Are you okay?"

"What?" Toni realized she must have been zoning out. "Yeah. Just waiting for the pizza to cool before I cut it. Could you hand me the scissors from that drawer?"

Boggs complied, then frowned at her. "Are you sure you're okay?"

Toni nodded. "It's probably just all the excitement of the last two days."

She cut the pizza and put the slices on paper plates, which Boggs carried to the living room. Toni joined her, handing Boggs a napkin.

"Not the normal few days, you know." Toni took a tentative bite of the pepperoni pizza. It was still too hot. "I mean, jeez, we decided to live together, then we bought a loft and two rooms of furniture. And oh, yeah. I found out you're a millionaire."

Boggs laughed. "I guess you're right." She was chewing. "But I trust your instincts. Are you feeling weird like when you thought someone was watching you a few months ago?"

Toni contemplated that for a moment. "Well, not like someone's watching me, no. But I do feel like something's wrong. Maybe it's just all the changes we're making." Even though she was discounting the feeling to Boggs, she was a little concerned. Usually when she'd had these feelings in the past, there was something to them. *It's just all the excitement*, she told herself.

They finished their pizza and chatted about their new loft. Toni pushed the feeling of dread from her mind. Boggs turned on the television and pulled Toni close. They stretched out on the couch and watched a baseball game. Toni felt safe and loved in Boggs's arms. She pulled Boggs's T-shirt out from her shorts and began to caress her stomach. Boggs moaned softly in response, which motivated Toni to explore more. She'd unbuttoned Boggs's shorts and had her mouth on her stomach before Boggs spoke.

"I guess I really don't care if the Cardinals win tonight or not." She pulled Toni on top of her and kissed her deeply.

Toni responded quickly. She felt like a teenager, barely able to keep herself from exploding. Her tongue was desperately searching Boggs's and her hands were pulling at her clothing. The T-shirt hit the floor, followed by her bra.

"Let's go upstairs," Boggs said breathlessly.

Toni jumped up and grabbed Boggs's arm. "Well, hurry up." She pulled and Boggs stood, albeit a little shakily. Her shorts dropped to her ankles.

"I'm at a bit of a disadvantage," she said, looking at her shorts on the floor then pointing to her chest.

"Just the way I like you." Toni held her hand and led her upstairs. Once they reached the bedroom she peeled off her own clothes and pulled down the quilt. "We only have a few weeks left with this bed, so we better make good use of it."

"I knew there was a reason I'm in love with you." Boggs rolled onto the bed and lay on her back with her arms and legs spread. "Use me."

Toni felt her whole body tingle as she crawled on top, her legs straddling Boggs's thigh. Toni kissed her passionately, feeling like she couldn't get close enough. She wanted to touch her, feel her, taste her. She wanted everything and the need was a burning fire inside her. Her hands were all over, trying to touch Boggs everywhere at once while continuing to rock against her leg. Her heart, mind and soul were filled with love for her woman, her partner, her best friend. But her body was overriding every other emotion and her climax came quickly and unexpectedly. She collapsed next to Boggs.

"Sorry," Toni said quietly, then giggled. "Didn't see that coming."

Boggs burst out laughing. "Didn't see that *coming*?"

Toni rolled her eyes. "Okay, well, I guess I did. But that was just a warmup." She smiled coyly and kissed Boggs's lips, then her neck, and began working her way down. Boggs protested for just a moment, but Toni held her where she was. As her hands and mouth found their target, Toni could barely distinguish her own moans from those coming from Boggs. There was no question, this was heaven on earth.

Chapter 14

Jan pulled into the parking lot of Toni's townhouse around midnight. She found Toni's little blue Neon at the edge of the lot in a spot marked with her address and was pleased to see that there was an empty parking space next to it. She pulled her car in, turned off the engine and waited. After ten minutes with no movement around her she got out, taking a plastic gas can out of the back. With work gloves on, she flipped the cap off the end of the nozzle and quickly poured the gasoline over the entire car. She'd done this several times before. When the can was empty, she returned it to her backseat.

She got back in her car and started the engine. She put down the driver's side window. She could smell the strong odor of the gas. Smiling, she lit a cigarette and took a long drag. She knew it wasn't healthy for her to smoke, but she didn't care and there was nothing like that first long drag. She backed out of the space and stopped when she was perpendicular to Toni's car. After another long drag from her cigarette, she shifted into drive and flicked the butt out the window. It landed on the trunk and instantly flames appeared. Any evidence from the cigarette would be incinerated.

Jan was pulling out of the parking lot when she checked her rearview mirror. The entire car was engulfed in fire. *Another job done well.* She was humming to herself as she drove home.

Once she was inside, she fixed herself a rum and Coke and reclined in her favorite chair. She lit another cigarette and called her boss. She tried to sound nonchalant when she told her about the fire, but on the inside she was jumping up and down. *God, I love my job.*

The sound of sirens immediately brought Toni out of her contented sleep. They were getting closer. She slipped out of bed, careful not to wake Boggs, and looked out the bedroom window. A fire truck was pulling into the parking lot.

"What's going on?" Boggs was sitting up, rubbing her eyes.

"Fire truck just pulled into the lot."

Boggs was fully awake now, looking on the floor, apparently for her clothes.

"They're downstairs," Toni said, grinning as she pulled on her own. By the time she got downstairs, Boggs was tying her shoes. Toni grabbed her cell phone and keys and Boggs picked up her fanny pack, which held her gun. They both went out the door.

The firemen were dousing the flames when they got to the lot. It took Toni about a minute to realize it was her car.

"Holy, shit! That's my car." She began to run, but Boggs grabbed her arm.

"I don't think there's much you can do now," Boggs said quietly. "I'm sorry."

Toni stood there, silently staring at her beloved car. When the fire was completely out, she approached one of the firemen. "Thank you," she said, saddened.

He smiled at her. "Your car?"

She nodded.

"I'm really sorry. You got an enemy or something?"

"What?" Toni didn't understand.

"Your car," he explained. "It was torched."

Toni was stunned for a moment. Of course it was torched, she told herself. Cars don't just burst into flames on their own accord. But why would someone want to hurt her? Set her car on fire? What would cause someone to do that? She racked her brain, trying to think of anyone she'd prosecuted who would be able to do that. Most of the serious criminals were still in prison, but maybe family members? It didn't make sense.

"Are you okay?" Boggs put her arm around her. "You said something didn't feel right earlier tonight. I guess you were right."

"But who'd do this?" Toni felt hurt. Not by just the loss of her car, but that someone would act out against her. "I guess I'm just too naïve." She was shaking her head.

"There's a cop," Boggs said, pointing across the parking lot.

They went over and gave the officer Toni's information. After finding out that she was an assistant prosecuting attorney, he called for the crime scene unit. Toni couldn't think of anyone in particular who would have done this, but she told the officer she'd look at her old cases. They sat on the curb and waited.

"I'm so sorry, babe." Boggs put her arm around Toni. "Did you have anything inside?"

Toni shook her head. "Not really. Maybe a couple CDs and a map." A tear rolled down her cheek. "And eighty cents."

Boggs kissed her on the cheek. "We'll be okay. I guess you're getting a new car. Any idea of what kind you want?"

"Oh, gosh, sweetie. I have no idea. I just want to know who

did this."

"Maybe it was random and had nothing to do with you."

"No. I don't think so. Just a feeling, but I think it was definitely for me." Toni scooted closer to Boggs, wondering how long it would take her insurance company to pay.

"I believe you." She held her closer. "We'll figure it out, promise."

As they sat on the curb, Toni felt the dread return. This wasn't the end, she just knew it wasn't. Even though Boggs had her arm around her, she didn't feel safe. And that scared her. She shivered, but not from the cool June breeze.

Chapter 15

Toni and Boggs arrived at work early on Monday morning. Even though they were together most nights, they usually drove separately. This morning Boggs drove them both. Once inside Metro, they went to their own offices. Toni had been at her desk for only fifteen minutes when Anne Mulhoney appeared.

"Are you okay?" she asked from the doorway.

Toni smiled and nodded. She respected her boss greatly and knew how busy she was. Toni was touched that she'd taken the time to stop by. "I'm fine, Anne. Thank you."

"I asked Vicky to look into your cases. She'll see if any are out of jail and check things out."

"Do you think that's necessary?"

"Absolutely," Anne said quickly. "I don't like the idea that some dirtbag thinks he can mess with one of my people. Don't worry about this. We'll find the guy." She smiled and left.

Toni felt a little better. She put in a call to her insurance agent and began working on her cases. By eleven o'clock she was so absorbed in work that she'd almost forgotten the ordeal from last night. The sound of the intercom startled her.

"Good morning, Ms. Barston. Ms. Boggsworth on line two for you," Chloe said. She was the receptionist at Metro and insisted on calling everyone either Mr. or Ms.

"Thank you, Chloe." Toni punched line two. "Hey, Boggs."

"Hi, babe. I was thinking, do you want to stop by a car dealer on the way home tonight?"

"I don't know. I won't get my check from the insurance agency for at least a couple weeks."

"But we can at least look and see what's out there," Boggs offered. "Do you have an idea of what you'd like to get?"

"I loved my Neon, but they don't make those anymore." Toni thought for a moment. "I kinda like the new VW Bugs. I for sure want something that has good gas mileage and is dependable."

"There's a dealer near my place," Boggs said. "Why don't we stop by there and at least take a look. Then we can stop at my place for some clothes and then go to your place?"

"I guess it wouldn't hurt to look." Toni was already pulling up the site on her computer. "Okay."

"I'll meet you at your office at five," Boggs said. "I've got to be out of the office for a while this afternoon. I love you."

"I love you, too." Toni was smiling as she hung up. Even though she still had that odd feeling, she considered herself the luckiest woman in the world. After looking at the new Bugs for a few minutes, she went back to work.

"You can't just buy a car. I mean, you can, but are you nuts?" Toni was standing outside the Volkswagen dealership talking to Boggs.

"But you need a car, babe. And I checked around on the

Internet and this is a good deal. I wouldn't suggest it if it wasn't. I'm pretty tight with money."

"Well, you could have fooled me." Toni was shaking her head. "Why don't we wait until I get the check."

"Because you need a car now," Boggs said matter-of-factly. "And you can replace the money in a couple weeks. Anyway, it's a great car and it's your favorite color, blue. And it's a five-speed." Boggs grinned. "You like it, don't you?"

"Of course. I love it." Toni was shaking her head. "You're crazy, you know that?"

"I know I'm crazy. What's your point? Come on, let's do it."

Toni hugged her so tight that Boggs let out a yelp. "Okay, but I'm paying you back as soon as I get my money."

Boggs shrugged. "Sure. You can pay *us* back." She grabbed Toni's hand and led her back into the showroom.

Thirty minutes later Boggs handed the salesman a check and he handed her the keys. They were standing next to Toni's new car in the dealer's lot when Toni's cell phone rang. She looked at the display. "It's Vicky."

After a few minutes of conversation, Toni hung up. She felt apprehensive.

"What's going on?" Boggs studied her.

"Vicky wants to have a powwow tonight. She said she's got some information, but she didn't want to get into it on the phone. They'll be over at my place in a half-hour."

"Why don't we meet at my house with all that's been going on?"

"I don't want to leave Mr. Rupert alone." Thinking of him right then, alone without protection, made her stomach lurch.

Boggs nodded, a serious look on her face. "You're right." She hugged Toni. "Okay. Well, if Vicky thinks it's important, it probably is." She looked at her watch. "You go ahead and go home. I'll swing by my place and feed the fish and get some clothes. I'll meet you there as soon as I can."

"Okay." She kissed Boggs and got in her car. As she drove home, she wasn't thinking about her brand-new car. The only feeling she had was one of dread. The last time Vicky called a powwow, it was because there was a crazy woman stalking her and she was in danger. And now someone had torched her car. This didn't look good and it certainly didn't feel good.

When she got to her parking lot she saw the scorched spot that had been assigned to her. Instead of pulling in, she parked in the visitor's section.

Toni entered her townhouse and quickly shut the door, putting on the chain. She reached down to pet Mr. Rupert and noticed her hands were shaking. This was ridiculous, she told herself. There was nothing to worry about. *I'm safe.*

She fed Mr. Rupert and started up the stairs to change. Fear gripped her. *There's no one here.* She held the railing tightly. She couldn't hear anything, but still she didn't move. Mr. Rupert appeared at her feet and she felt a little better.

"Come on, boy. Let's go upstairs," she said loudly, as though that would make her safe. She peeked into the bathroom. No one there. She tiptoed into her bedroom. Empty. Finally she pushed open the door to her walk-in closet. She let out a loud sigh.

"We're okay," she told him.

He nosed around the closet a few moments and, seemingly satisfied, hopped up on the bed and began to bathe.

Toni took that as a sign that everything was okay. She quickly hung up her blazer and dropped her slacks and blouse into the dry-cleaning pile. She pulled on a pair of olive cargo shorts and a white T-shirt. Normally she wouldn't have bothered with shoes, but she slipped on her favorite red tennis shoes and went back downstairs. She called Mr. Rupert to follow her, almost afraid to be alone in her own place.

She opened a beer and looked at her watch. It would be at least fifteen minutes before anyone arrived. She paced around the living room. She noticed her briefcase by the door and retrieved her wallet, keys and cell phone, putting them in her pockets. She never carried a purse. Now she was ready. For what? To run away? She didn't know, but she didn't want to be caught off-guard. She didn't know what to do, so she went back upstairs to check her e-mail.

Fifteen minutes later the sound of the doorbell made her jump. She ran downstairs and looked out the peephole. It was Boggs. She fumbled with the chain and yanked the door open, grabbing Boggs by the arm and pulling her inside. Boggs looked alarmed.

"Are you okay?" She scanned the room, looking for anything out of place.

Toni hugged her. "I just scared myself, I guess." She felt embarrassed.

Boggs put her bag on the floor and held Toni for a minute. "It'll be okay, babe. Honest."

Boggs had changed into jean shorts, a T-shirt and Tevas. She was wearing a white lightweight sweatshirt jacket. When she took off her jacket, Toni saw she was wearing her shoulder holster and breathed a sigh of relief.

Boggs gauged her reaction and grinned. "Armed and ready, babe." She went into the kitchen and got a beer, petting Mr. Rupert on the way.

Within ten minutes, everyone else arrived. Vicky, Patty and Johnnie were sitting on one side of the couch. Each had a beer, and Vicky and Patty had notebooks in hand. Toni and Boggs were on the other side of the sectional couch along with Mr. Rupert.

Toni pulled her legs up on the couch and wrapped her arms around them. She was still scared, but she wasn't sure why. Her closest friends were right here. Vicky was wearing shorts with a polo shirt untucked. Toni could see the bulge on her side and knew it was her service weapon in a pancake holster. Patty was also wearing shorts, but she had a fanny pack around her waist. Toni assumed her gun was inside. And Johnnie, of course, was wearing jeans with a pressed white Oxford shirt. The sleeves were rolled up partway. When she crossed her legs, Toni noticed her ankle holster. Seeing everyone armed made her feel a little safer.

"I guess you're all wondering why I called this meeting," Vicky said seriously.

Everyone laughed and Boggs threw a pillow at her.

"Seriously, though," Vicky continued, "we need to talk this out. First, we know that someone torched Toni's car. I've got the case, by the way." She looked at Toni, who smiled. "The crime scene guys didn't find anything useful. All we know is that it was soaked with gasoline. There wasn't a bomb or anything, so the guy probably lit a match or something. That tells us he was here at the time, then we assume he drove away. The guys canvassed the units around the parking lot and came up with nothing."

"So we're still at square one," Johnnie said.

"On this, yes." Vicky opened her notebook. "As you know, I've been looking into Kevin Tucker's past—"

"Hang on," Johnnie interrupted. "Fill me in here."

"Sorry. Tucker is the victim in Toni's murder case."

Toni gave Johnnie all the pertinent information and Vicky continued.

"We know now that Tucker was a dealer, mostly in the gay bars and strip clubs. We got some e-mails from Jim's computer. He's the son of the guy who killed Tucker. Apparently Jim and Tucker got involved romantically and Tucker convinced him to try ecstasy. Then there was talk of a new designer drug. That's what killed Jim."

"Did you get that from the tox reports?" Toni was curious.

"Yes, those came back today," Vicky explained. "So, I'm thinking we can maybe find the bigwig in this organization if we dig deeper into Tucker. I called Mike Johnson because he's got the case and I told him what I was thinking. He pretty much shut me down."

"That's where I come in," Patty said. "I've been assigned to Mike and we did the search of Tucker's apartment today. It was gross, by the way."

Vicky laughed. "That's why you make the big bucks now."

Patty rolled her eyes. "Anyway, Mike just stood there in the living room for a couple minutes. Then he said this was a waste of time. I figured it was some kind of test for me, so I put on some gloves and started nosing around. He just stood and watched me. When I found Tucker's computer I started to unplug it. He kinda freaked a little. Again I thought this was some kind of test, so I explained that we had to unplug it and take in the hard drive so the forensic people could look and see if there was anything there. He just nodded. That was the end of the search."

Vicky was anxious to continue. "Patty told me this early this afternoon and at first I thought maybe Mike was just getting lazy. You know, close to retirement or something. So I told Patty to ask Mike to look at whatever they found on Tucker's body."

"This was so cool," Patty interjected. "I acted like an excited 'new' detective, wanting to cover all the bases. He seemed pissed that I asked but showed me the stuff. The only things in the box were a wallet, car keys and a necklace. So I asked him about a cell phone, saying that almost everyone had one. He shrugged, so I looked at the inventory sheet and it had a cell phone listed. When I pointed this out he said it must have gotten lost. Then I asked if we should search his car since there were car keys there. Again he shrugged. Then his cell rang and he left. I put the box back and called Vicky."

"I knew there was a cell phone and I'd already gotten the phone records." Vicky took a sip of her beer.

The doorbell rang and Toni jumped. "Who is that?" After she said it she realized how stupid it was and felt her face burn with embarrassment.

"Oh," Vicky said. "I ordered pizza for us." She went to the door, paid the delivery guy and put the pizzas on the coffee table.

Toni got paper plates and napkins from the kitchen and Boggs brought out fresh beer for everyone.

While they ate, Vicky continued. "There were a lot of numbers, but one came up pretty regularly." She popped a piece of pepperoni in her mouth. Vicky always ate all the pepperoni first, then the rest of the pizza. "It's registered to an old lady in Arkansas who, by the way, is dead."

"Maybe it's his grandmother," Boggs suggested as she grabbed another slice of mushroom pizza.

"Then he's been calling *really* long distance for the last few years. She's been dead that long." Vicky laughed and took a drink of her beer. "Anyway, he doesn't have—or didn't have, I should say—any grandparents. They died before he was born. So, I'm thinking this person could be the boss, or at least someone higher up in the organization. I went to get a search warrant for Dead Granny's phone, and get this, Judge Crayton turned me down."

"On what basis?" Toni was confused. This certainly seemed enough to get a warrant.

"She said not enough probable cause and that was that."

"That makes no sense," Toni said, frowning. "The woman is dead and obviously she hasn't been making or receiving calls. Why wouldn't the judge issue a warrant?" She thought for a moment. "Unless she has a reason not to."

"Exactly what I thought," Vicky said. "So I went to Anne Mulhoney."

"Oh, my God," Toni exclaimed. "Do you think this is connected to Judge Smith and Butch?"

"Wait a sec," Johnnie said. "Let me see if I've got this right. You guys thought that the judge and that defense lawyer were being bribed a while back, right?"

Toni nodded.

"And Anne Mulhoney had you looking into that, off the record?"

Vicky nodded. "But I haven't gotten anywhere. I didn't have enough to get their phone records or anything. But Anne sensed for a long time that they were up to no good, so I've been digging for something solid. After I told Anne about Judge Crayton, she rewrote my affidavit for the warrant and went with me to Judge Baker. She signed immediately."

"So either Judge Crayton is in on this, or she has a different view of the Fourth Amendment," Toni said. "She said on Saturday that she was switching from civil back to criminal. Maybe she's just being careful."

"You saw her Saturday?" Boggs looked puzzled.

"Yes. She came over to say hello to Vicky at Patty's party."

"She stopped by the table and wished me a happy birthday," Patty said. "I thought that was odd, but cool."

"Do you know her?" Boggs still looked confused.

"I testified once in her courtroom when I first started. I think it was right before she transferred to civil. But otherwise, no. I don't know her." Patty shrugged.

"I think that's a little weird," Boggs said. "I think we need to watch her."

"I agree," Vicky said. "And so does Anne."

"What about the phone records for Dead Granny?" Toni asked.

"This is where it gets interesting." Vicky took another drink. "Dead Granny's been busy. She also called Tucker on a regular basis. A bunch of other numbers I haven't tracked down yet, but Judge Smith and Butch are on there. And there's another one that certainly sticks out. Mike Johnson."

"The detective?" Johnnie asked.

"One and the same," Vicky answered.

"Well, that makes things a little more complicated," Boggs

said. "We've got to be very careful. Hard to say who's involved and how deep this goes." She took a sip of her beer. "Hey, what about checking the GPS thing on the phone?"

"Already tried," Vicky said. "It's been disabled. All we know is that all of the calls came from Fairfield, according to the pinging off the towers."

Toni was shaking her head, unable to fathom the depth of corruption. "So Judge Smith and Butch were involved. But here's what I don't get. The case I was on with Butch a few months ago was a burglary. It had nothing to do with drugs."

"Maybe this organization is more than just drugs," Johnnie offered. "It could involve guns, prostitution or political crap."

"Maybe." Toni took another bite of her mushroom pizza and then looked at Vicky. "Hey. Remember a few months ago when you said one of your sources told you that Judge Smith was involved in kiddie porn? Could that be the connection?"

Vicky sipped at her beer. "Hmm. That's a real possibility."

"That makes sense to me," Johnnie said. "Organized crime within the world of bad porn. And by bad I mean kiddie or the snuff films."

"Snuff films?" Patty seemed confused.

"Those horrible things that involve the rape of a woman and then they actually kill her," Johnnie explained.

A wave of sadness and disgust swept the room and everyone fell silent. Toni shivered. After a deep breath, she shook those terrible images from her mind and got back to the topic. "And I get that and it seems possible," she said, "but how does this relate to me?" She looked at Vicky. "I got the impression when you called that you had some connection to me."

"We do. Well, sort of." Vicky pointed to Patty and took another drink of her beer.

Patty finished her last piece of pizza and put her plate on the coffee table. "Cathy called me this morning," she said. "You know, my sister Lori's friend?"

Everyone nodded.

Patty took a sip of beer. "The first thing she asked me was if you were okay, Toni."

Toni felt that dread again. Cathy's psychic abilities had proven to be accurate a few months ago when she knew she'd been in danger. "Had you told her about my car?"

"No, but she knew about it anyway. At least she knew there'd been a fire. She didn't know it was your car. Anyway, she told me that you kept coming to her mind and that she sensed danger."

Toni felt her heart beat faster. She'd been afraid when she came home tonight. But afraid with no real reason. As far as she knew then, the car was a random act. But now that Cathy felt she was in danger, Toni realized her fear was real. She wasn't sure what she should do.

Boggs put her arm around her. "It'll be okay, babe."

"Why are crazy people always fascinated with me. Jeez!"

Boggs held her tighter.

"There's more," Patty said. "Cathy told me that she was almost certain that the fire was related to drugs. She wasn't sure how, but that's what she was getting. And she said she felt like someone was obsessed with you. Not the same as last time, but still obsessed."

"Oh, jeez." Toni felt almost hopeless. She curled up closer to Boggs.

"Don't worry, babe," Boggs said tenderly. "We figured it out last time and we'll figure it out this time."

"That's right," Johnnie said. "You've got four reasonably intelligent women here to help you."

"And a psychic," Patty added.

"Thanks, guys." Toni smiled at everyone and kissed Boggs on the cheek. She felt a little better. "Now, let's try and figure this out." She sat up and took a sip of her beer. She sounded more confident than she actually felt. "If Cathy's right and this is all connected, maybe we can see how I fit in."

"Right," Boggs said. "Let's assume for starters that the guy who runs this organization had the judge and Butch on the payroll. And Mike."

"Or woman," Johnnie said. "We've found a lot more women heading up organized crime lately. And by we I mean the FBI."

"Okay." Boggs smirked at Johnnie. "Let's say 'the boss.' Anyway, the judge and Butch are killed because of Toni."

"Hey!" Toni protested.

"You know what I mean. Then one of his, or her, dealers is killed and Toni has the case."

"That's stretching it a little, don't you think?" Johnnie did not seem convinced.

"Well, maybe." Boggs thought a minute. "But it would put a crimp in the organization if one of your dealers is wiped out."

"Okay," Toni said. "If the boss person thinks I'm the cause of his, or her, problems, then maybe I could see the connection."

"But why torch your car?" Patty asked. "I don't mean to seem cruel or to scare you or anything, but why not just kill you? This is organized crime, right?"

"I agree," Johnnie said. "If we're talking real organized crime, they usually just get rid of a problem." She looked at Toni apologetically. "Sorry."

"That's okay." Toni smiled. "I agree. At least from what I know from my vast knowledge of this area. And by vast knowledge I mean that I've watched *The Godfather* one and two."

Vicky was tapping her fingers on her notepad. "What kind of person are we talking about, Toni? I mean psychologically?"

Toni leaned back on the couch with her beer. "Well, the stereotypical head of organized crime is usually very logical. They're very much like any CEO of a big company. The main difference is that the law doesn't apply to them. They do what they need to do for their business. And if that means paying a judge, then so be it."

"So how does torching your car come into play?" Patty asked.

"It would be a tactic to scare me, I guess. But that doesn't make sense here. I'm not involved in anything right now that would affect anyone's business. At least as far as I know. The only cases I have right now are pretty run-of-the-mill. You know— burglary, DWI and drug possession. I don't have any trafficking cases or kiddie porn. The only thing I have that relates is Kevin Tucker's murder."

"But what if this is a crazy person?" Boggs seemed serious. "Nothing personal, babe, but you seem to attract those kinds of folks."

Toni rolled her eyes. "Gee, thanks." She took another sip of beer. "But if we were dealing with another crazy person"—she made quote marks with her fingers—"and I use that term clinically."

Everyone laughed.

"And we appreciate your clinical expertise and correct psycho jargon," Vicky said. "Go ahead. What would they do?"

"Well, I could see them attempting to take something from me since I apparently took something from them. So, they take my car from me."

"And that would be the end of it?" Patty asked.

Toni shrugged. She had a feeling it would be much more than that.

"I don't like this," Boggs said. "What if things continue to go wrong with the organization. Or at least in the eyes of the boss. Then what?"

Toni shuddered. If they were really dealing with a person who had a true mental illness, it would be impossible to predict what they'd do next. And if Cathy was right in believing this person was obsessed with her, then anything that went wrong would be her fault. The last crazy person almost killed her. And Boggs. *Oh, my God. Boggs.* She shuddered again and this time Boggs must have noticed.

"What's wrong?" she asked.

97

Toni looked at all her friends. If she was in danger, then so were they. "If the boss thinks I'm responsible," she explained, "then every time something goes wrong, he or she will try to hurt me by taking something from me. First my car, then maybe my home or my friends." She looked down at Mr. Rupert, who was curled up next to her on the couch, and felt tears well up in her eyes. She pulled him onto her lap and kissed his head. "Or maybe even Mr. Rupert." She couldn't stop the tears now.

"Son of a bitch," Boggs yelled. She jumped up and began pacing. "What the hell are we going to do? We don't even know who 'the boss' is." She looked at Toni, who still had tears streaming down her face, and sat down next to her. "I'm sorry, babe." She put her arm around her. "We'll protect you and Mr. Rupert. Don't worry, okay?"

Toni wiped her cheek and snuggled in closer to Boggs. "I know," she said. "I just scared myself is all."

"We need a plan," Vicky said. "We need to check out Dead Granny. Maybe one of her relatives lives here. The phone number was issued to her when she was still alive, so that could be a lead."

"I'll take care of that," Johnnie offered. She got a notepad from her messenger bag and wrote down the specifics that Vicky gave her. "What about bank records from the judge and Butch? Do you have enough to get a warrant?"

"I don't think so." Vicky was tapping her pencil on her own list. "But I'll talk to Anne about it tomorrow. I'm thinking we'll stick with Judge Baker. Anne is confident she's okay."

"And I'll see if I can get anything from Mike," Patty said. "Maybe he'll slip up."

"Be very careful," Vicky instructed her. "Maybe just keep track of any phone calls he gets that make him leave the room, make note of the time. If it was legit, he wouldn't care if you heard."

"Isn't there something else I can do?"

"Follow up on the hard drive from Tucker's apartment," Vicky suggested. "Maybe there's something on there."

"I've got an idea," Boggs said suddenly. "If Tucker was the main dealer out of the gay bars, they probably replaced him. Maybe if we nose around we can find his replacement."

"We need to be very careful," Vicky reminded her. "We have no idea of who's involved."

"I bet we could trust Bert," Toni said. Bert Newton was one of the bartenders at the Cat's Meow, a mostly lesbian bar. Toni had always enjoyed talking to her.

"We could absolutely trust Bert," Johnnie said. "Remember? She said if she could ever help us out in any way that we should call her."

"That's right," Boggs said as she squeezed Toni's shoulder and grinned. "And she's got a huge crush on Toni."

"I'll talk to her later on tonight," Johnnie said. "She may have known Tucker. Do you have a picture?" she asked Vicky.

Vicky dug through her backpack, which was on the floor. "Here," she said, producing a copy of his mugshot and handing it to Johnnie.

"Well, you're certainly prepared, aren't you?" Johnnie said sarcastically.

"Always," Vicky said with a wink. "It comes in handy, especially on dates."

"What about Toni's protection?" Boggs looked concerned. "They know where she lives. We're moving to a loft, but not for another three weeks."

"What?" Patty sat up straight. "You guys are moving in together? How come you didn't tell us? This is so cool."

"We found the place Saturday," Toni explained. She described the loft to the others and for a few minutes she was completely caught up in the excitement, forgetting the reason they were all gathered tonight.

"And it's got an excellent security system," Boggs added when

99

Toni finished. "But what can we do in the mean time?"

"I can set up some cameras," Johnnie suggested. "On the front door and the parking lot. And we've got this laser thing that I can put on the door and windows. When the beam is broken it can set off an alarm or call a cell phone or do whatever you want. It's pretty slick."

"And how are you going to justify that?" Vicky asked.

"Well, I am the station chief here in Fairfield, you know." Johnnie grinned. "And this looks to me like organized crime, which then could be racketeering, which is a federal crime. Federal crime equals FBI, so I don't see a problem."

"That sounds good to me." Boggs finished her beer and got another round for herself and Vicky and Johnnie. "And I'll stay with Toni at night."

"Gee," Vicky said. "We'd hate to put you out, Boggs."

"Very funny. We need to pack anyway."

"What can I do?" Toni asked. "I feel like I'm letting you guys do everything." She thought for a moment. "Hey, maybe I can look for cases that Butch had and see who he was representing. Maybe that'll give us something."

"Good idea," Vicky said. "I'm going to update Anne and Captain Billings. He needs to know what's going on. He's already talked to Anne about the stuff with the judge and Butch, but he doesn't know the rest."

"Do you think Cathy would be willing to come over and talk to us?" Toni asked Patty. "Like she did a few months ago, see if she gets anything?"

"I'll call her and find out." Patty pulled out her phone. While she talked, the others made sure there was nothing else they could do for now. Patty closed her phone. "She can come over tomorrow night at six thirty. She has another appointment later on."

"Perfect," Toni said. "Maybe she can give us something to go on, some type of clue."

"I'm going to head over the the Cat's Meow and talk to Bert," Johnnie said as she picked up her messenger bag, pulling her pack of cigarettes from inside. "I'll have the cameras and the lasers set up tomorrow." She looked at Toni. "Do you have an extra set of keys?"

Toni went to the kitchen and searched through her junk drawer. After several minutes she located the keys and tossed them to Johnnie. "Is it just you coming inside?" She felt a little apprehensive about allowing a stranger into her home, especially with Mr. Rupert there alone.

"It'll be me and a tech," Johnnie said, an unlit cigarette hanging from her lips. "And don't worry, I won't let him out of my sight, okay?"

Toni smiled slightly, feeling embarrassed about her paranoia. "Thank you."

"Okay," Vicky announced as she got up. "Everyone's got their jobs to do and we'll meet here tomorrow by six thirty. What about food? I won't have time to go home and eat."

"How about if I pick up sandwiches for us at Subs-R-Us?" Toni grabbed a pad of paper to take orders. "I've got plenty of beer and soda. What do you guys want?"

They placed their orders and Vicky stopped at the door. "Hey, what about your car?" She looked at Boggs. "Are you driving her to work?"

Toni answered for Boggs and smiled. She'd completely forgotten about her new Bug. "We got a new car after work." She kissed Boggs on the cheek. "It's in the parking lot now."

"Is that your Bug?" Patty asked. "I noticed it when I pulled in. It's so cute. How does it drive?"

"Great, I guess." Toni shook her head. "I don't think I even noticed. Vicky called just as we were getting ready to leave the dealer."

"Is it in your spot?" Vicky asked.

Toni shook her head.

"Good. Does it have plates or just temporary tags?"

"Temporary. The old ones were sorta burned."

"I'd suggest you pick up the new plates tomorrow and continue to park in the visitor's section. At least for now, okay?" Vicky hugged her on her way out.

After they all left, Toni and Boggs picked up the beer bottles and pizza boxes and took them into the kitchen. Toni noticed her hands were shaking and she just stared at them. Boggs looked over and quickly wrapped her arms around her.

"I know you're scared, babe. But it'll be okay. We'll figure this out. We always do." She kissed her. "Let's get our minds off it for a while," she suggested. "It's still early. I've got some boxes in my SUV. Why don't I go get them and we can pack some stuff? I'll take these pizza boxes out to the Dumpster and be right back."

"That sounds good," Toni said. "We'll be out of time before we know it." She opened the front door for Boggs and quickly locked it behind her. *This is stupid. Why am I so scared? She'll be back in a minute.* She waited by the door, looking out the peephole. Nothing. *What's taking her so long?* Toni's heart was racing. She started to pace and patted her pockets, making sure her phone, wallet and keys were still there. This was ridiculous, she told herself. What good would those things be? So she could run out to the parking lot like an idiot and jump in her car? *I need a gun.*

A noise outside made her jump. She felt a knot in her stomach and she froze. What was that? She tried to make her legs move, tried to get back to the door so she could look out, but nothing on her body seemed to work.

Another loud bang.

"It's me, babe," Boggs yelled.

Toni felt her whole body go limp, but she managed to unlock the door. Boggs was balancing at least six empty boxes and had apparently kicked the door with her foot. "Sorry," she said as she took some of the boxes from Boggs.

"You look a little pale," Boggs said as she set down the remaining boxes. "Are you okay?"

Toni sighed and plopped down on the couch next to Mr. Rupert. "I keep scaring myself," she admitted. "And I feel so stupid. You were gone two minutes and I panicked. I want a gun."

Boggs joined her on the couch. "Okay. We can get you a gun. In fact, because of your job, you can carry a concealed weapon if you want."

"Do you think I'm being too paranoid?" Toni was feeling embarrassed and ashamed of her behavior.

"Not at all," Boggs said tenderly. "Not at all. You're just being careful. Now, if you'd never handled a gun before, I'd be a little leery. But I don't see a problem. Metro's already done a background check on you, so you'll probably only have to pay for the permit. We can do it tomorrow, okay?"

She hugged Boggs. "Thank you, hon. It means so much to me that you understand." She jumped off the couch and grabbed a box. "I feel better already. Let's do some packing."

They spent the rest of the evening packing books, knick-knacks, CDs and some of Toni's kitchen items. Boggs retrieved several more boxes and by eleven o'clock Toni was exhausted. All of the boxes except one were neatly labeled. The remaining box had items to donate, including several duplicate CDs. They were sitting on the floor in the living room.

"That wasn't too bad," Toni said as she sipped her lemon water and Boggs taped the last box shut.

"We got a lot done." Boggs opened her own bottle of water and drank half. "I think we should celebrate." She scooted closer to Toni and kissed her softly. "In fact, I think we should celebrate every night." She caressed Toni's face and kissed her again, this time more passionately. Her hands began to wander and she was able to unbutton Toni's shorts without breaking stride. When her hand reached inside, Toni moaned softly.

"Don't you want to go upstairs?" Toni whispered.

"No. I'm busy," Boggs said, continuing to kiss her. Somehow she managed to pull up Toni's T-shirt and unhook her bra without removing her other hand from inside Toni's shorts.

Toni attempted to touch Boggs somewhere, anywhere, but her position made it impossible. "I want to touch you. Let me touch you."

Boggs removed her mouth from Toni's breast and smiled. "I'm busy" was all she said before returning to her nipple.

Toni breathed deeply and sighed, enjoying every sensation. "Okay, but if you get carpet burns, don't blame me." She thought she heard Boggs chuckle before she lost all awareness except for the feel of Boggs's hands and mouth on her. All thoughts of crazy people and paranoia left her and the only thought in her mind when she climaxed was how much she loved Boggs.

Chapter 16

Toni awoke on Tuesday morning feeling a little disoriented. She opened her eyes and saw boxes. She shook her head and sat up. She couldn't believe that she'd slept through the night on the living room floor. She was as naked as a jaybird and there was a blanket and pillows from the couch next to her. She blinked a few times and saw Boggs through the opening to the kitchen holding up a cup of coffee.

"Do you want a cup before you shower?" she asked. "And by the way, you look great in the morning."

Toni got up off the floor, not bothering to cover herself, and went to the kitchen. "I'll take a cup to go, thank you." She kissed Boggs, noticing she was already dressed. "I'm assuming the shower is free?"

"Yes, unless Mr. Rupert is still up there." She handed a cup of coffee to Toni and kissed her. "Last night was frickin' unbelievable," she said, grinning.

Toni took a sip of her coffee and headed upstairs. "If you think last night was good, just wait until tonight," she called from the stairs. "I'm in charge."

Boggs popped into Toni's office at around one o'clock and glanced at the new license plates on her desk. "I see you got the new tags."

"Yeah. I went next door to city hall. I didn't know until today that there was a DMV office there." She turned away from her computer and smiled at Boggs. "And I've got a list of Butch's clients for the past two years. A lot of big names. I don't know if it'll help us at all, though."

"You never know." Boggs sat in the only available chair. "On a different subject, I've got the paperwork for your gun permit." She held up the papers. "But you have to take a firearms safety course."

Toni frowned, but then she remembered. "Hey, I took the course. I took it my last semester in law school for research for a class." She quickly looked up the phone number for the shooting range where she took the course and requested a copy of her certificate to be faxed to her office. Five minutes later it was in her hands.

"If you've got some time we can walk over now and pay the fee. I talked to Captain Billings this morning and he said they'd give you a temporary permit immediately because of the circumstances."

Toni checked her daily calendar. "I don't have anything in court this afternoon, so let's go ahead." She grabbed her wallet and checkbook from her briefcase. As they headed down the hall she saw Anne Mulhoney.

"Hi, Toni. Boggs. Are you two going to lunch?"

"No," Toni said, holding up the papers. "Gun permit."

106

"Good idea," Anne said. "Do you have a gun yet?"

"No," Toni said. "I thought we'd go somewhere after work tomorrow."

"Do you have anything on the docket this afternoon?"

"No, why?" Toni asked. "Do you need me to do something?"

"Not at all." Anne smiled. "Why don't you take the rest of the afternoon and go over to Tom's Gun Shoppe after you get your permit. I'll call him and tell him you're coming and he'll give you a good deal."

Toni raised an eyebrow. She had no idea that her boss was familiar with guns.

"My husband Bill and I like to shoot," she explained. "And Tom's a friend of ours. Go ahead. I'm sure you'll feel better once you get one. Of course, you've got Boggs here."

Boggs nodded and smiled at the recognition.

"Thank you, Anne," Toni said. "I appreciate it."

As Anne walked away, Toni was shaking her head. "I couldn't ask for a better boss. Let me go ahead and get my things from my office and then we can leave after we get the permit." She got her briefcase and blazer and picked up the list of clients she'd compiled.

By four o'clock that afternoon Toni was the owner of a Smith & Wesson M & P Compact nine-millimeter pistol. It had a three-and-a-half-inch barrel with both front and rear sights and weighed only a little over twenty-one ounces empty. The overall height was four-point-three inches. The magazine held twelve rounds, with one in the chamber. She also had a pancake holster with a thumb break for safety.

"They've got a range in the back if you want to give it a try," Boggs suggested. "It'd probably be good if you got a feel for it, you know?" She bought an extra box of ammunition and paid for a booth.

Toni loaded the magazine with ease and slapped it into the butt of the pistol. She put on safety glasses and ear protection and looked downrange at the target. It had been many years since she'd practiced, but she felt comfortable and confident. She raised her weapon and looked down the sight. It was helpful having a rear sight. She took a deep breath, letting out half before squeezing the trigger. There was just a slight kick, less than she'd expected. Her shot was a little off-center. She frowned. She was a bit rusty. She tried again. Perfect. Ten more shots hit dead center. She took off her ear protection and turned to look at Boggs.

"It feels good," she said. "Good balance, not as loud as I expected." She picked up the spent cartridges and realized that having a gun in her hands made her feel much safer. Why, she didn't know. She had no idea if someone was actually after her, and even if that was true, she had no clue who it was. Still, a gun made her feel less vulnerable.

Boggs was just staring at her, her mouth wide open.

"What?" Toni was puzzled. "Why are you looking at me like that? Do I have something on my face?" She reached up and brushed her cheek.

Boggs burst out laughing. "No, you don't have anything on your face, babe." She was shaking her head. "I know you said a while ago that you were a good shot, but holy shit! You're amazing."

Toni felt her face flush. Even though she was proud of her marksmanship, compliments usually embarrassed her. "Um, thanks." She looked at her new pistol. "Oh, I guess I should get a gun cleaning kit."

Boggs helped her gather her things. "I've got one at home, babe. Let's stop there so I can feed the fish and we'll clean your gun."

Toni glanced at her watch, then smiled at the woman she adored. "Okay. That'll still give us enough time to pick up the subs and get back to my place by six." She took Boggs by the hand and headed to the parking lot.

Chapter 17

The woman finished some work at her desk in the study and glanced at the clock on the wall. It was nearly five o'clock, so she fixed herself a glass of Famous Grouse. After stirring the Scotch three times, she tapped her finger on the rim and licked the liquid. That first taste always soothed her. She took a generous swallow and centered the glass on her coaster.

She shook her head. Since her brief meeting with Toni on Saturday night, she couldn't stop thinking about her. At times she was so filled with rage at how this one bitch completely screwed up her organization, she'd find herself fantasizing about torturing her. But as soon as that vision crystallized in her mind, she'd find herself wanting Toni for herself. Both emotions were intense and the competition between the two was driving her to drink more than usual. She hoped Jan could get Toni's e-mail address soon.

She finished her drink in two quick gulps and fixed herself another. She was halfway through that one when Davey called. Her brother described the new designer drug he'd created as a cross between ecstasy and GHB. He'd tried it out on his girl-friend the night before and now went on and on about how well it worked. Created in both liquid and pill form, he seemed proud of the fact that he put a big *D* on the pills. He also informed her he needed more ingredients to do the next batch. She wrote down what he needed and congratulated him. She'd have Jan get him the ingredients he needed and also pick up what he had later on tonight.

After hanging up, she made a few entries into her computer to reflect her expected costs for the next batch of drugs. She replayed Davey's description of the effects of D, as he now called it. Maybe she could use it on Toni. She thought about how won-derful it would be if Toni willingly went to bed with her. And if Davey was right, the sex would be absolutely mind blowing. She could have almost four hours of fun and Toni would have no idea the next day. The idea excited her and she was grinning as she fixed herself a third drink.

She returned to her tall, dark leather chair and leaned back, closing her eyes and once again fantasizing about Toni. *But what if something goes wrong?* She opened her eyes and sat up straight. She reached for the lead glass tumbler and took a long swallow before she realized her mistake. She set the glass back on its coaster and stared at it. *Oh, my, God! I drank first.* Her heart was beating wildly and her hands were shaking. She couldn't remem-ber the last time that happened. How could she have been so stupid? She tried to replay the last few minutes, desperately hoping that she had, in fact, stirred the drink three times and tapped her finger twice. *This can't be happening.* She knew in her heart that she'd forgotten. This wasn't good. Bad things would certainly happen now and it'd happened because she was think-ing of Toni. She ran her fingers through her hair five times but felt no relief. *Fuck. Fuck. Fuck.*

She was panicking and started to pace. This was a bad sign, she told herself. Once it started, everything else would follow and her life would be ruined. She had crossed the room four times and was about to sit back down when she realized that she must make it five. After the fifth time she felt a little better. She knew she must somehow make this right. Shaking, she picked up her glass and heard the ice cubes rattle as she carried it to the small sink at the bar. She emptied the glass and washed it. Then she washed it again, and again. She dried it thoroughly and set it down next to the three matching tumblers. She washed her hands while counting to thirty, dried them, then picked up her glass again, carefully putting in three ice cubes and filling it exactly right with Famous Grouse. Her hand was still shaking as she carried it back to her desk and sat down, putting the drink in the center of the coaster.

She stared at the glass for several minutes before finally stirring it three times with her left index finger. She tapped the rim lightly twice and licked the Scotch from her finger. She took a deep breath before lifting the glass to her lips. She felt the smooth burn of the Scotch going down her throat and her body finally began to relax. It would be okay now, she told herself. She just needed to be more careful.

By the time she finished the drink she had her plan. She wasn't quite sure of the details yet, but she knew that she'd have Toni in her bed very soon. She fantasized about what all that would entail as she waited for Jan to arrive.

Chapter 18

Toni and Boggs arrived at her townhouse around five thirty. They were carrying two twelve-packs of beer, a twelve-pack of Diet Mountain Dew, six sub sandwiches, five empty packing boxes, a small duffle with Boggs's clothes and Toni's briefcase. Boggs had one of the empty boxes on her head and they were laughing as Toni unlocked the front door. They'd just maneuvered themselves inside when an alarm sounded and Toni dropped the soda and stared at Boggs. Boggs put down all her stuff and began looking for the keypad. She found it on the wall behind the door and quickly punched in some numbers and the room fell silent.

"Shit," Toni said, relieved yet laughing. "That'll get your adrenaline pumping. I completely forgot about Johnnie setting that up today."

"Me, too." Boggs closed the front door and picked up the

beer and soda. "She called me this morning and asked what code we wanted. I think you were in court." She told Toni the code sequence while she put the drinks in the fridge. She opened a beer for herself. "You want a beer?"

Toni was petting Mr. Rupert and reassuring him. "Yeah. A beer sounds good. I'm going to run up and change and check my e-mail real quick."

Toni changed into jean shorts and a big T-shirt and slipped on a pair of red argyle tennis shoes. She looked at her feet and grinned.

"What do you think, Mr. Rupert? Pretty cool, huh?"

Mr. Rupert sniffed her shoes and looked up at her with his mouth open.

"You think they smell bad?"

She laughed at his response and clicked on her e-mail. She scrolled through them, deleting most of them without reading them. There was an online newsletter about mental illness that she decided she'd read later and a note from Aunt Doozie. She read that one, jotting down the flight information. Mr. Rupert meowed loudly, rubbing his huge head against her leg.

"Okay, buddy." She scratched his head and followed him downstairs.

Boggs had stacked the empty boxes in the corner of the dining room and was now in the kitchen getting out chips and napkins. Toni noticed her briefcase near the door and remembered her new gun was inside. She pulled it out, along with its holster, and quickly slipped it on her waistband, pulling her shirt over the top. It felt a little strange but she immediately felt safer.

Back in the kitchen she and Boggs piled all the subs on a plate, keeping them in their wrappers because the type of sub was written on the paper. She carried them into the living room and set them on the coffee table. Boggs followed with the rest of the things and handed Toni an opened beer. Toni plopped down on the couch.

"Oh, shit." Toni reached back and adjusted her gun.

Boggs grinned. "It takes a while to get used to wearing it," she said as she lifted her own shirt and pointed. "I usually wear it here, just behind my right side."

"I'm such a dork." Toni laughed. "It's like I'm playing cop or something. But still, I feel a little better having it. And, of course, I have you." She pulled Boggs down on the couch and kissed her. Unfortunately they were interrupted by the doorbell.

Toni looked out the peephole, saw all four guests and let them in. Each was carrying some type of food or drink.

"Did you all ride together?"

"No," Vicky said. "Believe it or not, we met in the parking lot." She went to the kitchen to put her beer in the refrigerator. "Hey, Toni. Did you get your tags today?"

"Crap," Toni said, shaking her head. "I did, but I forgot to put them on."

Johnny was still standing near the front door, petting Mr. Rupert. "I'll put them on for you."

Toni thanked her and retrieved them from her briefcase.

Johnnie pointed to the keypad. "Did it work okay?"

"Scared the shit out of me," Toni replied. "Good thing Boggs was with me."

Johnnie laughed. "Sorry about that. But I didn't want to leave the code on a message for you." She frowned at Boggs. "Why didn't you tell her?"

"I forgot," Boggs said. "Anyway, I was with her all afternoon."

Johnnie rolled her eyes, lit a cigarette and went out to the parking lot with Toni's new tags for her Bug.

"Ugh." Boggs sighed and shook her head, while looking at Toni. "Agent Perfect strikes again."

Toni kissed her on the cheek. "That's just how she is, hon. Don't worry about it."

"But sometimes I feel like she thinks I can't take care of you. Just pisses me off. You know she still has the hots for you."

"Well, she can keep her hots to herself. I'm in love with you, so there." She kissed her quickly on the mouth this time and went to the couch where Patty, Vicky and Cathy were already seated. Patty and Cathy were drinking soda and Vicky had just opened a beer.

"Cathy said we can start as soon as Johnnie comes back," Vicky announced. "Then we can eat and strategize."

Mr. Rupert joined them on the couch and they chatted until Johnnie returned. Cathy asked everyone to relax. She said a short prayer and began, looking at Toni.

"Okay. I'm still getting that there is a person who is extremely obsessed with you and I sense danger. I'm also seeing numbers, but I have no idea what that means. Random numbers like two, five, thirty. The feeling is that this person has some control issues."

Toni felt frightened. This could be anyone and she'd have no idea. How could she protect herself from an anonymous person? She scooted closer to Boggs and linked her arm in hers. "Do you get anything else, Cathy?"

Cathy was quiet and closed her eyes. After a few minutes she smiled, then looked at Toni. "This is strange, but there's one more thing. I have a strong feeling that you met or came into contact with this person not long ago, within a couple weeks. Sorry, that's all I have for you today."

"Wow," Toni said. "That's amazing. Thank you so much. You helped us so much the last time, and you were incredibly accurate. I'm sure we'll be able to figure this out." Even to her own ear, she sounded much more positive than she felt.

Cathy blushed. "It's not me, really. I just give what I get. I hope it helps." She took a sip of her soda. "Now, on to other important topics. Have any of you seen the new bartender at the Cat's Meow? And do you know if she's single?"

Everyone laughed and Toni began handing out the subs. While the women ate, they talked about the new bartender, the upcoming Pride Day festivities, the softball team and, eventually, Toni and Boggs's new loft. After about an hour, Cathy had to leave.

"Thanks so much for the food and company," she said as she stood to leave. "This has been so much fun. It's rare that I get a chance to just sit and chat with friends. Let me know the next time you all go out and if I can, I'd love to join you."

Toni assured her that they would and after she'd gone, she cleared off the coffee table and brought fresh drinks for everyone. They had their notebooks ready and Toni retrieved her own notes from her briefcase and joined them on the couch.

Vicky took charge. "Okay, first let's share what we have and then we'll talk about the info we got from Cathy. I talked to Anne this morning and she still doesn't think we have enough to get warrants for bank records on Judge Smith or Butch. She's going to run a few searches and see if she gets anything interesting on Judge Crayton. That's all I've got."

"Well, I ran dry myself," Patty said. "The forensic computer guys haven't touched Tucker's hard drive yet. They said it might be another week before they can get to it. And Mike took the afternoon off. I had a burglary this afternoon, so I didn't get anything else done." She looked apologetic.

"Don't feel bad," Toni said. "The only thing I got was a list of Butch's clients over the last couple years." She handed the list to Vicky. "There are a lot of big names on there, but no one that stood out to me." She shrugged. "Oh, I did accomplish one more thing. I got a gun today." She lifted her shirt and turned. "See?"

"Captain Billings gave her a temporary concealed-carry permit," Boggs added. "And you should've seen her at the range. Shit. And I thought I was a good shot."

Toni felt her face flush. "It was only at twenty-five yards," she insisted. "And it's got great balance. Nice gun."

Boggs hugged her. "I don't think it was the gun, babe." She looked at the others. "She shot dead center, every shot."

"I missed one," Toni admitted.

"An inch off dead center is not a miss." Boggs laughed. "My woman's an ace," she teased.

"Hey, Toni," Patty said, "will you go to the range with me sometime? I really need the practice and maybe you could give me some tips." She looked hopeful.

"I'd love to." Toni smiled at her. "It'll be fun. Maybe this weekend, okay?"

Patty nodded excitedly.

"What kind of gun?" Johnnie asked.

Toni told her and she asked to see it. Toni carefully removed it from her holster, easily popped out the magazine and expelled the cartridge in the chamber before handing her the gun, butt first.

Johnnie smiled. "You've been shooting a long time, huh?"

"Mostly in high school and undergrad," Toni said. "I haven't really shot in a long time."

"Well, you handle it better than most instructors I've seen." Johnnie held the gun, pointing it down at the floor. "Wow. This does feel good. And it's a nine millimeter, just like my duty weapon. This would be a nice off-duty pistol." She looked down the sights. "Would you mind if I loaded it so I could feel the weight and balance?"

Toni handed her the magazine. "I think we can trust you," she said, chuckling.

Johnnie got up and went toward the front door. She put in the magazine, chambered a round and removed the magazine. She held out her hand and Toni gave her the extra cartridge, which she quickly snapped into the magazine. After reinserting the clip she leveled the gun toward the door in a shooting stance. "This is really nice. I think I might get one. How about if I join you and Patty at the range? I'd like to try it out." She engaged the safety and handed the gun back to Toni.

Toni double-checked the safety and returned it to her holster.

"Sounds like fun. And I'd like to try your duty weapon if that's okay."

"Maybe we can all go on Saturday," Boggs said.

Toni noticed that Boggs seemed a little jealous and she couldn't blame her. A few months ago Johnnie had made it abundantly clear that if Boggs weren't in the picture, she'd be the first in line. And Johnnie was very smooth, that voice like butter. Even though Toni had felt a connection with her, it was Boggs who held her heart and soul. She snuggled closer to Boggs. "I would love that, honey." She felt Boggs relax just a bit.

"Okay, ladies." Vicky drank the last of her beer. "Back to business. What did you find out, Johnnie?"

Johnnie had gone to the kitchen to get a beer. When Vicky held up her empty bottle she got one for her and asked the others. Back on the couch she opened her beer and began. "I went to see Bert last night and she was thrilled to be able to help us. Or help Toni, I should say."

Toni rolled her eyes and the rest laughed.

"Anyway, I showed her Tucker's picture and she recognized him immediately, said he came around a couple nights a week. She'd assumed he was selling ecstasy."

"How come she never reported him?" Patty asked.

"She said he never caused any problems and he was a nice guy. When I told her that the drugs had caused an overdose she freaked out a little. I had to assure her that she wasn't in trouble at all."

"I'm glad you did that," Toni said. "She's nice and I wouldn't want her to think that we're after her."

"Yeah. She looks hardcore, but she's on the up and up. I asked if I could use her as kind of an informant of sorts. She liked the idea."

"Does she think Tucker's been replaced?" Boggs asked.

"She hadn't noticed anyone, but she wasn't looking. Apparently Tucker had a routine, come in on Friday and Sunday nights like clockwork. So she'll keep an eye out this weekend and let us know."

"What about Dead Granny? Did you find any relatives here?" Vicky asked.

"Still working on that. Dead Granny had four kids and who knows how many grandkids. Hopefully, I'll have something to go on by the end of the week. I have an agent working on that." Johnnie paused. "And the cameras here are all set, one outside the front door and one in the parking lot. They're set on a twenty-four-hour loop. The windows and the front door are wired. If the alarm isn't shutoff in thirty seconds, a signal is sent to the police and all of our cell phones. We'll get a text message that says 'Toni Alarm.'" She gave them the shutoff code. "Not too original, it spells out *Toni*."

Everyone nodded.

"Okay," Vicky said. "Let's talk about what Cathy told us."

"Oh, wait," Boggs said suddenly. "I completely forgot. Remember the anonymous letters that Toni's been getting?"

"You know who that is?" Toni asked. She'd been getting these letters for almost six months now. They started innocently, just saying how wonderful she was, and they were all signed "Till We Meet Again." A few months ago gifts began arriving, and she'd gotten a chocolate rabbit and Peeps near Easter. Although there was never anything threatening, she thought they were creepy. She didn't even open them anymore but instead gave them directly to Sam Clark, the chief investigator at work and Boggs's boss.

"Sam found the guy," Boggs continued. "The last box had an angel statue inside, wrapped in newspaper. Sam noticed it was from a small town in rural Missouri so he called the chief of police down there. Get this, the police chief knew exactly who it was. The guy's name is Buford Monroe and he's sixty-seven years old. He tells everyone who'll listen that he thinks you're great. Must have seen you on TV. You remind him of his daughter who died a few years ago. His other daughter lives here in Fairfield and when he comes to visit her, he mails something to you. That's why the postmarks are always from here. He's totally harmless. Another mystery solved."

Toni slumped back on the couch. "Well, that's a relief. That's really sweet, don't you think? That I remind him of his daughter? And to think we thought he could have been a killer a few months ago."

She smiled, then realized that there was still an obsessed person out there. "Okay, what about Cathy's info? She said something about random numbers. That kinda makes sense if we're talking obsessive-compulsive. These people tend to count in order to calm down, or they have to do something like wash their hands a certain number of times. Maybe that's what it means."

"What exactly is obsessive-compulsive?" Patty asked.

"Basically with this type of person, it starts with some kind of small obsession, like maybe germs. Then, for example, they'd need to wash their hands. Not once, but many times. In their mind, they'd need to wash five times or to a count of twenty, or they're not clean. And the thought process is irrational. To them, if they don't go through that routine, something very bad will happen to them. They're not always sure what that bad thing is, but they are certain it will happen. As the illness progresses, they engage in more and more compulsions, or behaviors. In really bad cases, they may not even be able to leave their house because of the number of rituals they must complete before they go. Or maybe their hands will be horribly chapped, almost to the point of bleeding, because they have to wash them so much."

"My God," Patty said, shaking her head. "That's terrible."

"I know." Toni was frowning. "I had one client when I was a psychotherapist who had to check the lock on her back door fifteen times, wash her hands twenty times, check to make sure the stove was off ten times and test her answering machine ten times. It took her almost two hours to get out of her house and once she left, she worried constantly that she'd missed something. It was really sad."

"Maybe it will be easier to find this guy if it's really bad," Patty offered.

"Possibly," Toni said. "But most of these folks hide their illness pretty well."

"At least it's something to look for," Vicky said.

"Y'know, Cathy said that you met this person recently, or at least saw them," Boggs said, looking at Toni. "Can you think of anyone you met in the last few weeks?"

Toni thought for a moment. "I met your Aunt Francie last week, but I don't think that's it." She laughed.

"No," Boggs agreed. "She might be a little eccentric, but I don't think she's the one."

"Let's see. I met a new defense attorney last week, Derek Lemon. And we got a new secretary. Oh, I met Judge Crayton at Patty's party. And we're already watching her. Do you think that's who it is?"

"She's definitely on the list," Vicky said as she wrote in her notebook.

"And I met the owner of Gertrude's Garage, Doris something."

"Doris Jackson," Vicky said. "And that was odd, if I remember. She said hello and then just left."

"There was somebody else, too. What was her name?" Toni could picture her, tall and blond, but the name was a blank.

Vicky thought for a minute. "Nancy Manford was there. Oh, that's right. Karen Young. She used to work at a bank and I met her when I was investigating an embezzlement case."

"She said she worked freelance now, in advertising," Toni added. "I think that's all the people I've met in the last few weeks, but maybe I don't even realize that I've met this person. You know, like when you go to a store or restaurant and someone helps you. They might know who you are because of your credit card, but you don't know them."

"That makes it even harder," Boggs said. "But since we don't have anything else to go on yet, let's focus on who we've got."

Vicky looked at her list. "We've got that defense attorney Derek Lemon, Judge Crayton, Doris Jackson, Nancy Manford, Karen Young and the new secretary. What's her name?"

"Velda Schmirnoff."

"You're kidding," Vicky said.

"Serious." Toni said. "She's kinda tall with long dark brown hair. Her face is rather long, but she's super funny and nice."

"Nice means nothing," Vicky quipped. "Anyway, I think we should start with a background check on each of them. Then maybe we can make some connection between one of them and Dead Granny."

"Let's get pictures of each of them," Patty suggested. "I can pull their driver's license photos tomorrow. Maybe Bert's seen one of them before."

"Good idea," Vicky said. "I think Cathy was right when she told Patty that the car fire was tied to drugs. If we can figure out the drug connection, it should lead us to the boss. I hope Bert can help us there, because no one is going to come up to one of us in the bars and try to sell us something. I think they hit the younger crowd." She looked at Patty. "You're young enough, but you were on the streets too long and I'm afraid people know you're a cop."

"Hey," Toni said, "why don't we get Jessie involved? She's younger than any of us and has only been on the force a couple months." Jessie Taylor had helped them out a few months ago right after she graduated from the police academy. She'd been an MP in the army prior to that and proved to be the perfect choice when they needed a bodyguard for Toni. She posed as Toni's cousin and did a good job.

Vicky pursed her lips. "I could ask Captain Billings to loan her to us for a few weeks like he did before. I'm sure she'd love to do some more plainclothes work." She was nodding to herself. "Yeah, that could work. She would fit in perfectly with the bar scene and we still have the fake ID we set up for her before. She was supposed to be a grad student. Good idea, Toni. I'm going to call him right now."

While Vicky was on the phone with Captain Billings, Toni stretched out, putting her feet on the coffee table with Mr. Rupert on her lap. "I guess we've covered all the bases, at least for now."

Boggs put her arm around Toni and pulled her closer. "I suppose, but I hate this not knowing crap. I sure wish we knew who we're dealing with." She kissed the top of Toni's head. "It'd be nice if we were already in our new place. We'd have the security cameras everywhere."

"What kind of system does it have?" Johnnie asked.

Boggs described it in detail while Toni rubbed Mr. Rupert's head. Patty had opened a fresh beer and was just sitting back down on the couch when Vicky ended her call with Captain Billings.

"He thinks we're on to something," Vicky announced. "As long as Jessie says okay, he'll assign her to me for a few weeks. I'm going to call her now." Five minutes later she was smiling. "She's totally on board. I gave her the basics and I'll fill her in on the rest tomorrow."

"Perfect." Toni picked up her beer from the coffee table and took a sip. "I agree that if we can just find the drug connection, we'll figure this out."

"We will," Vicky said. "Okay. Johnnie will work on the Dead Granny angle. Patty's going to get photos of the people on our list so far and we'll get those to Bert. Let's see." She looked at her notebook. "We've got Derek Lemon, Judge Crayton, Doris Jackson, Nancy Manford, Karen Young and Velda Schmirnoff. I'll do background checks on all of them. What else?"

"I'll do some more digging into Kevin Tucker's life," Boggs said, "but without Mike Johnson knowing. I'll see if I can find another boyfriend or something."

"I guess we're good," Vicky said as she finished off the last of her beer and took it to the kitchen. "Unless something else comes up, let's meet again on Friday and catch up then."

Everyone nodded in agreement.

"Oh, yeah. I almost forgot," Vicky added. "The Eat for Pride thing is going on tomorrow night. If you go to one of the sponsoring restaurants or bars, they'll donate fifteen percent of your check to an AIDS foundation. Both Gertrude's Garage and the Cat's Meow are on the list."

"Perfect." Toni grinned at Boggs. "I guess we're eating out tomorrow night."

The women left and Toni locked the door and reset the alarm.

"I feel a little better knowing that we've at least got something to go on," she said as she cleaned up the empty beer bottles from the coffee table. "If what Cathy said was right, and I'm betting it is, then we've got five suspects. We should be able to figure this out, don't you think?"

"I know we can, babe," Boggs said as she finished off her beer. "And if Bert can figure out who took Tucker's place, we should be able to make a connection between him and the boss." She grabbed an empty box from the corner of the living room. "Want to do some more packing?"

"Sure. Let's head upstairs and pack some of my clothes." Toni picked up an empty box. "We can at least pack all my winter things."

Boggs got the rest of the boxes and followed her. "And I was thinking of us maybe getting another cat. You know, a friend for Mr. Rupert. What do you think?"

Toni stopped at the top of the stairs and turned around, grinning. "I think Mr. Rupert would love to have his own cat for a pet." She laughed, then hugged Boggs fiercely. "I love you. Now let's get to work."

Chapter 19

On Wednesday morning Jan was sitting at her kitchen table, drinking her third cup of coffee. She was trying to figure out a way to get Toni's e-mail address. She Googled her to no avail and there was no e-mail listed for the prosecuting attorney's office. Frustrated in her inability to come up with a plan, she began thumbing through the morning paper. In the entertainment section, she saw an article about Eat for Pride. Within minutes she had a plan. A half-hour later she was printing off sign-up sheets for an imaginary organization that helped the pets of people living with AIDS. She knew there was such an organization, but she altered the name. The sheets asked for people to help and had a place for their names and e-mail addresses. On the top of each page was a picture of a puppy and a kitten.

Jan looked at the finished product. It was perfect, really tugged at the heartstrings. Hell, she might even sign up.

Although it was far from a sure thing, at least she had a shot. If this didn't work she might have to just go up and ask Toni. She looked at her work again. She'd put these sheets at both Gertrude's Garage and the Cat's Meow and pick them up tonight around ten.

Late Wednesday night the woman was continuing to obsess about Toni. The thought of having her in bed had invaded her thoughts constantly for the last few days. Now that her second plan was set in her mind, she was just waiting for Jan to arrive so she could give her the details. She smiled, making herself a drink and centering it on the coaster without looking. She sat in her tall, dark leather chair and sighed deeply. This would be absolutely perfect, she told herself. She stirred the Scotch three times with her left index finger and tapped it lightly twice on the rim. She savored the drops on her finger. Her eyes were closed and she was reliving her latest fantasy of Toni when she heard the front door open. A few minutes later Jan appeared in her study. She opened her eyes and motioned toward the bar. Jan made herself a drink and grabbed the ashtray from the bar before sitting.

"I've got a job for you."

Jan nodded and lit a cigarette. "I got the e-mail address." She gave a quick explanation of how she obtained it.

The boss sat up straight and her eyes got wide. She could feel her heart beating faster. She held out her hand and watched as Jan put the scrap of paper there. She stared at it, knowing it could get her closer to Toni. She curled her fingers around it and closed her eyes. She could already imagine sitting in her chair, watching Toni. She licked her lips and slowly opened her eyes.

"Okay, now here's my other plan," she said, coming back to reality. "I'll give you the basics and you can figure out the details. I want you to set up a meeting between Doug and Toni. Have him call her and say that he's got information or something. Make sure she's alone. Have them meet at a bar. Then we'll spike her drink with Davey's new drug. I've got some here in liquid form." She took a sip of her drink and smiled. "Then you step in and help Toni. According to Davey, she'll probably seem a little drunk, but not too bad. You can bring her to me. It should only take about fifteen minutes for the drug to work, so you'll need to be close by. She won't remember anything once the drug takes effect. It'll last maybe four hours, according to Davey, but to be safe, you should take her back in three."

Jan nodded. "What about Doug?"

The woman took another sip of her drink. "You'll have to take care of that. And we'll have to find a replacement, but I think it's worth it." She smiled, dreaming of her rendezvous with Toni.

Jan put out her cigarette and immediately lit another one. "I've got a couple guys in mind," she said as she slowly exhaled the smoke. "I lined them up in case Doug didn't work out." She took another drag and grinned. "And I guess he didn't."

The woman finished her drink and glanced at Jan, who immediately made her another. After she set it down on the coaster, she returned to her chair.

"When would you like this done?"

"Tomorrow is good for me. Would that be a problem?"

"I don't see why," Jan said as she put out her cigarette. "I'll take care of everything and call you when I have a set time." She emptied her ashtray into the metal can and washed it and her glass, then picked up her old backpack. "Do you have the drug?"

The woman retrieved the vial from her desk drawer and handed it to her. Jan put it safely into her backpack and left.

The woman leaned back in her chair, took a sip of her drink and closed her eyes. In less than twenty-four hours she'd have Toni in her bed. She grinned in anticipation, then called Davey, telling him she had the e-mail address. He told her he'd be over in fifteen minutes.

Forty-five minutes later Davey pushed away from her desk. "It's all set for now. The e-mail will look like it's coming from that fake place Jan made up. There's an attachment with a picture of a kitten. When she opens it, we're in. Then you'll get a message on your screen. Once you get it, call me and I'll come over. It'll give me her system specs. If she's got a webcam I'll be able to activate it. Otherwise, I'll just set it up so you can read her e-mails. If she does have a webcam, once my program is in place, we'll get a message that says 'accept.' All we do is click on that and a screen will open. You should be able to see and hear everything."

"What does the e-mail say that you sent her?"

"Just a thank you," Davey said.

The only thing she could do was smile.

Jan flipped open her cell phone with one hand and lit another cigarette with the other as she sat in her recliner. Doug answered on the third ring.

"Hi, Doug. I've got an easy job for you and it pays a cool thousand."

After a few minutes of explanation and instructions, everything was set. Doug would call Toni tomorrow morning at work. He'd ask to meet her at Homer's, a small tavern that Jan knew and tell her that he had information about Kevin Tucker. Jan would be in the bar, but he wasn't to acknowledge her. He could tell Toni anything he wanted about Tucker—it didn't matter. Jan planned to meet him a half-hour later in the alley behind the old candy factory and give him the money. When she hung up she couldn't help but grin. He'd seemed eager to please her. Tomorrow would be a great day. She was going to drug and kidnap a woman and then kill a guy. It had been a while. Yes, tomorrow was definitely going to be a good day. She was humming as she fixed herself a rum and Coke.

Chapter 20

Toni was sitting at her desk on Thursday morning when Chloe buzzed her. "There's a Mr. Doug Bradley on line three for you."

"Thanks, Chloe." Toni wondered who that could be. She punched line three. "This is Toni Barston."

"Um, hi. I need to talk to you. It's super important. I have information about Kevin Tucker."

"Okay. It's Doug Bradley, right?" She was jotting down notes.

"Yeah, that's me. Meet me at two o'clock at Homer's and I'll tell you everything I know." His voice sounded shaky.

"Can't you just tell me now?"

"Uh, no. Not on the phone. I need to tell you in person, okay? I gotta go. I'll see you there at two."

The phone disconnected and Toni stared at the receiver. Hmm. The guy was probably scared, she thought. Homer's was only a few miles away. She looked at her calendar and saw she had nothing on the docket this afternoon. Maybe this Doug guy could give her the information they needed to crack this case. And if he had enough information, maybe Anne could offer him immunity from prosecution. She called her boss first and then Boggs to fill her in.

"I don't think you should meet this guy by yourself," Boggs said. "I can rearrange a couple things and go with you."

"No. I'll be fine. It's in a public place. I don't want to scare the guy off. If I can get enough information, I'll try to convince him to talk to Vicky."

"I don't know," Boggs said. "But, well, I guess as long as you call me as soon as you're done, okay?"

"I will. Promise." Toni was smiling. She loved the fact that Boggs worried about her. "I'll call you as soon as I get back. I love you."

"I love you, too, babe."

Three hours later Toni turned into the small parking lot of Homer's tavern and noticed there were only six other vehicles in the lot. Who went to a tavern in the middle of the afternoon? she wondered. People who worked the night shift maybe? Lovers wanting a secret rendezvous? Maybe sneaking off to a place where they could hold hands and make plans? She shook her head, brushing off her vivid imagination. She parked her new Bug in a spot closest to the door and went inside. It took her eyes a minute to adjust to the darkness of the room, but when she did, she saw a couple sitting at a far table, engaged in what looked like a serious conversation. Maybe she was right about a rendezvous, she thought. Listening closely, she could hear people talking in a backroom, but she couldn't see them. There was also a woman seated at the end of the bar reading a newspaper and a young man about twenty-five years old at the other end of the bar. He was drinking a beer and looked nervous. She assumed he must be Doug and went over.

"Are you Doug?" she asked.

"Yeah," he whispered. He pointed to the barstool next to him and Toni sat.

An old man appeared behind the bar. He looked like he'd been a fixture at the tavern since its inception and she grinned. If ever there had been a man who matched the name of Homer, it was him.

"What can I get ya, miss?"

He smiled and she could see that he had unfortunate teeth, the kind that didn't realize they were intended to be part of a matched set. One stuck out at a rather odd angle. Still, he seemed warm and friendly and she smiled back at him. "I'm fine, thanks," she responded. The old man frowned. "Well, I guess Sprite would be good." She didn't want to be rude.

He flashed another tooth-filled smile and looked at Doug, who nodded at his almost empty beer. He returned a few minutes later with the two drinks. Toni thanked him and paid for both, slipping her wallet back inside her blazer pocket. Homer disappeared in the back and she turned to Doug.

"Now, what would you like to tell me?" she asked.

Doug got off his barstool and went to the window, motioning her to follow him. When she was at his side he pointed to a car in the lot.

"See that Pontiac there?"

She nodded, not understanding his point.

"That belonged to Kevin Tucker." He stared at the vehicle for a few minutes and she wondered what his point was. Doug went back to his barstool and Toni followed, still puzzled. "I got spare keys," he explained. "I used to hang out with him and stuff. After he got himself killed, I just went ahead and borrowed it." He took another long swallow of his beer and began telling her about his friendship with Kevin.

131

She had listened politely for almost twenty minutes and had finished her soda before she finally stopped him. "What about Kevin?" she asked. She knew if she didn't interrupt him soon, he'd probably talk all afternoon and never say anything worthwhile. Her patience was running thin.

"Oh, well, I know he sold drugs because there's some in the car," he said.

Finally. God, she thought he'd never get to the point. She stood up with the intention of going out to the car with him and she felt herself sway. She steadied herself by grabbing the bar. She felt dizzy. "Is it still in the par?" She giggled. "I said par." She giggled again. "I meant car, but I was thinking Pontiac." She laughed so hard she almost fell down.

"Yeah, they're still in the car." Doug seemed oblivious to her condition and headed for the door. Toni attempted to follow. *What's wrong with me?* When she got to the door, she felt the support of a woman's hand on her arm. *Her hand feels soft.* Doug was already halfway across the parking lot when she crossed over the threshold of the door and stumbled. The woman tried to catch her but it was too late. Toni crashed into a cement planter headfirst and landed on her butt on the sidewalk. She giggled as she put her hand to her head but stopped when she realized she was bleeding. She felt the blood streaming down her face and tried to get up. She stumbled several times before she was able to stand, and then leaned against the planter. *What the hell happened?* She scanned the parking lot. Doug was nowhere to be seen. And neither was the woman. She made her way back into the tavern, holding onto the wall as she went. Once inside she slid down the wall and sat on the floor. Nothing was making sense.

"Homer!" she yelled, and then giggled. Never in her life could she have imagined calling out that name, unless maybe to a dog. "Homer!"

The old man ran to her side and pressed his bar rag against

her head. "Miss, are you okay?"

"I think I'm bleeding," she answered nonchalantly. Then she giggled again.

Homer went back to the bar and she thought she heard him phone 911. He got a clean rag and returned to Toni's side, handing her the replacement. "Here you go, miss. I called for help. They should be here any minute. What's your name?"

She thought for a minute. "Um, my name? It's, um, Toni. Yeah. My name is Toni." She fumbled for her wallet inside her blazer pocket but couldn't seem to get it out. The process made her giggle once again.

Within minutes the ambulance arrived and two paramedics came into the tavern. The man looked at Toni, then at Homer. "Hey, Homer. What happened? Have too much to drink?"

"Hi, Billy. Nope. She only had a soda."

The paramedic lifted the rag and looked at the wound. "You're going to need some stitches." He cleaned the gash in her head and applied a butterfly bandage to close the wound.

His partner was filling out the paperwork. "What's your name?" she asked.

Toni giggled again. "My name is Toni."

Billy looked at Homer. "Are you sure she isn't drunk?"

"Only had a soda," Homer repeated. "She's only been here maybe twenty minutes. She met some young kid here, but he left. Maybe he slipped her a Mickey."

The paramedics helped Toni to the ambulance. She was inside the emergency room in ten minutes. Amazingly a doctor looked at her right away. "How did this happen?" he asked.

Toni blinked several times and smiled. "I was bleeding." She giggled.

The doctor looked at the paramedics. "Is she drunk or on something?"

Billy shrugged. "The bar owner said she only drank soda but he thought somebody might have spiked her drink. The only thing we got out of her was her first name. Toni."

"Are you allergic to any drugs?"

"I don't know," Toni said, grinning.

The doctor shook his head. Just then a nurse came into the room. "Ms. Barston? What happened?"

"You know her?" the doctor asked.

"Sure," the nurse said. "This is Toni Barston. She's a prosecuting attorney and was almost killed by that maniac last fall. I treated her then." She went over to Toni's side. "Hi, Ms. Barston. It's Sally. Remember me?"

Toni looked at the nurse and just grinned.

"This seems wrong to me," the nurse said. She glanced at the paramedics. "Where did you pick her up?"

"At Homer's," Billy replied. "He said she met some young kid there. Maybe got slipped a Mickey or she was doing drugs is all I can figure."

Sally shook her head. "I'll pull her old chart and see if she's allergic to anything, and then I'm going to call her work. I think something's not right here."

After finding out she wasn't allergic to any medications, the doctor stitched her up. She was dozing when Boggs arrived.

"Oh, my God. Toni! Are you okay? What in the hell happened?"

Toni opened her eyes and grinned. "Hiya, honey. Whatcha doin'?"

"Shit. Nurse!"

A nurse, not Sally, arrived in seconds, looking somewhat alarmed.

Boggs flashed her investigator's badge. "We need to run a tox screen on her. She's been drugged."

The nurse hesitated.

"I'm sure of it. She was meeting with an informant and something obviously went very wrong." Boggs softened her tone. "Please?"

The nurse smiled and disappeared, returning a moment later to take a blood sample. Boggs pulled a chair up to the bed and sat next to Toni. She held her hand. "You'll be fine, babe. Just rest." Toni closed her eyes and drifted off.

As soon as she saw the gash in Toni's head, Jan had gotten in her car and gone to her boss's house. She wasn't looking forward to this conversation. Her boss didn't like bad news or sloppy work, and this was both. She took a deep breath and opened the front door. She climbed the stairs to the study.

"There's been a problem," she said as soon as she saw her.

The boss was sitting in her desk chair. Jan could see that she had on nice slacks and a pressed blouse. She'd been ready for her date with Toni and Jan could smell the overly musky fragrance of cologne that her boss preferred. The woman pointed to the bar. "Make me a drink," she growled. She didn't suggest that Jan make one for herself.

Jan fixed her a drink and picked up the ashtray. She placed the drink carefully on its coaster and then sat in one of the club chairs. She lit a cigarette and waited until her boss took her first sip.

"Toni fell outside the bar and cut her head pretty bad. She needed medical attention, so I didn't bring her here." Jan waited for a response.

The woman took a healthy swallow and glared at Jan. "You hurt Toni? How the hell could you fuck up so bad? How hard was it to bring her to me?" She slammed her fist on the desk. "Now what are you going to do?" She ran her fingers through the right side of her hair five times.

Her boss was breathing very fast and Jan watched her do that hair thing five more times. "I'll have her for you in a week or so." She put out her cigarette and immediately lit another. "I'll find another way."

The woman seemed furious. "What about Doug?"

"I'm meeting him in a few minutes. And I've already set things up with John Clarkson to take over the bar scene. I gave him the supply this morning. He's done some work for my cousin in Little Rock and he's reliable."

The woman gulped the rest of her drink and slammed it down on her desk. She ran her fingers through the right side of her hair five more times and then slammed her fist again. "Make me another drink, then get the hell out of here and fix things."

Jan put out her cigarette and washed out her ashtray. She made her boss another drink, centering it on the coaster. "I'll call you tomorrow and give you an update."

The woman merely grunted and turned to check her laptop to see if Toni had opened her e-mail yet. Jan left without saying anything else.

Once in her car she lit another cigarette. She'd seen her boss mad before, but this was new. Her obsession with Toni Barston was getting out of control and that hair thing was driving Jan nuts. If she'd just chill out a little, things would get back to normal in no time. This thing for Toni was going to be a problem and Jan wasn't sure how she was going to handle it. But at the moment she had another chore to complete.

Jan turned into the alley behind the old candy factory and saw Doug sitting in Kevin's Pontiac about halfway down. She pulled alongside him so the driver's side windows faced each other.

"Hey, Jan."

"Hi, Doug." She grinned at him. "You did a great job. I've got a new phone number, so why don't you hand me your cell so I can program it in for you?"

Doug handed her his phone. "Thanks."

Jan looked at the phone. It was the untraceable throwaway phone she'd given him just a week ago. She put his phone on the passenger seat of her car and picked up her gun. Without saying another word, she leveled her nine millimeter at his head and fired. He was looking right at her when the bullet hit the center of his forehead. There was a look of disbelief on his face, and then he was gone. Jan placed her gun under her seat as she drove away. She was home in ten minutes. She fixed herself a rum and Coke and ordered a pizza. She flipped on the television while she waited for the delivery boy and wondered how she'd get her boss back on track.

Boggs was sitting next to Toni's bed, still in the emergency room. She'd only left once to get a cup of coffee from the vending machine. She'd called everyone and was sick with worry.

Toni was still dozing when Vicky arrived at the hospital. She grabbed a chair and pulled it next to Boggs.

"How's she doing?"

Boggs was holding Toni's hand. "She's been sleeping off and on. I had them run a tox screen." She glanced at her watch. "It's been almost an hour."

"I'm going to find out what's taking so long." Vicky had just stood up to leave when the doctor and the nurse came in the room.

"We got the results," the doctor said but stopped and looked at Vicky. She flashed her badge and he nodded. "There's a mixture of gamma-hydroxybutyrate and methylenedioxymethamphetamine."

"What the hell is that?" Boggs asked.

"It's basically a blend of ecstasy and GHB, the date rape drug."

"Is she going to be okay?" Boggs felt sick. She couldn't stand the thought of someone taking advantage of Toni.

"It should wear off in about two or three more hours. She'll probably have very little memory of what happened and might feel a bit of a hangover. The laceration on her forehead isn't too bad. We put in five stitches. She should have those removed in a week."

"Can we take her home now?" Boggs wanted to get her home and tucked into their own bed. She needed her to be safe.

The doctor nodded, wrote a prescription for pain medication and left the room. Sally, the nurse, remained. "She'll be okay." She got a wheelchair from the hallway and pushed it near the bed. "She'll probably continue to doze off and on, but that's okay. She's in no danger." She shook Toni gently. "Ms. Barston, time to wake up."

Toni slowly opened her eyes and blinked several times. "Oh, hi." Her deep blue eyes searched for Boggs. "Hey, what's going on?"

"We're just going to take you home, babe." Boggs helped her sit up. "The nurse here is going to let you ride in a wheelchair."

Toni seemed alarmed. "I'm in a hospital? What happened?" She looked at her slacks and touched the bloodstains on her pants. "I'm bleeding?"

Boggs smoothed her hair and gently took her hand. "You're okay, babe. You cut your head, but the doc fixed you up."

Toni touched her forehead and the bandage. "It hurts."

Both Boggs and the nurse helped Toni into the wheelchair. She looked a little confused but complied easily. As Boggs wheeled her out, Sally handed Toni's blazer to Vicky. Boggs had already retrieved Toni's wallet. Thank God nothing seemed to be missing. Her credit cards were there as well as forty-seven dollars.

Vicky dug in the pocket, finding the keys to Toni's Bug. "I'll call Patty and go pick her up," she told Boggs. "Then we'll swing by Homer's and get the car. We'll meet you at Toni's place. And I'll give Johnnie and Jessie a call too. Oh, and I'll take care of the prescription."

Grateful for the help, Boggs nodded and wheeled Toni out through the ER, Vicky following close behind. She was so mad at herself. She should have gone with Toni to that tavern. If she

had, none of this would have happened. Maybe Johnnie was right, and she really couldn't take care of Toni. She felt tears begin to well when she realized what could have happened to Toni and she quickly blinked them back. She needed to be strong now. Whoever was after Toni would have to get through her first. As they approached the automatic door, she double-checked her weapon. "Vicky, you stay here while I get the car. And don't let *anyone* talk to her. Understand? *No one.*"

Vicky had just closed her cell phone. "I'll be right here, hon. Don't worry."

Boggs hesitated. She wasn't sure she could leave Toni there in the wheelchair.

Vicky must have noticed her apprehension, because she pulled the side of her blazer back and tucked it behind her holster. She put one hand on her gun and the other on the back of the wheelchair. "We'll be fine. Go get the car," she ordered.

Boggs did as she was told. Once through the automatic doors, she literally ran to her car, hitting the unlock button at ten feet away. She hopped in, slammed the door shut and promptly dropped the keys on the floor. After picking them up, she fumbled getting them in the ignition. Her hands were shaking. *Damn it.* She tried again and they slid in easily. She started her SUV and took a deep breath. *Jeez. Get ahold of yourself, girl.* Normally she was cool and calm in a crisis, but when it came to Toni, she was a mess. She'd never felt this way about anyone and she had an overwhelming need to protect her by taking her somewhere far away. She shook it off and tried to focus. Pulling up in front of the entrance, she threw the car into park and hopped out. Vicky was wheeling Toni toward her.

"I think she should ride in the backseat," Vicky said. "She keeps dozing off."

Boggs opened the back door and gently shook Toni. "Come on, babe. Time to go home."

Toni opened her eyes and smiled, while Vicky and Boggs

helped her into the backseat. Vicky buckled her in and Boggs got in the driver's seat. By the time she closed her door, Toni was lying down.

"I'll see you over there," Boggs said through the open passenger window. She navigated slowly and carefully to Toni's townhouse, her eyes darting from the road to the backseat, to the rearview mirror. Satisfied they hadn't been followed, she pulled into a visitor's spot and helped Toni to the front door.

Once inside, Boggs quickly closed the door, locked it and punched in the security code. Mr. Rupert came running to greet them.

"Hiya, buddy." Toni leaned down to pet him and almost fell.

Boggs steadied her. "Come on, babe. Let's go upstairs and get you changed." She guided Toni up the stairs with her arm around her waist for balance. "Okay, you take off your clothes and I'll get you some shorts and a top."

As Toni unbuttoned her blouse, Boggs again saw the bloodstains and her stomach turned. Why the hell would someone drug Toni? she wondered. And whoever it was, she was determined to find them and make them wish they'd never seen the light of day. She opened a drawer in the dresser and pulled out a pair of khaki cargo shorts and a white T-shirt. When she glanced back, Toni was standing next to the bed, completely nude, petting Mr. Rupert. Boggs chastised herself for the thoughts that immediately came to mind. This was not the time for that, she told herself.

"I think you can put your bra and underwear back on," she said. "Unless you want to take a shower." She noticed dried blood on her face and neck. "Yeah, I think maybe a shower would be good. Are you feeling up to that?"

"I'm not feeling great, but I think a shower would make me feel a little better." She smiled weakly.

Boggs glanced at her watch and figured that the drug would be wearing off in about an hour. She thought that Toni would

feel both better and worse. "Just don't wash your hair," she offered. "And if that bandage gets a little wet, we'll just put a fresh one on, okay?" Sally had given her extra gauze and a roll of white tape.

Toni looked confused. "Bandage?"

Boggs led her into the bathroom and showed her in the mirror.

"Oh, God," Toni exclaimed when she saw her reflection. "That's attractive." She touched the area around the bandage and winced. "How bad is it?"

"They put in five stitches," Boggs said. "But the nurse told me the doc is really good." She smiled as her gaze trailed up and down Toni's body. "And I must say, you're looking pretty hot right now."

Toni blushed. "Well, thank you very much. And I'll be happy to go to the eye doctor with you so you can get glasses." It was the first time she smiled like her old self.

Boggs started the shower for her and waited while the water warmed up.

Toni stepped into the shower, holding onto the wall to steady herself. "Will you stay up here with me?"

Boggs could tell that she was frightened, the gravity of the events just beginning to sink in. "Of course, babe. In fact, I'll get in with you." Boggs quickly disrobed and joined her. She turned the showerhead and let the warm water cascade over them. She soaped up a washcloth and gently washed the blood off Toni's face and neck. Toni was still unsteady on her feet. "Just hold on to the bar, babe."

Toni did as instructed as Boggs continued. She loved her more than she'd ever loved anyone and the urge to protect and comfort her was overwhelming. When Toni was clean, she turned off the shower and grabbed a towel, patting her dry where they stood. Then she got out and placed a fresh towel on the lid of the toilet.

"Just sit here for a minute, babe." She helped Toni out of the shower and sat her down.

Boggs quickly dried herself and dressed. She retrieved Toni's clothing and helped her get dressed.

Toni again saw herself in the mirror and she reached up to touch the bandage. "What happened to me?"

Boggs checked the bandage and noticed it was wet. She sat Toni back down and gingerly replaced it. "You cut your head."

"But why can't I remember? Did I get knocked out?" She looked at her feet. "I need shoes."

Boggs helped her into the bedroom. "Are you feeling better after your shower?"

"Yeah, a little. My brain seems a little less foggy, but my head is pounding."

"Vicky's going to fill the prescription and bring it over," Boggs said. "That should help."

Toni sat at her desk and put on her shoes. She glanced at her laptop. "Let me check my e-mail and then you can tell me what the hell happened." Boggs watched her scroll through the list, ignoring most. "Hey, I got an e-mail from that place that helps pets of people with AIDS." She opened it. "It's just a thank you for your interest. It says they'll send more information later. There's a cute picture of a kitten."

"That's great," Boggs said. "I think that's a wonderful thing. And speaking of pets, I was browsing the Web site of Stray Rescue this morning and I saw this great little guy." She was grinning.

"Let's go downstairs and you can tell me all about him. I'm parched."

Boggs got them both a diet Dew and they sat on the couch. "He's only ten weeks old and he's mostly gray with white on his chest and all four paws."

"I thought we were going to wait until we moved."

"I know, but he's adorable. And here's the clincher. He's a

Cinderella cat."

"A Cinderella cat? What the hell is that?"

"He was adopted originally from the humane society, but the people brought him to Stray Rescue with some stupid excuse. Allergies or something. His tail was broken and the doc had to amputate it. Now his tail is only about two inches long."

"Oh, my God," Toni said. "That's horrible." She was shaking her head. "Hey, wait a minute. Was all that information on the Web site?"

Feeling only a bit sneaky, Boggs grinned but said nothing.

"I didn't think so." Toni laughed. "You already called them, didn't you?"

"Just to get more information," Boggs admitted, recalling the conversation with the lady at Stray Rescue. "But I'd never do anything without talking to you first."

Toni leaned over and kissed her on the cheek. "So when do we meet this little guy?"

"How about Saturday after we go to the range? I, um, already filled out the online application form."

"Perfect," Toni said. She looked over at Mr. Rupert, who was sitting on the coffee table. "I think you're about to get your very own cat. Would you like that, buddy?"

He meowed once and then yawned.

"Now tell me what the hell happened today."

Boggs had just finished telling Toni what she knew when the doorbell rang and she let in Vicky and Patty.

Vicky draped Toni's blazer over one of the dining room chairs. "I don't know if your cleaner can get the blood out of this," she said. "And I've got your pain meds." She held up the small white sack. "Are you ready for one of these?"

Toni nodded and Vicky tossed her the bag.

"Do you need more to drink?" Vicky was already in the kitchen with the refrigerator open. With Toni's reply in the negative, Vicky got a beer for herself and one for Patty. She came back into the living room. "I hope nobody minds, but I ordered pizza again. We can start talking as soon as Johnnie and Jessie get here." She plopped down on the couch next to Toni. "How are you feeling? Still woozy?"

Toni smiled. "Not nearly as bad as before. Now it's mostly just this." She lightly touched the bandage and took one of the pain meds. "But why don't I remember?"

"It's the drug, babe, but you're okay now," Boggs said.

Patty opened her beer and sat on the other side of the huge couch. She took a healthy swallow. "I brought your Bug over and I stopped by your office and got your briefcase." She pointed to the dining room table where she'd placed it.

"Thank you so much," Toni said. "To all of you. Thank you."

The doorbell rang again and this time Patty answered it. It was the pizza delivery guy with Johnnie and Jessie standing behind him.

"I've got it," Boggs said as she headed to the door. She paid and carried the four large boxes to the coffee table. "Jeez, Vic. Hungry?"

"Shut up and get us some plates," Vicky said, chuckling. "I couldn't decide," she added. "Anyway, I'm hormonal."

Boggs gathered the paper plates and napkins as well as beer for Johnnie and Jessie. She noticed that Johnnie had taken her spot on the couch next to Toni, and Jessie was sitting on the other side. She glared at Johnnie but kept her mouth shut. This wasn't the time or place, she thought. But jeez, why did she think it was okay to plop her butt next to Toni? Johnnie thought she was God's gift to the FBI and to all women. Boggs knew she still had it bad for Toni. Boggs shook her head. It pissed her off. She sat next to Patty on the other side, putting the plates and napkins on the coffee table. As everyone grabbed slices of their favorite kind, she tried to let her anger go. Maybe she wasn't doing that great of a job protecting Toni. Look at what had happened today. What if that guy had taken advantage of her? *Shit.* She took a deep breath and tried to focus on the task at hand.

Boggs glanced over at Vicky and laughed. "Why do you pluck off the pepperoni? I've been watching you do that for years."

"It's all about the process," Vicky said. "So shut up. It's one of my best qualities."

The woman sat at her desk, staring at her laptop. She'd already checked her bank balance and occasionally she'd play a game of solitaire or perhaps mah-jong, but mostly she was waiting for that window to pop up indicating that Toni had opened the e-mail and the attachment. Frustrated, she made herself a drink and slowly went back to her desk. She set the heavy glass tumbler on the center of the coaster and stared at it for several minutes. Finally she stirred the Scotch three times with her left index finger, tapped it twice on the rim and slowly licked the drops. She sighed deeply and took a healthy swallow, feeling the wonderful burn inch down her throat. She *needed* to see Toni, to feel her, to know her inside and out. After a second sip, she let her gaze drift back to her laptop and her pulse quickened. There it was. A small window on the screen notifying her that Toni had opened that special piece of mail. She was so close now. She grabbed her cell phone, trembling as she dialed Davey's number. Her excitement was quickly turning to anger when she heard his phone ring for the fourth time. *Where the hell is he?* She needed him right now. He answered on the fifth ring, right before it would have gone to voice mail.

He rang her bell twenty minutes and one drink later. Davey was sitting in her desk chair, his fingers flying over the keys, while she hovered over his shoulder.

"This is perfect," he said after about fifteen minutes. "Her firewall and antivirus software are crap. I've logged in as administrator and you now have full access to her e-mail. Just click here." He pointed to a small icon at the bottom of her screen.

"What about the camera?"

"She's got a webcam built into her system." Davey began a detailed description of its properties, but she stopped him mid-stream.

"Can I see her?" She noticed her hands were shaking as she set her drink back down on the desk.

"Oh, sure. Just click on this icon here." He pointed to an icon that looked like a miniature camera. "Here, I'll show you." He clicked on it and a window popped up, about three-quarters the size of her own screen.

She stared at the laptop, then pulled him out of the desk chair, taking his place. "It looks like her bedroom." Half of her bed and a chair in the corner were visible. She continued to stare. "But I don't hear anything. Isn't there sound?"

"There's sound. But the microphone isn't that great on these models. You'll only be able to hear things that are in that room, and maybe in the next room."

Just then she saw a huge black and white cat jump up on the corner of the bed and stare at the screen. "Look," she murmured, trying to talk without moving her lips. She slowly pointed to the screen, trying not to startle the cat. "Are you sure he can't see me?" She clenched her teeth, barely moving her lips.

"I'm positive. Here, watch." He screamed at the laptop and the large cat didn't move. "See? If he could see or hear us, he'd have run away."

The cat jumped from the bed to the desk and his face filled the screen. "When he moved it was all jittery," she said.

"That's because the resolution is crap. She needs a better webcam."

"Can I keep this up all the time? Even when I do other things?"

"Sure. Just minimize it, and it'll still be in the corner." He demonstrated. "If you close it, it'll disappear and you'll have to click on the icon again to see it. You can do that if you don't want

146

someone to know you're hooked up." He winked at her.

"Thanks, Davey. You're amazing. Is there something I can get for you?"

"Well, there is this really cool Mac I've had my eye on for a while, but it's pretty pricey." He shrugged.

"Is it under fifteen grand?"

"Hell, yeah."

"Do you need my actual credit card or can you order it online?" She still couldn't take her eyes off her laptop, fascinated by the inside of Toni's bedroom.

"Online," he said.

She pulled herself away from the screen just long enough to write down her credit card information for him. "Here you go. Order whatever you want, up to fifteen grand. Just let me know the total, okay?" She trusted him inherently and knew he'd never do anything but order computer things.

"Wow. Thanks, sis. You're the best. I'm going to go home right now and order it. Is there anything else you need me to do?"

"Just keep up with our supply and I'm good." She stood up and hugged her brother. "Now go on, get yourself a new system. And thanks."

He grinned like a little kid and hurried out the door. She made herself another drink and sat back down in front of her laptop. *It's in her bedroom.* How lucky was that?

Boggs had polished off three slices of her favorite—beef and bacon—but noted that Toni hadn't even finished her first piece. Not a good sign, she thought.

"I know I need food, but I still feel a bit sick, like a hangover I guess." Toni sipped at her soda. "I guess I drank too much."

"You didn't drink, sweetie. It's the drug."

"The nurse there told us that you might feel that way most of

147

the evening," Vicky said. "Can you tell us what you remember?"

Toni shook her head. "God, the drug. I keep feeling like I drank." She looked at Vicky. "What did you just ask me?"

"What do you remember?"

"Well, Doug Bradley called me this morning, telling me he had information about Kevin Tucker. I met him at Homer's at two."

"We've got an APB out for him now. Do you remember any vehicles in the parking lot," Vicky asked.

Toni seemed to think for a moment, her face slack, as if she really was hungover. "Things are so fuzzy. I'm sorry."

Johnnie put her arm on Toni's shoulder. "Don't worry about it. You're doing great. Just tell us whatever you remember."

The gesture didn't escape Boggs. She felt her anger rise and noticed she was clenching her fists. *Let it go. She's just being supportive.* She took a deep breath and tried to focus on what Toni was saying.

"Well, I think there were six cars in the lot. I remember wondering who in the hell goes to a tavern in the middle of the afternoon." She laughed. "Oh, wait. Doug was driving Kevin Tucker's Pontiac. He pointed to it from the window."

"Hang on one sec," Vicky said, flipping open her phone. "I'm going to call Captain Billings so he can put out the word to look for Tucker's car." A couple minutes later she said, "Okay, go on. Can you remember any other people there?"

"Well, there was Homer." She smiled. "And I think there was a couple at a table and a woman at the other end of the bar. And I could hear people in the back somewhere." She took another sip of her soda. "I saw Doug at the bar. He looked nervous and was drinking a beer, so I went over and introduced myself."

"Did you have a drink?" Johnnie asked.

"Yeah, well, I ordered a Sprite. But it tasted okay," she said apologetically.

"It doesn't have any taste, babe. You'd never know." Boggs

said. "Was there anyone else near you, besides Doug?"

"No. At least I don't think so. We got our drinks and he rambled about his friendship with Kevin."

"And he told you about having Tucker's car?" Vicky asked.

"Yeah. No, wait. He showed me. He pointed out the window."

"So you went over to the window from the bar?" Vicky was sipping her beer and sat up straighter.

"That's right. After Homer brought us our drinks, I paid for them. Then Doug went over to the window and motioned for me to follow. He pointed to the car in the lot, then we went back to the bar and he just started rambling."

"I bet that's when your drink got spiked," Boggs said, imagining the scene. "Did you see anyone leave the bar or walk around?"

Toni shook her head. "I can't remember much. It's all so hazy. But I wasn't really paying attention to anyone but Doug. Damn it. How could I have been so stupid?"

Again Johnnie touched Toni's shoulder. "Don't blame yourself. It could have happened to any of us. That shit has no taste and if it's in liquid form, it doesn't take long to kick in."

That was the second time she touched her, Boggs thought. She gritted her teeth. *What the hell?* Did she think she could just move in on Toni like this with her sitting across the room? She glared at Johnnie and apparently Vicky noticed because she shot her a look and mouthed, "Cool it." Boggs bit back a retort and tried to let it go.

"But why would this guy want to drug you?" Jessie asked. "Am I missing something? I mean, why drug someone and then disappear?"

"I have no idea," Vicky said. "And I don't think you're missing anything." She smiled at the young officer, who blushed in response.

"He probably ran because you got hurt," Johnnie offered.

"Wait," Toni said. She sat on the edge of the couch. "I vaguely remember someone else. Like there was someone else with Doug and me as we went outside. Was there anyone there with me when the ambulance came?"

"No," Vicky answered. "I talked to Homer and he said you were just sitting on the floor inside when you called for him. So that would make sense to me. If someone was working with Doug, they wouldn't stick around. Maybe that's the person who's obsessed with you."

"We have to find out what happened before the ambulance arrived," Jessie said. "Because you can't remember. How much time went by? He gave you a date rape drug and maybe . . ." Her voice trailed off and her hands flew to her mouth. "I shouldn't have said that. I'm sorry, I mean . . . I'm sure nothing happened."

Toni paled and her hand went to her chest as though she was trying to cover herself. "Did he . . . did he rape me?" Her voice was barely above a whisper and the room was silent.

"No, sweetie," Vicky said. "There wasn't time. Homer said you left and then called for him in less than five minutes."

Toni seemed to relax just a bit.

Oh, my God. He could have raped her, Boggs thought. And she wasn't there to protect her. *I'm going to kill that son of a bitch.*

"God, this is all so creepy," Toni said. "I don't even want to think about what could have happened if I hadn't gotten hurt." She reached for her soda with trembling hands and promptly spilled it all over her shirt. "Jeez." She reached for napkins. Jessie quickly wiped up the spilled soda. Toni looked at her soaked shirt. "I guess I need a clean shirt. Back in a sec."

Toni slowly climbed the stairs. *Someone gave me the date rape drug.* She shuddered. Entering her bedroom, she saw Mr. Rupert sitting on her desk, staring at her laptop. "Hey, buddy. What are you doing? Ordering something online?" She rubbed his head and peeled off her wet T-shirt, tossing it in the hamper. She glanced at the screen saver with its tropical fish swimming. She rarely turned off her computer and the screen saver would come on after twenty minutes of inactivity. "Oh, I see. Your very own fishtank." She dug in her dresser drawer and found another T-shirt. She watched the online fish swimming back and forth for a moment, then pulled on her shirt. She rubbed his head, kissed him, then headed back downstairs.

"What did I miss?" she asked as she sat down close to Boggs on the couch.

Boggs kissed her on the lips and possessively put her arm around her. "We've decided that you're not allowed to go anywhere by yourself," she said. "And I think that includes the bathroom."

Everyone laughed. "Well," Vicky said, "I guess that means you'll have to accompany Toni to the bathroom at work. And if I recall correctly, you've done that on occasion."

"And we almost got caught." Toni chuckled. She snuggled a little closer to Boggs. "And I still can't walk past there without thinking about that kiss, even months later."

"Ugh. You guys make me sick." Vicky reached over and patted her lightly on her arm. "And I love it."

A phone rang, playing Rod Stewart's "Tonight's the Night," and everyone laughed. Vicky glanced at the display on her phone. "It's Captain Billings." After a cryptic, one-sided conversation, she disconnected. "They found Doug Bradley. He was behind the old candy factory in Tucker's car. Dead. One shot to the head."

Toni was shocked. She'd just been talking to him hours earlier.

"I guess his usefulness was over," Johnnie offered. "Did they find anything else?"

"Nope," Vicky said. "And no cell phone, which is odd. I'm guessing that whoever he worked for had him set up this meeting with Toni. After that, they had to get rid of him. I sure wish Homer's had cameras in the parking lot. That would have been helpful."

"What's our next step?" Jessie asked.

Vicky glanced at her. "You're going to hit the bars. Friday, Saturday and Sunday nights. See if you can't find someone selling ecstasy or something like that. Use the cell Johnnie gave you to snap a photo if you can. And you'll have to remember not to acknowledge any of us when we're around, okay?"

"Got it." Jessie was beaming. She seemed excited at the prospect of doing some more undercover work.

"You'll use the identification that Johnnie gave you before, and I'll give you some marked buy money. One of us will be at the bar with you, and you'll have to wear a wire. Captain Billings has already talked to Johnnie about this, right?"

"Yeah. We're doing a joint deal here," Johnnie said. "Since we don't know how far this thing goes in the police department, we don't want cops in on it. I'll have two agents on the other end of the wire. We're going to be on between nine at night and two in the morning, all three nights."

"I guess we're good for right now," Vicky said. "We need to meet tomorrow night before Jessie goes to the bars. I'll have the background checks on our suspects by then and maybe Johnnie will have some info on Dead Granny."

"That sounds good," Toni said. "How about if I get Chinese food for us? It's the least I can do for all you guys are doing for me." She grabbed a pad of paper and took the orders from each of them.

Boggs glanced at her watch. "It's almost seven. I need to get some clothes and feed my fish. Can one of you guys stay here with Toni while I go?"

"I'll be fine, hon. You'll only be gone maybe thirty minutes."

"No way, babe."

"I agree," Vicky added. "Until we know who's behind this

crap, we're not letting you alone for even thirty minutes."

"I'll stay with her," Jessie said quietly. "If it's okay with you." She looked at Toni. "I haven't seen you in quite a while since I've been on nights."

"That would be great," Toni said, smiling at Jessie. She liked her and wouldn't mind catching up. "You guys go on, and Jessie and I'll hang out, okay?"

They all agreed and within five minutes, Toni and Jessie were alone in the living room. Jessie had stayed with Toni for several weeks a few months ago when she was acting as a bodyguard of sorts. Jessie had kindly cleaned up the coffee table, putting the leftover pizza in the fridge. She joined Toni on the couch, bringing with her a fresh beer for herself and a soda for Toni.

"I am so wiped out," Toni said as she stretched out on one side of the couch. "I could probably fall asleep in minutes if I closed my eyes." She thanked Jessie and opened her soda. "Tell me what's been going on with you."

Jessie opened her beer and sat cross-legged on the opposite side of the couch. They'd been talking for about ten minutes when Jessie suddenly sighed and took several gulps of her beer. "Well, I told my folks." A pained expression crossed her face.

"Didn't go too well, huh?"

"They pretty much disowned me. And I've been cordially uninvited to the yearly Fourth of July gathering." She took several more gulps of her beer. "I guess I knew it was coming, but I was hoping it wasn't."

"I'm so sorry. I know that must be very hard for you. Do you have any brothers or sisters?"

"I've got a younger brother who's pretty cool about it and an older sister who thinks I'm going to hell." She laughed. "Oh, well. I never really cared for her anyway."

"How about coming to our Fourth of July party? I don't have any of the specifics yet, but there'll be plenty of food, drink and friends."

"That sounds really nice." Jessie seemed to relax. "Where will it be? Here?"

"Oh, no. Boggs and I bought a loft down in the warehouse district and we close in two weeks. We'll have just enough time to unpack before the party."

"That is so exciting. I'm happy for you." She took another sip of her beer. "Um, would it be okay if I brought a friend?"

Toni grinned. "A friend? Have you met someone?"

Jessie blushed. "We've only gone out twice, but I'm hopeful."

"Tell me everything. Where did you meet her?"

"She transferred down from St. Louis about two months ago. We're on the same shift." Jessie took a sip of her beer. "She's wonderful," she added with a sigh.

Toni watched the dreamy look on Jessie's face and smiled. It reminded her of herself when she thought of Boggs. "Did you tell her about this assignment?"

"No. I didn't know if I should or not, but I'm sure she's okay."

"I'm sure she is, but just to be safe, you better ask Vicky, okay? In fact, since you're going to be out at the bars with a fake ID, I think maybe you should go ahead and call Vicky now." As Jessie dialed the number, Toni whispered to her, "What's her name?"

A smile exploded on Jessie's face. "Helen." She closed her phone five minutes later. "Vicky said I could tell her I'm working on a special task force, undercover. And if she sees me, she shouldn't acknowledge me unless I speak to her first."

"She'll understand, I'm sure of it," Toni offered. "In fact, why don't you go ahead and call her now. I'm going to go upstairs and put on my jammies and crawl into bed. Is that okay? I'm just really wiped out."

"Oh, sure. Thanks for talking to me and inviting me to your party." She had her phone in her hand and glanced at it.

Toni understood her excitement, waiting to call her girl. "Go on, call her. I can't wait to meet her."

Toni slowly climbed the stairs and as she rounded the corner, she saw Mr. Rupert still sitting on the desk, staring at her laptop. "I didn't know you liked the fish so much, buddy. Soon you'll have your own tank."

She pulled off her clothes, realizing how tired and achy she felt. She stood for just a moment, feeling exhausted from just taking off her clothes. After a heavy sigh, she dug in her dresser for an oversized T-shirt with a picture of a cat bowling on the front. She felt strange, but she couldn't put her finger on it. Probably from those drugs, she thought. And she'd taken those pain meds too. God, no wonder she felt like crap. But how long would those other drugs be in her system? Would she still feel like this tomorrow?

Curiosity overcame her and she sat down at her desk. "Beep beep, Mr. Rupert. Mom's gotta do some work."

He seemed reluctant to move his large self, but after a little nudge, he hopped over to the bed and watched her from that vantage point. She Googled *ecstasy* and *GHB* and read everything she could. After about fifteen minutes, she realized that there were a whole host of symptoms she may experience in the next few days. The whole thing left her feeling depressed and she chuckled to herself. Depression was one of the possible side effects, along with fuzzy vision, inability to focus, memory problems and fatigue. Well, she had all those right now. *Great.* One Web site did say that some people experience no bad effects. Hopefully, that would be her.

Feeling overwhelmed, she clicked off the site and checked her e-mail. She decided there was nothing that couldn't wait and closed the window. She debated playing a game of solitaire while waiting for Boggs to return but decided to just go to sleep. She turned off the light on the desk and crawled into bed. The blinds had already been closed and the room was dark. Mr. Rupert snuggled next to her and she wrapped her arm around him before falling fast asleep.

The woman frowned as her view of Toni went dark. And even though she was disappointed it had ended so soon, it had been one of the best nights of her life. She'd gasped out loud when she saw Toni standing there completely nude. Her entire body had reacted and she yearned to be close enough to touch her as she let her fingers lightly touch the screen. Even now, when she closed her eyes, she could see Toni standing there. So close and yet so unobtainable. At least for right now. She knew that very soon she'd be able to hold Toni close and really caress that wonderful body.

She played that twenty minutes of bliss over and over in her mind. When Toni had first sat down, she was horrified at the small bandage on her forehead. The area surrounding the white gauze was red and puffy. She was furious with Jan for having caused damage to Toni. She decided she'd need to handle that later.

She remembered seeing Toni chuckle shortly before she turned out the light. The woman closed her eyes and desperately tried to recall what she'd done right before Toni had smiled. After about ten minutes, she realized that she'd run her fingers through her hair on the right side five times, then three more. It was at that exact moment that Toni had smiled. The woman smiled herself and decided that five times plus three was critical. She repeated the routine and went to bed.

Chapter 21

Toni opened her eyes on Friday morning and smiled. Mr. Rupert was sleeping next to her on his back, with his rear feet in the air and his front paw resting on her chin. He was snoring. She rubbed his belly and he stretched his toes in response but continued to snore. She reached over him and touched Boggs's cheek lightly and watched as she slowly opened her eyes and rolled over on her side, facing Toni.

"Good morning, babe." Boggs pulled herself up, putting her head on her hand, and smiled. "How are you feeling?"

"Much better than last night." She gingerly touched the bandage. "This is still pretty sore, but not bad."

"You and Mr. Rupert were sound asleep when I came up. I went back down and talked to Jessie for a while. She's a great kid. I'm glad you invited her to our party. Can you believe we'll be in our new place in two weeks?"

Toni sat up in bed, pulling her knees up and wrapping her arms around them. "I really can't believe it. It doesn't seem possible, and we've still got so much to do. But I am *so* excited." She looked at her clock. "It's still way early. How about going out to breakfast before work? My treat. For some reason I'm starving this morning."

Boggs grinned. "Sounds great. You jump in the shower first and I'll feed Mr. Rupert and make us some coffee." She cocked her head and winked. "Unless, of course, you want to shower together."

Toni laughed. "Although that sounds wonderful, I'd rather save that for when we have a few hours to spare." She got out of bed and headed for the bathroom. "Can I have a rain check on that?"

"Mmm. Maybe I'll just stay here and think about that," Boggs said.

Toni peeled off her T-shirt and threw it at her.

Boggs caught it and held it to her nose. "Mmm. Smells good."

The woman sat in her tall, dark leather chair with a steaming mug of coffee in front of her. She was staring at her laptop, watching as the early morning sun began to lighten Toni's bedroom. She'd gotten up well before dawn and was on her third cup of coffee. She felt her body tingle when she thought she saw movement beneath the covers. That was twenty minutes ago.

"Time to wake up, sweetheart," she said aloud. She took another sip of her coffee and placed it in the center of the thick square coaster. Remembering her realization from last night, she ran her fingers through the right side of her hair five times, paused for a moment and did it three more times. She was instantly rewarded by seeing Toni move her hand and touch that huge cat. Then she saw the hand reach farther, outside the view of the camera. There was a rustling noise, then loud and clear she heard another woman's voice.

Oh, my God! There was another woman in bed with her. How could that be? She shoved her chair away from the desk. But Jan said she lived alone. The woman shook her head in disgust. Some things couldn't be trusted to others, she chastised herself. Her hands balled up as she thought about what she could possibly do to punish Jan. Her mind was racing when suddenly she realized that she was missing what was going on. She scooted closer to her laptop and strained to hear every word, every nuance.

She watched intently until there was no sound and no movement. She was frustrated and angry, thinking that someone else was sharing Toni's bed. She'd run her fingers through her hair five times, then three more, when it suddenly hit her. That other woman had basically propositioned Toni, asking her to shower together. And Toni refused. The woman smiled. Yup. Toni had flat out refused. She felt a little better and took a sip of her now cold coffee and grimaced.

After reheating her coffee downstairs in the kitchen, she tried to remember what Toni had said and not just the way she looked, although that was almost beyond belief. She'd never seen someone wake up in the morning looking that good. Even though her hair was sticking up and she wore a ratty looking T-shirt, Toni was positively radiant. *What had she been saying?* She closed her eyes to concentrate, but the only thing she could see was Toni's body when she'd stood in front of the laptop the night before. She shook that image from her mind and tried to focus on the words she'd heard this morning. Toni talking about moving, she recalled. In two weeks. *Damn it. I don't have much time.* She went back to her study, called Jan and then Mike, anxious to put the wheels in motion. Then she tapped into Toni's e-mail and began reading each and every one.

⚬᙭᙭᙭ᴖ

Toni made it through her day on autopilot, grateful that she didn't have any court appearances. Martin had agreed to plead guilty to voluntary manslaughter but his court date wasn't for several weeks. She'd had difficulty concentrating on her work all morning and had to write and then rewrite several documents. Her boss, Anne Mulhoney, stopped by around ten o'clock and told her to go home, but she insisted on staying. She muddled through the rest of the day, but by three thirty, she gave up all hope of accomplishing anything more.

Frustrated, she pushed her chair back from her desk and put her feet up on an open drawer. "I am so worthless today," she muttered to herself. She grabbed a legal pad and began to list the things left to do before they moved into their new loft. She'd made note of all the places she'd need to put in a change of address and was just starting to list the utilities when Boggs poked her head around the corner.

"Hi, gorgeous. Busy?"

Toni grinned and waved her inside. "Not at all. I've been totally useless today. In fact, I was just making a list of address changes. What should we do about the utilities?"

Boggs sat in the only available chair and stretched out her legs. "Well, I think we should have utilities, babe. They come in handy."

"Very funny. I meant whose name?"

Boggs laughed. "I know, I was just giving you a hard time. I asked Aunt Francie to take care of that for us. All utilities are in both names and they'll be turned on the twenty-ninth. Is that okay? I guess I should have asked you first."

"Oh, sweetie, that's perfect. Now I can cross that off my list, although I do need to notify them about stopping service at my townhouse."

Boggs nodded. "Me, too. But right now I'm ready to get the hell out of here. Can you leave now?"

"Well, I'm not doing anything worthwhile here. Anyway,

Anne told me to go home hours ago." She grabbed her blazer and briefcase.

"How about going to my place first. We can do some packing and I can feed the fish and get some clothes together. And laundry again. Before we leave we can call in the order for Chinese food. How does that sound?"

"Like heaven," Toni said. "Especially if you offer me a huge glass of wine."

By six fifteen they were back at Toni's with a huge box of Chinese food. Boggs was pouring them each a glass of Riesling while Toni went upstairs to change.

"Are you still staring at your computer fishtank? Did you touch the keyboard to make it go?" She rubbed Mr. Rupert's cheek and kissed his head before stripping down to only her bra and panties and digging in her drawers for clothing. After pulling on an obnoxiously bright neon yellow T-shirt and gray shorts, she sat down at her desk. "Beep beep, Mr. Rupert. Let me check my e-mail." He moved just enough so that she could reach the keyboard and she quickly scanned the list, deleting most without even reading them. It took her less than two minutes and she was heading back downstairs, calling her boy to follow her. "Come on, buddy. We're having Chinese food tonight. It's one of your favorites."

The doorbell rang just as she hit the bottom step and she looked through the peephole, opening the door for Jessie. The rest of the gang arrived within five minutes of one another. They sat in the living room, their plates overflowing with a variety of Chinese specialties. As always, Vicky's plate was flooded with soy sauce. If you wanted to sample her food, you had to be quick. After they'd all finished and Mr. Rupert was taking the last of her beef and broccoli, Toni and Boggs gathered the dishes and got everyone a fresh drink. On their return everyone was opening and eating their fortune cookies.

"I'm stuffed," Vicky announced. "I feel like my Halloween costume. And my fortune says *Don't take in too much*."

Boggs and Toni laughed hysterically along with Vicky while the rest of them just stared.

"Vicky dressed up as a sumo wrestler for Halloween last year," Toni explained, still giggling. "Guess you had to be there."

"Anyway," Vicky continued, "I've got the background checks on our list of suspects." She dug in her backpack, pulling out her notebook.

"And I made copies of everyone's driver's license photos," Patty said while handing them out. "I put them all on one sheet."

There were a few giggles as they looked over the sheet. "Jeez," Toni said, eyeing the mugshots. "Not the most flattering, are they?"

"No one really looks like these photos," Vicky said. "I bet you don't."

It was a deliberate challenge, and Toni laughed. "You're right about that. My eyes are squinty and my hair is a lot longer on my license." She laughed again. "At least my weight stays the same regardless of how much I actually weigh."

Vicky was smiling. "Exactly. I picked a weight that I was happy with, even though I haven't weighed that little since college." She opened her notebook. "Okay, here we go. First is Nancy Manford. We had the info on her from a few months ago. She's single, according to the state of Missouri. She's had two DWIs, six convictions for disturbing the peace and a stalking charged that was dropped last fall."

"I think that was when Rachel broke up with her," Toni offered. "Talk about being bitter. She almost spits out her name when she talks about her."

"Next we have Judge Mildred P. Crayton," Vicky continued. "I wonder what the P. stands for? Anyway, no convictions, no surprise. Single. She's a member of the bar, of course, and a consultant for Lambda Legal Defense. But now that she's back on the criminal docket, she's taken a leave of absence at Lambda. That's it on her."

"I ran her through the database at work," Johnnie added. "Nothing there."

"Okay, next is Doris Jackson. Also single. She owns Gertrude's Garage. One DWI back in 'eighty-eight. She also owns a small investment firm. That's it for her. Did you get anything, Johnnie?"

"Nope."

"Karen Young. Again, single. Two speeding tickets back in 'ninety-nine. That's it. She used to work fulltime for one of the Bank of Missouri branches as a VP in advertising. Now she's just on the board. Derek Lemon had four speeding tickets and one drunk-as-a-skunk while in law school. He works for a huge firm downtown. Married with two kids. Last is Velda Schmirnoff. She's also single and had an involuntary manslaughter prior. Apparently she fell asleep at the wheel and crashed, killing a guy. Turns out he was in a stolen vehicle, fleeing police. She got straight probation. That was back in 'eighty-four."

"That's terrible," Toni said. "Poor woman."

"Don't let that fool you," Boggs countered. "It could be any one of these people who had your car torched."

"True," Toni admitted. "Even though this information was interesting, I don't think it gets us any closer to the boss. God, this is so frustrating."

Patty's phone rang before Toni could say anything more. After only a couple minutes, she disconnected. "That was Cathy. She said she's certain that the person we're looking for is a woman."

"Well, that eliminates Derek," Vicky said. "Unless there's something we don't know about him."

"I ran dry on Kevin Tucker's love life," Boggs said. "I talked to some neighbors and they say he had a different guy all the time. He hadn't talked to his parents in ages, so I'm pretty much at a dead end there." She sighed.

"Well, I found out some info about Dead Granny's kids," Johnnie said. "Sad life. Husband died in the 'seventies. They had two girls and two boys. One of the girls died years ago, as a teenager during childbirth. Dead Granny raised the baby—a girl—and we have no idea where she is. I talked to one of the other grandkids and she said that she works for some big company in a big city and sends them money sometimes. Always a money order, so there's no way to trace those. She knew her first name was Jan, but that's about all she knew. Not very informative."

"Dumb as a box of hair, huh?" Vicky asked.

"Pretty much, yeah. Anyway, one of Dead Granny's boys has been in prison for over twenty years for murdering his wife, and the other boy is in the Army, stationed in Germany right now. The last girl still lives in Little Rock in Dead Granny's house. She works as a waitress at a truckstop there. She's the one I talked to."

"What about the other grandkids?" Patty asked.

"The Army brats are both in college back East." Johnnie flipped through her notepad. "Prison dad had four kids. Dead Granny helped raise them with the help of the mother's family. The oldest died in a car accident in 'ninety-nine. The second is married to a realtor there in Little Rock and has three kids. The third isn't working and he's had a few run-ins with the law, mostly small stuff like burglary and possession of marijuana. He's been out of trouble for several years and seems to have an income, but no job. My guess is he's dealing drugs or stolen merchandise. The last kid is doing a stint in county lock-up for his fourth DWI."

"Do any have a connection to Fairfield?" Jessie asked.

"Well, before Cathy said it was a woman, my bet would have been on the third boy. No one has a concrete connection here, so that leaves the last one, Jan. We're trying to find out more about her. I've asked an agent down there to talk to all the kids and see if they can come up with a last name. Back then, who knows what would have been put on the birth certificate since the mother died in childbirth. Could have been the father's name or the mother's. Hard to say."

"Well, at least it's something to start with. Everything else seems to be a dead end, or at least no information to go forward with."

Mr. Rupert jumped up on the coffee table at that moment, meowing loudly. He sat in the middle and continued to talk. "What's the matter, buddy?" Toni asked.

Everyone watched him as he continued to meow and paw at a napkin. "Do you think he's hungry?" Jessie asked.

"He's always hungry." Toni was puzzled. "But he had supper and licked our plates clean." She reached over to pet him and he jumped toward her at the same time, knocking over Jessie's soda and soaking her khaki pants.

Napkins flew as they tried to soak up the spill. Boggs got paper towels from the kitchen. Mr. Rupert was pacing back and forth on the couch.

"He seems upset about something," Toni said as she tried to soothe him.

Jessie was blotting her pants.

"Come upstairs with me," Toni said, grabbing Jessie's hand. "We'll get those pants washed out and dried in no time."

Up in her bedroom, Jessie emptied her pockets and took off her pants, handing them to Toni. "I can do it," she protested.

"I'll do it for you. You can slip on a pair of shorts or sweatpants while they dry. Dig through the drawers for something." Toni went into the bathroom to wash the soda out of the pants just as Jessie's cell phone rang.

"Hi, Helen. Are you getting ready to go to work?"

Toni closed the door to give her some privacy and worked on

the pants.

When she came out from the bathroom a few minutes later Jessie was closing her phone. "I see you found some shorts. Let's go down and I'll put these in the dryer. They should be dry in about twenty-five minutes or so."

Back downstairs, the gang discussed options and guesses about who could be behind this mess. By the time Jessie's pants were dry, they'd all run out of ideas. Johnnie was taking the first shift at the bar and Patty the second.

"I guess that's it for tonight, ladies," Vicky said. "Are you all still going to the range tomorrow?"

"Absolutely," Patty said. "If you're still up for it, Toni."

"Sure. Let's meet there at ten. Is that okay with everyone? And Jessie, you're welcome to come along. We're going to try out my new gun."

"Okay. That sounds like fun and I could always use the practice."

After everyone had left, Toni plopped back on the couch. "I'm beat tonight, hon. How about we just veg a bit and watch a movie or something."

"Perfect. I'll start some laundry and then be right there. Do you have anything upstairs in the hamper?"

"Yeah, I'm sure I do. Want me to go?"

"No. You stay right there and I'll take care of it. Do you want something to drink?" Boggs asked.

"A soda would be nice." She stretched out on the couch with Mr. Rupert curled up next to her. She was feeling exhausted from both the aftereffects of the drug and the stress of what was happening. The throbbing in her head was getting worse. She glanced at her watch and calculated that it had been at least two hours since she'd had any wine. "Hey, hon? Could you bring me a pain pill? The bottle's in the kitchen."

Boggs was in the kitchen headed toward the small laundry room. "How long since you had wine? I don't want that to mix."

"Two hours, hon. I checked."

"Okay." She brought the medicine out and then checked under the bandage. "It's a little puffy still and starting to turn a lovely shade of purple."

Toni swallowed the pill with a swig of soda. "Thanks. I like to be fashionable, so purple is good." She rolled her eyes.

"How about some popcorn? I know we ate a huge amount of Chinese food, but I'm hungry again."

"That sounds good to me." Toni started to get up, but a hand on her shoulder stopped her.

"Let me take care of things tonight, babe. I'll throw in the laundry and make the popcorn. Do you want plain, butter or Parmesan cheese?"

"Mmm. Parmesan sounds yummy."

"Be ready in a minute, babe. You just stay there with Mr. Rupert and surf the channels. See if you can find something for us to watch. I kind of like being home with you on a Friday night."

Even though Toni's head was pounding, her heart was filled with love for Boggs. She couldn't believe that in two weeks they'd be in their new home together and starting their new life. If they could just figure out who this crazy obsessive person was, things would be absolutely wonderful.

Chapter 22

The woman was sipping her Famous Grouse when she first saw Toni Friday evening. Most of the time it had been that huge cat staring at her. She gasped when she saw Toni standing there in just her bra and panties. She'd felt her heart begin to race and she'd quickly run her fingers through her hair fives times, then three more. She was rewarded by having Toni sit down in front of her laptop, even though she was now wearing clothes. The bandage on her forehead made her cringe. The vision of Toni lasted only a couple minutes, but it had been worth the wait. When she heard her tell the cat they were having Chinese food, she picked up her phone and ordered some for herself. It was almost like they were having dinner together.

After eating at her desk, she continued to have the window on her screen open in the corner. She checked her bank balance and then her stocks. She was playing a game of solitaire over an hour later when she heard voices. She immediately maximized the screen and saw another woman in Toni's bedroom. She was much younger than Toni and was getting clothing out of a drawer. *This is who she's sleeping with? This child?*

She leaned in closer when she heard a phone ring. She listened closely as the girl made a date with someone named Helen for tomorrow. They would meet at the girl's apartment, but tonight she'd be going to the Cat's Meow, driving a white Toyota Celica, not her own car. *What?* This girl was going to live with Toni yet she'd made a date for tomorrow? *What a bitch.* She could hardly contain her rage. When the webcam went silent she fixed herself another drink, her hands shaking. After centering it carefully on the thick square coaster, she slowly stirred the Scotch with her left index finger three times, then tapped it twice on the rim. After licking the amber liquid from her finger, she took a long swallow. She sighed deeply, set her drink down and began pacing, trying to decide what she wanted to do. She'd made five passes across her study, but it wasn't helping. She went to the small sink in the bar and began scrubbing her hands while counting to thirty. She rinsed, dried and began again, this time with hotter water. She scrubbed with her apple-scented antibacterial soap again and again until she felt the tension begin to leave her body. By the time she was done, she'd made a decision.

Jan answered on the third ring.

"I need you to do something tonight," she announced.

"Sure, boss. What do you need?"

"I want you to torch a car and maybe hurt a girl. She's driving a white Toyota Celica and will be at the Cat's Meow tonight. She's young, about five foot eight, I'd guess, and lean. She's got short dark brown hair with that messy style."

"Do you know her name?"

"No. She's Toni's girlfriend and she's cheating on her. Call me when you finish, okay?"

"No problem."

169

Jan sat in her recliner and sipped at her rum and Coke. Even though she was a little worried about her boss's continued obsession with Toni Barston, she was thrilled at the collateral jobs she'd gotten. She was trying to decide on her best options. She knew that the Cat's Meow had no cameras in the parking lot, so she'd just need to be careful and not let anyone see her. She decided that she'd drive her throwaway car, as she referred to it, a junker that she'd bought last year and couldn't be traced to her. She kept it in a garage in the alley, two doors down from her house. The license plates were expired and she'd used brown paint to make them look dirty, obscuring the sticker. She thought that was pretty clever.

At around ten thirty, Jan walked to her little garage and unlocked her 1990 Honda Civic. It started with no problem. She grabbed a full gas can and a can of spray paint and headed to the bar. Luckily there was only one white Celica in the parking lot and she parked in one of only two spots open, two spaces down. She lit a cigarette and watched. Nothing seemed unusual or out of place. She knew she wouldn't be able to hurt the girl tonight. She had no real idea what she looked like and it was too risky inside a crowded bar. The car would have to be it for now, assuming it was the right one. She got out with the spray paint in hand. In less than a minute, she'd spray-painted the word *cheater* on the pavement next to the white car. She was humming as she worked and slid back in her car.

She smoked another cigarette and waited. A few people drove by the bar and several parked on the street. She waited about ten more minutes and casually got out, this time with her gas can. It took her only another minute or so to completely soak the car. She returned to her own car and sat another few minutes, waiting for the gas to seep in a bit further. She lit another cigarette and backed out of her spot. As she drove past the white car, she took another drag and flicked the cigarette out the window. It landed on the trunk and almost immediately flames rose and the smell of burning gasoline reached her nose. She pulled out of the parking lot with the sight of fire in her rearview mirror.

Jessie had been in the Cat's Meow only about twenty minutes and hadn't seen anything out of the ordinary. She spotted Johnnie sitting at the bar smoking a cigarette, chatting with several people. Just then she got up and made her way toward Jessie, bumping her slightly as she passed and whispering, "Outside."

Jessie waited a couple minutes, wondering what was up, then went outside. Her car was in flames and she held back a gasp.

Johnnie was waiting for her. "Just act like it's your car, but don't freak out too much. The police and fire department are on the way. Give them the ID I gave you. Take a cab home when you're done. I'll be there."

Jessie nodded and on shaky legs went toward the car. The fire truck had just pulled up and within five minutes the fire was out. The cars on either side were damaged, but the white car was burnt to a crisp. She saw the word *cheater* on the asphalt and quickly snapped a picture with her phone.

By the time she'd given her information to the police, there was a crowd of people outside, huddled in groups of three or four. Some were beginning to go back in and others were trying to see who owned the car. Many were pointing at the spray-painted word and Jessie imagined they were all grateful it wasn't their car. When everything was done, she called a cab and went home.

Johnnie was smoking a cigarette and leaning against the doorway of the four-family flat when she walked up. Once inside, she allowed herself to relax.

"What do you think that was about?" she asked Johnnie as she headed toward the fridge.

"No idea right now. The agents in the van didn't see anyone." She sat down in a recliner in the living room and accepted Jessie's offer of a beer. "It may have just been a mistake and there's some angry woman out there whose ex-girlfriend drives a white Celica. But it looked like the same kind of torch as Toni's car and I really don't believe in coincidences. I called Vicky to let her know. Who besides us knew you'd be at the Cat's Meow tonight?"

Jessie felt herself stiffen as she thought back over the last twenty-four hours. "The only person I told was Helen, but I'm sure she didn't do that. She's not like that, really."

"I know," Johnnie said gently. "But just to make sure I checked and she was on a call at that time. She didn't do it."

Jessie let out a sigh of relief.

"Are you sure you didn't tell anyone else? Maybe just in passing?"

Jessie thought again, feeling like she'd made a huge mistake and let everyone down. But she *knew* she hadn't told a soul besides Helen. Hell, she didn't even know anyone else well enough to tell them anything. "I swear, Johnnie. I didn't tell anyone else." Her voice caught in her throat.

"Okay, I believe you. But maybe someone overheard you. Where were you when you told Helen?"

"I was on the phone. She called me when I was upstairs with Toni when I got soda on my pants."

"What cell phone did she call you on?"

"My real phone, not the one you gave me to use at the bars."

"Okay. Don't worry about this. You didn't do anything wrong. This is either a huge coincidence or we've got a real smart crazy person working here. Get some sleep and I'll see you tomorrow at the range."

They finished their beer and Johnnie went home, leaving Jessie to wonder if she'd still have a job in the morning.

❦

The boss hung up her phone and grinned. Even though Jan hadn't hurt the girl, the added bonus of spray-painting *cheater* was wonderful. She fixed herself another drink and stared at the window that showed her Toni's darkened and quiet bedroom.

Toni and Boggs were watching a movie when they got the call from Johnnie. Relieved that Jessie hadn't been hurt, Toni tried to play off what this meant. She snuggled closer to Boggs and held Mr. Rupert tightly on her lap. She allowed Boggs to move away only long enough to double-check the alarm. Even though Boggs did her best to reassure her that she was safe, her sleep was infrequent and restless the entire night.

Chapter 23

Despite the car fire the night before, they agreed to meet at the firing range at ten o'clock as planned and talk about their strategy afterward. They took turns trying Toni's new gun and there was no question that Toni could outshoot them all. She tried Johnnie's gun and then fired Boggs's a few times. It didn't seem to matter what she was shooting, she always hit dead center. After about an hour, they put away their weapons and met in the parking lot.

"Why don't we go out for breakfast?" Johnnie said.

"Wouldn't you rather talk somewhere more private?" Boggs asked.

"Well, I don't know if Toni's place is safe," Johnnie replied.

Toni felt her whole body go rigid. "What do you mean?" she asked quietly, gripping Boggs's arm.

"I'm sure everything's okay, but let's just go to Aunt Hattie's.

She's got great food and I'm sure it won't be crowded this time of day."

Toni nodded. Aunt Hattie's was a hole-in-the-wall kind of place inside an old warehouse. If you didn't know exactly where it was, you'd miss it for sure. The only sign was tiny and made of wood, barely discernible from the building itself. They arrived in several cars and made their way inside. It was actually quite quaint with about twenty tables, each with its own candle and mismatched silverware. The same waitress who had waited on Toni every time she'd been there led them to a large table in the back. There were only two other people in the place.

"Would you ladies like breakfast or lunch?"

After everyone agreed on breakfast food, the waitress gave them menus and asked who wanted coffee. They all did and she left to get the pot.

"You can stop drooling, Jessie," Vicky snickered.

Jessie blushed and quickly looked down at her menu.

The waitress usually wore a flannel shirt that looked like it had been shrunk in the dryer. It stuck to her like Saran Wrap and was usually unbuttoned dangerously low. Today she had on that same type of shirt, only the sleeves had been cut off at the shoulders. Apparently this was her summer look. She returned a minute later with a steaming pot of fresh coffee and filled their mismatched cups. After taking their orders, she gave Jessie a wink and sashayed away. Vicky giggled again.

"Any news about last night?" Toni asked.

"The crime lab guys think it's the same guy as your car, although that's just a hunch. No hard evidence." Vicky sipped her coffee.

"And I'm thinking maybe your place is bugged," Johnnie added, lighting a cigarette.

"If that's true, then whoever it is must know everything that we've been saying so far." Toni was beginning to panic. The thought of someone hearing her inside her own home was almost too much to bear. She felt almost naked. That and the fact that someone had given her a date rape drug made her skin crawl.

Boggs put her arm around the back of Toni's chair and lightly rubbed her shoulder. "We'll figure this out, babe. I'll call Aunt Francie and see if we can get the closing date moved up. It's not like we're waiting on anything. The place is empty." She pulled out her cell phone and made the call as the waitress brought their food. After disconnecting, Boggs took a sip of coffee. "She said she'd call the owner and see what she could do."

They each dug into their breakfast, which was far more than one person could possibly eat. They'd each gotten some type of omelet that came with hash browns, bacon, biscuits, fruit and orange juice. Toni was about a third of the way through her cheese and mushroom omelet when something dawned on her. "Hey, why would this person torch Jessie's car and write *cheater*? I'm with Boggs. If they wanted to take something away from me, wouldn't it make more sense to torch Boggs's car?"

"That's true," Vicky admitted. "Tell us exactly what you said to Helen," she instructed Jessie.

"Well, she told me to be careful and then I asked her over for dinner tonight." Jessie blushed slightly.

"No, silly. About the car." Vicky was smiling.

"She asked me where I was going and I said the Cat's Meow. Then she asked if I was driving my car so she'd know not to give me a ticket and I told her I was driving a white Toyota Celica."

"That's it," Toni exclaimed. It made sense now. "Whoever is listening in is hearing only what's said in my bedroom."

"Well, I bet that's interesting," Vicky raised an eyebrow.

Toni felt her face get hot. "Because otherwise," she continued, ignoring Vicky's remark, "they'd know I was with Boggs. Whoever heard this thought that I was seeing Jessie and then she made a date with another woman. That's where the cheater part comes in. It's the only thing that makes sense, don't you think?"

She took another bite of her omelet.

"That makes me feel both better and worse," Boggs said as she dug into her hash browns. "But it does make more sense. So, what do we do, sweep the room for bugs?"

"Or maybe we could use that against them," Vicky said, "If they don't know we're on to them, then maybe we could have Toni say she's going to be somewhere alone and see who shows up."

"Hey, I don't think we should use Toni as bait," Boggs argued. "This is way too dangerous."

Toni actually thought it was a good idea but held her tongue.

"But we'd be right there," Johnnie said. "I think it might work."

Boggs's phone rang. "Aunt Francie," she mouthed. After two minutes she disconnected and was grinning. "She said we can close on Monday at nine thirty in the morning. She's going to call the movers for us and see if we can get them to change the date and take care of the utilities." She pulled out some papers from her wallet. I'm going to call the furniture people real quick and see if I can change them." After several calls she took another bite of hash browns. "Well, the bedroom set can't come until Tuesday, but the mattress and living room stuff is all set for Monday afternoon. If nothing else, we can at least stay there Monday night."

"This is just all too weird," Toni said. "Shit. I've got a preliminary hearing at nine on Monday." She looked at Boggs, not sure what she should do.

"Do you have anything else in court on Monday?" Boggs asked.

Toni racked her brain. Prelim. *Shit.* What else? She couldn't think straight. "I don't think so, but I'd have to look." She felt incompetent, not knowing her schedule.

"Let me call Anne." Vicky pulled out her phone. "She needs to know that Toni's place has been bugged." After a few minutes, she closed her phone. "Anne said she'd do the prelim for you and that you're not to come in until Wednesday. She's very concerned about your safety. She's going to call Captain Billings and let him know what's going on. As soon as we figure out what we're going to do, I'll let both of them know."

Toni was suddenly frightened. Having her boss insist she stay away worried her a little. *Does she think I'm overreacting? Or does she think I'm about to be killed?* She felt a cold chill go through her body and she put her fork down. The thought of food suddenly made her queasy.

Johnnie, sitting across the table, reached out and touched Toni's hand. "We'll figure this out. You're safe with us."

Toni smiled weakly, and Boggs gave her a reassuring squeeze on the shoulder.

"We need to assume that your place is bugged, at least in the bedroom. But to be safe, let's not talk about anything regarding this in the entire place." Johnnie pulled out her phone and hit speed dial. She gave Toni's address and a few instructions then hung up. "I've got an agent sitting on your place until you're completely moved."

Boggs sipped her coffee, her brow furrowed. "You know, I'm now in a 'trust no one' mode, so I'm thinking we need to double-check the movers and the furniture delivery people."

"I agree," Vicky said. "Give me the info." She pulled a notebook out of her backpack and wrote everything down. "Now we've got to figure out what they already know. Since this shit started, tell us everything you can remember that you did in your bedroom."

Toni felt her face get hot once again. She remembered one particular night when she'd been rather aggressive and vocal in bed. *Oh, my God!* If anyone heard her, she'd just die of embarrassment. She lowered her eyes for a moment and when she looked at Boggs, she was grinning like an idiot. Obviously she remembered that night. *Jeez.* Toni looked at the rest of the group, who were all grinning. By now she thought her face was probably the color of a ripe tomato.

"I don't think we need *those* details," Vicky said, chuckling. "Of course, it might prove to be entertaining."

"It was pretty hot," Boggs offered, then hugged Toni. "But seriously, I'm sure we talked about moving."

"That's right." Toni was relieved that the topic had moved away from that particular night. "In fact, I remember us saying something about we'd be in our new place in two weeks."

Patty shook her head. "Then we have to think that they're going to step things up. Did you ever discuss where?"

Toni was shaking her head. "I don't think so, but I'm not sure. You know how it is, random conversations when you wake up or when you're getting dressed." When she glanced at Johnnie, she received a quick wink. Her face flushed again.

"I'm pretty sure we never talked about the location in the bedroom," Boggs said. "The only time we did was to you guys in the living room."

Johnnie was drumming her fingers on the table. "Well, I think we should check the place out before you move in, just to be safe." She wrote the address down. "What about bank people, or the title company? Karen Young works for a bank."

"I'm sure we're good on the bank people," Boggs said. "I'll let Aunt Francie know that we need to be very discreet. She'll know what I mean." She made the call.

Toni smiled and nodded at Boggs, realizing that she hadn't mentioned there was no loan. Did Vicky even know they were buying the house with cash?

"What about your parents?" Patty asked. "Do they know any-thing?"

"Nope. I told them that we were going to look at houses and that we'd found one, but I never told them where."

Boggs had just gotten off the phone. "What about Aunt Doozie? Did you tell her?"

"Sure, but I don't think I told her the location." She thought for a minute. "Oh, yes, I did. I told her it was in the warehouse district." Her shoulders slumped as she realized that information might put them in danger. "Oh, wait. I didn't talk to her on the phone and I'm sure we weren't webcamming." She was trying to remember. "That's right. I didn't say a word. I e-mailed her." Relief flooded her.

"Then unless you were talking out loud when you were typing," Vicky said. "I think we're okay."

"What about the party?" Jessie asked. "Have you asked people? Told them the address?"

Toni and Boggs looked at each other, shaking their heads. "I mentioned it to Sam," Boggs said.

Jessie shot her a puzzled look.

"Sam Clark. My boss. But I didn't give him the address, just told him to tell his wife, Betty. I don't think I've mentioned it to anyone else." She shrugged at Toni.

"I told my aunt, but only in an e-mail."

The waitress appeared and took everyone's plates. She returned a minute later with a full pot of coffee, filling their cups and leaving the check on the table. The restaurant was still pretty empty.

"We need to do two things now," Vicky said as she added cream to her mug. "First, we need to get you two out of that townhouse immediately. Too many fires for my taste. Second, we need to flush these people out."

"We can stay at my place," Boggs said.

"Let's go under the assumption this woman is obsessed with me," Toni said. "She thought I was with Jessie, so she torched her car. To make her feel better, we'll need to have me break up with Jessie. Maybe that way she won't feel as pressured to act. Then I can announce, to myself, that I'm going out somewhere. I'm betting that she'll attempt to make contact."

"I don't know," Boggs said. "That sounds a little dangerous to me."

Toni's mind was racing. She was afraid to go home now, but she had to go and get Mr. Rupert and some clothing. If fire was a solution for this woman, the next logical place would be her home. The thought of anything happening to her boy terrified her. "I need to get Mr. Rupert." She was beginning to panic again.

"I've got an idea," Vicky said. "You and Jessie will go back to your place. Throw enough stuff in a bag for a few days. Then have an argument and kick Jessie out. She'll take your stuff and leave. Then you announce where you're going. Put Mr. Rupert in a kennel and leave."

"Wouldn't it look odd to take a cat out? In case they're watching, I mean," Jessie said.

"I'll say I'm taking him to the vet for his yearly shots," Toni said. "And then we're getting the hell away." Once she knew that Mr. Rupert was safe, she'd feel a little better.

"Now where should we have Toni go?" Patty asked. "Somewhere where we can keep an eye on everything."

Vicky finished the last of her coffee. "A bar wouldn't make sense. Toni wouldn't go there by herself and anyway, there won't be many people there in the afternoon and tonight everywhere will be packed."

"That's right," Toni said. "It's Pride weekend. What about me going there? To the park? It would look normal for me to wander around and look at the booths and stuff."

"By yourself?" Boggs put down her mug. "No way."

"I could wire her," Johnnie offered. "Along with the wire I'd put a transmitter on her. We'd know exactly where she is every minute. I think it could work. We could all hear everything and mingle around. As long as Jessie isn't around, we should be okay. I'll have agents in the van on the outskirts of the park. We've already got the van set up for the surveillance at the bars for Jessie." She looked to the group for a response.

181

Vicky nodded. "I think it's worth a shot. We'll have Toni on our radar the whole time. Then tonight we'll watch Jessie at the bar to try to get a handle on the dealer."

"And I know who I'm looking for, right? One of our suspects." Toni took a deep breath. "I'm up for this. As long as I know that Mr. Rupert is safe."

"But it could also be someone else," Boggs argued. "Like when Doug called you."

"I won't feel safe until this woman is caught," Toni responded. "And I'm sure it's a woman because of what Cathy told us." She squeezed Boggs's hand. "And you'll be there." She looked at the rest of them. "Let's do it."

Johnnie and Vicky immediately got on the phone. Toni borrowed a piece of paper from Vicky and began listing the things she wanted to take.

Vicky closed her phone. "Okay, which car did you bring?"

"We took my car," Boggs said.

"Okay. Then Jessie will drive Toni home. We'll all meet at Boggs's place at three to get the wires set up." Vicky looked at Johnnie for confirmation. She nodded.

They all put money on the table for the bill and left. Outside, Toni hugged Boggs. "I'll be there in less than an hour, hon. I love you."

Boggs kissed her quickly. "I love you, too. Be careful."

As Jessie was driving, Toni noticed she was gripping the steering wheel like it was about to fly off. She grinned. "Don't be nervous. I'll give you cues as to what to say. I think if you act like it was no big deal that you cheated on me, it'll go smoothly." Jessie's eyes got big and Toni laughed.

"I would *never* do that," Jessie said.

"Oh, sweetie, I don't think that." She touched her arm. "We just need to make it believable. Just act like an ass and it will be fine."

Jessie finally relaxed. "Okay, I can do that. I'll just pretend I'm my sister."

Jessie parked and they both took a deep breath before Toni opened the front door to her place. She keyed in the code and locked the door. Checking her list, she went to the laundry room and grabbed a duffle bag. She motioned for Jessie to follow her upstairs, putting her finger to her lips.

Toni went into her bedroom, nodded to Jessie and began. "I can't believe you think it was okay for you to go out with someone else."

Jessie grinned. "Hey, what's the big deal? It's not like we're married or anything."

"But we're supposed to move in together," Toni countered. "That means we're a couple. What were you thinking?"

"So I slept with someone, what's the problem? I love you. I don't love her."

Toni was standing near her walk-in closet and she almost giggled. She composed herself and threw the duffle bag onto the bed. "That's it. You're such an ass. Take your crap and leave." She took several things from her closet and started packing the bag. Then she went to her drawers and began digging, pulling out everything she thought she might need. Then she gathered all her things from the bathroom. Once the bag was full, she handed it to Jessie. "Now take your shit and leave."

Jessie took the bag. "God, you're such a bitch." Then she mouthed, "I'm sorry," grinned, grabbed Toni's briefcase and left.

Toni waited until she heard the front door slam shut, then began mumbling about what an ass she'd been, believing that someone actually loved her. She took Mr. Rupert's carrier from her closet and called to him. "Come on, buddy. Time to go to the vet." She noticed her voice was shaky. *Perfect. She'll think I'm upset, not scared to death.* Mr. Rupert sniffed his carrier, then went inside and curled up. She took a deep breath. "Too bad you can't come to Pridefest with me this afternoon, buddy. But it's way too hot out there with all your fur. Guess I'll have to go stag. Well,

time to go to the doc. I want to be at the park by four o'clock."
She touched her gun that was under her T-shirt, looked around
her bedroom and started out. She felt the urge to run but managed to control it. At the last minute she closed her laptop and
tucked it under her arm.

The woman frowned when the screen went black. *Damn it.
She must have closed it.* Even though she was disappointed, she
was thrilled that Toni had dumped that woman. And she was
going to be at Pridefest *alone*. Perfect, she thought. She'd call Jan
and see if she could drug her again. It wouldn't be unusual to see
someone a little drunk at Pridefest. Happened all the time. She
grinned and made the call.

Boggs was waiting outside her apartment when Toni and Mr.
Rupert arrived. She ushered them inside, set the laptop on her
computer desk and hugged her. "How did it go?"

"I think we're going to be nominated for an Oscar," Toni said,
chuckling. "But I'm so glad to be out of there. It gave me the
creeps standing in my bedroom." She opened the door on the
carrier and Mr. Rupert poked his head out. "This is our new
temporary home, buddy." She smiled as he headed straight for
the 55-gallon fishtank. Boggs had put a chair in front of it so he
could sit and watch at eye level. "Shit. I completely forgot about
his litter. I've got to run to the store." She headed to the door,
but Boggs stopped her.

"I've already got one," she said. "I put it in the half bath."

"You're the best," Toni said as she hugged her. She picked up
her huge cat, took him to the bathroom and set him down.
"There's your new facility." He sniffed once, touched the litter
with his paw and meowed. Then he ran back to the living room
and took his place on the chair again, staring at his fish. Toni fol-

lowed him out and laughed.

"You know, babe," Boggs said, glancing at her watch, "we've got about two hours before everyone gets here." She was grinning.

Toni felt her face get hot.

"Oh, I wasn't thinking that," Boggs said. "But I wouldn't mind a repeat of the other night." She winked. "But I was wondering if you'd like to go over to Stray Rescue and see that little guy."

Toni was still flushed, remembering the same night as Boggs, but she pushed that from her mind. "That sounds great. If we decide we want him to join our family, I think it would be best if we waited to bring him home until Tuesday, don't you think? That way he won't have so much chaos."

"Sounds good to me, babe. Let's go. Do you think Mr. Rupert will be okay for a bit? I've got food and water for him." She pointed to bowls in the kitchen.

"I'm betting he'll still be sitting there when we get back." She rubbed his big head and kissed him. "Be back in a little bit, buddy."

They were greeted at Stray Rescue by a woman named Harriet, who was sitting behind the front desk, trying to fill out some paperwork. Three large cats were helping her, one attempting to grab the pencil from her hand. She smiled at them warmly.

"Hi. My name is Boggs and this is Toni. I called about the little Cinderella kitten."

"Oh, he's such a doll," Harriet said. "Come on back to the cat room." She led them through several doors and Toni heard the sounds of cats, dogs and who knew what else. The cat room had about twenty-five kennels. Some of the cats were lounging around on cat condos and an overstuffed chair. There were several toys strewn about. "Some of the older cats like to be with each other," she explained. She opened a kennel, took out the

little gray and white cat and handed him to Boggs.

Toni watched as Boggs's eyes filled with love. The little guy was only about twelve inches long. His gray fur had been shaved from his tummy down to his legs. The fur on his back two paws was untouched, making it look like he had white fluffy socks. His tail was about two inches long, and it moved around in a circular motion. His eyes had a look of surprise on them, but he was purring loudly in Boggs's arms.

"Oh, my God," Toni said as she reached out to pet him. "He's adorable." He licked her hand in response to the compliment. Boggs handed him to Toni and he immediately snuggled into her arms and continued to purr. She lightly kissed his little head and he meowed. It sounded more like a squeak. "I don't know about you, but I'm sold. I think he belongs with us." She looked at Harriet. "Is it possible for us to wait until Tuesday to bring him home with us? We're going to be moving on Monday and I don't want to traumatize him too much."

"That would be fine," Harriet said. "We've already approved your application."

"You won't let anyone else take him, will you?" Boggs asked.

"Oh, no, honey. He's yours. I think he likes you both."

Toni kissed him again. "We'll be back in three days, little guy. Don't worry. And you'll have your very own big brother." She put him back in his kennel. "This is hard," she said to Boggs. "I don't want to leave him here."

"Me either, babe. But you're right about all the commotion and stuff of moving." She put her finger in the kennel and he licked it. "See you soon, little guy."

They went back out front and Boggs gave Harriet the adoption fee. Even though it was only supposed to be sixty dollars, she handed her two hundred. Harriet frowned at her in confusion.

"That's for his boarding fee," Boggs said with a grin. "Since he's ours now, that's for his room and board."

Toni squeezed Boggs's arm. What a great feeling to be able to donate to a great shelter. While Boggs signed a few forms, Toni noticed a flyer from the organization that cared for pets of people with AIDS. Something about the flyer looked wrong, but she couldn't put her finger on it. Boggs touched her arm, letting her know she was done, and they left.

"Let's stop at the pet store before we go home," Boggs suggested. "We need to get some new toys and stuff."

Once there, Boggs made a beeline toward the cat condos. They had all shapes and sizes and she stopped in front of one that was six feet tall.

"This looks perfect," she said. "It's got a little fort on the bottom, lots of shelves, a tray on top, and there's toys hanging. Let's get it for the boys."

Toni giggled. "Do you think it's big enough?"

Boggs frowned. "Do they have any bigger ones?"

"I was kidding, hon. This is huge." She looked at the price. "And it costs a fortune."

"But since we're getting new furniture, shouldn't they? Do you think it will fit in my SUV?"

"I'm sure we can make it fit."

Boggs rushed off and got a flat cart and the two of them hoisted it up. "Jeez. This thing weighs a ton," Boggs said. "I guess we don't have to worry about it falling over."

They wheeled it through the store, stopping to add a container of catnip, fuzzy mice toys, a stick with a string and feathers attached, two new food dishes and a bag of kitten food. "You know Mr. Rupert will probably eat this," Toni said. "But I'm sure he could use a few extra calories." She laughed at the image of Mr. Rupert even bigger.

After paying for their haul, and spending at least fifteen minutes trying to get the condo in the back of the SUV, they headed home. It took another ten minutes to get it into Boggs's apartment. When they came in the door, sure enough, Mr. Rupert was still sitting in his chair, watching the fish. He seemed to be most enthralled with the albino frog that would swim for a moment and then stop and float. Toni went over and offered her hand to him, knowing it would smell like their new little kitten. He sniffed for several seconds and looked at her. He looked around the room for a bit, then jumped down to investigate the condo. Boggs offered her hand and he sniffed again, then went in search of the new animal. After finding no one new, he climbed to the top of the condo and stretched out, or as much as he could with his twenty pounds of fur on an eighteen-inch square platform.

"I think he's happy," Toni said. "And it was good for him to get a whiff of his new cat." They left the rest of the toys and goodies in the bag.

Boggs got them each a soda and glanced at her watch. "We've got over an hour before anyone gets here. Want to do a bit of packing?"

"Absolutely," Toni said, taking a quick drink. They got started and within an hour they had most of the kitchen done and all of the pictures and candles in the living room packed. Toni began on the CDs. "You know, I think you're the only one left on this planet that still has a reel to reel." She laughed. "But then again, I'm the only one with a waterbed."

"I know." Boggs groaned. "I'm trying to put all the music I had on tape onto CDs. It takes a while to do it and I never seem to have time."

"Why don't we work on that tonight and tomorrow. After we do the Pridefest this afternoon, we don't have anything else to do except pack. Oh, and you've got a softball game tomorrow. What time do you play?"

Boggs checked the schedule next to her computer. "It's at noon, but I could skip this week."

"No way. It'll be a nice distraction. And anyway, I love watching women run around in shorts."

"You're sounding more and more like Vicky every day," Boggs said. "So tomorrow we'll do some more packing and I'll break down my computer system. I want to move that myself." Boggs had a very sophisticated system with equipment whose purpose utterly baffled Toni.

At three, Jessie arrived first, carrying the duffle with all of Toni's clothes and her briefcase. The rest came within ten minutes of one another. Toni changed into a pair of olive drab cargo shorts, a gray T-shirt with six flamingos embroidered in the rainbow colors and leather Tevas. She'd taken off her gun per Johnnie's instructions. Satisfied, she came back out to the living room.

"We need to put the wire on," Johnnie said, motioning for her to pull up her shirt. Johnnie hooked the small battery pack to the inside of her shorts, with only the small clip visible on the outside. She ran the wire up, stopping at Toni's bra and looked at Boggs, who came over and completed the task. The wire went under the bra and hooked on the strap where it attached to the cup. Toni pulled her shirt back down.

"How does it feel?" Johnnie asked.

"Not bad. Weird, but not bad. Why can't I wear my gun?"

"Because we want you to mingle and be close to people," Johnnie said. "And wearing a gun isn't second nature to you yet. Anyway, we'll be there and we'll all be able to hear everything you say. Except for Jessie, of course." Johnnie handed the others small units that resembled Bluetooth phones. "These receivers will pick up Toni's wire," she explained. "They're also like walkie-talkies. All you do is press the button while you talk and we can all hear you. Let's test them. Toni, go into the bathroom and talk quietly."

Toni did as she was told, catching a glimpse of everybody slipping the devices onto their ears. Toni began to sing "The Spy Who Loved Me."

Everybody was laughing when Toni came back in the room a

few minutes later.

"What's so funny?"

"This is great," Vicky said. "We can talk about you and you can't hear us."

"How fun for you," Toni said sarcastically. "Just make sure you have my back, okay?"

Boggs hugged her tightly and whispered, "I'll make sure you're safe, babe. And tonight, we'll *really* celebrate."

Vicky giggled. "Can I come over and celebrate with you?"

Toni felt her face get hot and even Boggs blushed.

"I think the mic works pretty good," Johnnie said. "So don't forget to take it off when you get home tonight." She winked at Toni. "And here, put this in your pocket, but please don't spend it." She handed her what looked like a nickel.

Toni examined it and then shrugged.

"It's the transmitter," Johnnie explained. "It will track you."

"Oh, now that's really cool." She fingered the small coin and slipped it in her pocket. "So I'm supposed to just wander around Pridefest and see if anyone approaches me? Is that my job?"

"Basically, yes. We'll also be wandering around, but when you see one of us, just say hi. Two-minute conversations at most. We want you to appear alone."

"And you think this will work?"

"Well, so far it's just a shot," Vicky said. "We need to flush this woman out, and if she thinks you're available, maybe she'll go for it. Are you ready?"

"As ready as I'll ever be," Toni said with a sigh. "Let's go."

Toni drove her Bug to the park and found a spot near the entrance. As she drove around she'd spotted the van that would be keeping track of her. She squelched the urge to say hello.

"That would have been bright," she said, then realized that everyone could hear her. *Be careful what you say or you'll sound like an idiot.* She headed for the long row of vendors, keeping her eyes out for one of the suspects. Nancy, Judge Crayton, Doris

Jackson, Karen Young and Velda. She'd etched those names in her memory. The first booth had every T-shirt imaginable and she looked at all of them. Suddenly she felt an arm go around her waist and she froze.

"Hiya, Toni," Nancy sang out.

Toni felt herself relax slightly and she turned around. "Hey, Nancy." She gave her a quick hug. *Nancy is bizarre, but it can't be her, can it? Obsessed with me? No way.*

Nancy grabbed a woman from behind Toni. "This is Laura, my date," she explained.

Toni shook her hand. "Nice to meet you, Laura. Have you guys been here very long?" *Hmm.* Laura seemed quiet and rather harmless.

"About an hour," Nancy said and Laura nodded. "There's a great band starting in another hour, we'll save you a spot if you want. Are you here by yourself?"

"Yeah, going stag," Toni said, shrugging. She hoped that Nancy wouldn't ask about Boggs. She didn't. They waved and off they went.

Toni went back to looking at the T-shirts. "I think we can cross Nancy off the list," she whispered. "And I sure feel sorry for Laura." She smiled to herself and headed to the next booth. She could just imagine Vicky agreeing with her about Nancy's date.

After she'd perused about a quarter of the vendors, Toni felt odd, as if she was being watched. *Well, duh. I am.* She looked around for Boggs, Patty, Vicky or Johnnie and saw none of them. This was creepy. They could see her and hear her but she couldn't see or hear them. She tried to keep calm, but the feeling of dread was beginning to overwhelm her. No wonder they said she couldn't carry her gun. She was no good at this. *What's wrong with me? I'm safe.* She saw a booth that sold candles and wandered over. There were several that she thought would look great in their new home. Just because she was bait doesn't mean she couldn't shop, right? She found a large three-wick pillar candle and a simple silver candleholder and bought them. While the vendor was wrapping them up for her, she saw both Judge Crayton and Karen Taylor standing near a food booth. She took her bag and headed toward them.

"Hi, judge, Karen. Great day for the fest, don't you think?" *Pretty smooth, Toni.*

"Well, hello, Toni," Judge Crayton said, smiling. She shifted her bottle of water to her left hand, wiped her right on her shorts and extended it. "Please, call me Mildred."

Toni shook her hand and noticed it was dry and chapped. Hmm. Excessive handwashing?

"Good to see you, Toni." Karen smiled. "What happened to your head?"

"Oh, just a little tumble. Nothing seriously injured except my pride."

Toni put her hand out. Karen seemed to hesitate just a moment, then shook it.

"I'm sorry to hear that," Judge Crayton said.

"Is the food here good?" Toni asked them, wanting to change the subject.

"It's the best," Judge Crayton said, pointing to the sign. It was the Gertrude's Garage booth. "Their pink lemonade is wonderful. Why don't I get one for each of us?"

Toni noticed that Doris Jackson was tending the booth and she nodded. There were also a couple other women working there. She *was* thirsty. *What's the harm?* "Sure. That sounds wonderful, judge."

Judge Crayton frowned.

"Sorry. I mean, thanks, Mildred."

"Do you want regular or tart?"

"Regular is good for me," Toni answered.

Judge Crayton nodded and looked at Karen. "I'll have the tart."

Judge Crayton ordered three pink lemonades, two tart, and three orders of wings. "Let's sit over at that table." She motioned behind the booth where several picnic tables were set up.

As Toni sat down, she spotted Johnnie leaning against a tree several yards away. There was a beautiful young woman talking to her, but she could tell that Johnnie was only half listening, mostly concentrating on Toni. *Thank God.* Judge Crayton and Karen came carrying the food and drinks. Karen handed one of the lemonades to her. It had a big *T* on the side of the white Styrofoam cup, written with a marker. "Is this one tart?"

Karen shook her head. "No. When Mildred was ordering, she said, 'Toni wants regular,' so the woman put a *T* on it." Karen sat across the table and Judge Crayton sat next to her.

Toni took a sip of her pink lemonade, sweetened just right. "This is really good," She sampled the wings, nice and spicy. "It's true. Trish does make the best wings in town," she said. They chatted for about fifteen minutes and she wondered if one of them could be the one. Several women said hello as they passed the picnic table. Both Karen and the judge seemed normal enough, but one never knew.

Suddenly she didn't feel right. She brushed her forehead and noted that she was sweating. *God, is it hot or is it me?* She felt sweat dripping down her chest, into her bra. *Oh, no.* What if this thing shorted out? Would her bra burst into flames? She began to panic and searched the crowd for one of the gang, but found no familiar faces. *I'm being ridiculous.* She took another drink. *I feel funny. Just like . . . oh, shit.*

"Are you feeling okay?" Judge Crayton asked. "You don't look well."

Both Judge Crayton and Karen were now towering over her. She felt like she was swimming underwater. She was cold and hot at the same time, frantically searching the crowd for a friendly face. She needed help. Why weren't they coming? She was nearing desperation when a hand gripped her arm. *Who is that?* It felt familiar. Suddenly there were people all around her. Someone was helping her to her feet. Everything was blurry and swirling around her. She was moving in slow motion, but nothing made sense. *Help me!* Someone was leading her away. Away from the crowds and away from her friends.

"First Aid here," a disembodied voice said.

The crowd parted and she felt the hand ease its grip and drop from her arm.

"Let me help you, sweetie," the voice said.

Toni was scared to death. Someone was trying to lead her away, take her and do something horrible to her. *The date rape drug.* She felt lips press to her ear and she froze, terrified. She tried to move away, move any part of her body but it wouldn't cooperate. *God, help me.*

"It's me. Vicky. You're okay."

She blinked several times, but everything and everyone was blurry and the ground was moving beneath her. *What did she say?*

"Sweetie, it's Vicky."

Toni's body went limp and she collapsed to the ground.

Boggs was waiting by her SUV silently praying, waiting for Vicky to arrive in that damn golf cart with Toni. She'd heard Vicky on her headset and knew that Toni had passed out. She saw them flying through the park and her stomach felt queasy. The cart slammed to a stop in front of her. Patty ran from somewhere and the two of them grabbed Toni and got her into Boggs's SUV. Seconds later Toni was leaning out, throwing up.

"Did you get the drink?" Boggs said, clicking the button on her earpiece. The answer was yes and she threw the car in gear and off they went. They were at the hospital in record time.

Once inside the emergency room, Boggs found Sally, the nurse who'd treated Toni the last two times she'd been in the hospital. They were taken into a treatment room almost immediately where Toni promptly threw up again. Sally took a blood sample to run a tox screen. Forty-five minutes had passed and Toni had gotten sick two more times. Sally had started an IV with fluids in an attempt to flush her system. Boggs was holding Toni's hand as she dozed off and on while Patty sat in a chair nearby. Sally and a doctor came in minutes later and the doctor was holding the chart.

"We got the results back from the tox screen. I'm Claire Henson." She shook hands with Boggs and nodded at Patty. "There was a highly concentrated form of gamma-hydroxybu-tyrate in her system. Thankfully she vomited most of it out, but there's still a little left in her system. We're running fluids and I'd like to keep her overnight for observation."

"Is she going to be okay?" Boggs could barely whisper, she was so choked with fear.

"She's going to be fine," the doctor said. "We just want to make sure she's fully hydrated and there are no ill side-effects. Sally will get her settled in a room." She smiled and left.

Within the hour, Toni was sleeping in her hospital room. Boggs hadn't left her side. Vicky and Johnnie had arrived and along with Patty, they sat in chairs next to Toni's bed.

"There's no question that the drug was in the lemonade and it was super concentrated," Johnnie said. "But the question is who put it there. Judge Crayton suggested the drinks and paid for them, Doris Jackson prepared them, and Karen Young carried them to the table. And it was clearly labeled as Toni's drink."

"We need to watch all three of them very closely," Vicky said. "I've already filled Captain Billings in on what happened. Did you talk to him yet?" she asked Johnnie.

"Yeah, on my way over here. I've got two agents on each woman. This is insane. One of them drugged Toni right under our noses." She slammed her messenger bag down on the floor. "I'm going into the office before I go to the bar tonight and see if I can find anything on this missing grandkid of Dead Granny.

Maybe we can find something that connects to Fairfield."

"Or maybe Jessie can find the dealer tonight," Patty said. "I'd be willing to get him in a room alone to find out what we need to know."

"Hopefully it won't come to that," Vicky said. "But I'm getting a little worried here. Whoever this obsessed woman is, she's stepping it up."

"We're not using Toni as bait again," Boggs said quietly. She'd made up her mind. "I won't stand for it, and if that means we have to move away, then so be it. I'm not risking her life again."

Vicky put her arm around Boggs's shoulder. "Don't worry, sweetie. Until we find this psycho, Toni won't be put in danger again. I promise."

Boggs nodded slowly and continued to caress Toni's arm. Toni's eyes opened and she tried to sit up.

"Just relax, babe. We're all here and you're safe."

"Can you raise my head a little," Toni said weakly.

Boggs pushed the button and rearranged the pillows. "Is that better?"

Toni nodded. "What the hell happened?"

"The lemonade was spiked, but you threw up most of it."

"I don't feel so good."

Boggs quickly grabbed an emesis basin, just in case.

Toni smiled. "No, I don't think I'm going to need that, but thank you." She looked at the IV in her arm, then back to Boggs.

"The doc said they're giving you fluids to flush your system and hydrate you."

"Okay. Can I go home after that?"

"They want to keep you overnight," Boggs said.

"I'd rather go home as soon as this is done," she said, pointing to the hanging bag. "I don't feel safe here."

"If the doc says it's okay, then you can go home."

"I'm not as fuzzy and confused as I was last time."

"I think that's because you threw up so much and they're giving you saline," Vicky said. "Are you just feeling sick to your stomach?"

"Yeah, mostly. And tired. But I do remember something from Pridefest. When I shook hands with Judge Crayton, her hand was rough and chapped. Maybe that's from excessive handwashing."

"Interesting," Vicky said. "And she's the one who offered to buy the drinks, and she denied my search warrant before. Maybe she's the one, but I don't want to rule the others out until we're sure."

"I agree," Johnnie said. "I'm going to head out." She grabbed her bag. "Let me know if you guys go home, okay?"

Vicky and Patty left soon after, leaving Boggs alone with Toni. After checking twice with the doctor, Boggs told Toni they could go home in two hours.

Jan sat in her boss's study sipping her rum and Coke. She'd smoked at least five cigarettes as she listened to her boss repeat over and over how close they'd come.

"If that fucking Detective Carter hadn't been working First Aid, we'd have Toni here right now," she said for the fourth time. She rattled the ice cubes in her empty glass.

Jan refilled the drink and made another for herself. She noticed her boss doing that hair thing again and again. If she didn't get over this Toni obsession, Jan thought, the entire organization was going to fall apart. She had to do something, although she didn't yet know what. The woman kept checking her laptop screen and there was a black square window in the corner. "What's that?"

The boss finished her routine of stirring her drink and waited until she'd taken her first sip to respond. "It's a webcam that Davey set up for me. Whenever Toni's laptop is open and turned on, I can see her."

Jan was intrigued. "Can she see you?"

"No. I can hear and see from the camera in her computer, but she has no idea. That's how I knew that girl was cheating on her and that they were going to move in together. And how I knew she'd be at Pridefest alone this afternoon." She smiled.

"This could be the way for me to find a time to grab her," Jan said. "And the next time there will be no mistakes. Let me know if she says anything about where she's going."

The boss smiled, but Jan wasn't doing it for her anymore. She was doing it for herself. Twice something had interfered with her plan and it wasn't going to happen again. She prided herself on doing good work, and this crap with Toni had been sloppy. Next time there would be no complications and she'd deliver.

Chapter 24

Toni woke up in Boggs's bed Sunday morning and it took her a minute to get her bearings. Mr. Rupert was snoring next to her, but Boggs was nowhere to be seen. She rubbed Mr. Rupert's tummy and he opened his eyes and meowed. "Good morning, buddy. Where's Boggs?"

"I'm here, babe," she called from the bathroom. She appeared a moment later wearing only a towel. "How are you feeling?"

"Good now. The only thing better than seeing you in just a towel in the morning would be if you dropped the damned thing and got in bed with me. As long as you give me ten minutes in the bathroom first."

Boggs grinned. "That's a deal. While you're in the shower, I'll make us some coffee. It'll be waiting for you as soon as you're done, okay?"

Toni didn't even respond. She got out of bed, winked at

Boggs and headed to the shower. She was careful with her bandage but still needed to put a fresh one on. The puffiness was gone but the bruising was worse. Wearing only a towel, she returned to the bedroom to find Boggs sitting on the bed dressed in a T-shirt. There were two mugs of steaming coffee on the nightstand. Toni took a sip and grinned. "God, this hits the spot. There's nothing like starting a morning off with Kahlua and cream in your coffee. What's the special occasion?"

"Well," Boggs said, sipping her own coffee, "it's the last Sunday in an apartment."

"Works for me. I'm so excited about moving into the loft," Toni said. "For a number of reasons." She drank a third of her coffee and sighed. "You know, honey, aside from the fact that someone is trying to hurt me, I feel like I'm the luckiest person in the world." She kissed Boggs on the cheek. "I've got you, Mr. Rupert, our new little boy, and we're about to move into our own home. I don't think I've ever been happier."

Boggs set her mug on the nightstand and wrapped her arms around Toni. "I feel the same way, babe. I've been lucky enough to have a few bucks stashed away, but I was never really happy or content until I met you. Thank you."

This time when they tumbled back into the bed, they took their time and enjoyed every touch and every caress. It was, Toni thought, more about expressing their love and gratitude for each other than a physical release. That came as a bonus.

After Boggs's softball game, which they won, they spent the rest of the afternoon transferring music from the reel-to-reel player to CDs and packing. Toni made burgers on the tiny Smokey Joe grill on the patio and they ate their dinner amongst the many boxes. Afterward, Boggs began packing up her elaborate computer system and Toni sat on the couch with her laptop. She checked her e-mail and was pleasantly surprised when she heard the familiar ding of her webcam.

"It's Aunt Doozie," she said to Boggs, then turned to the

screen. "Hiya, Aunt Doozie. What's up?"

"Oh, I was just checking in to see how the packing is going. You've got less than two weeks, you know."

"Less than that. In fact, we're actually moving tomorrow. A little change in plans." Toni was grinning.

"Oh, my gosh, honey. Are you ready?"

"We've just about finished all the packing, and the movers will do all the heavy work. We just have to point."

"Are you taking that ancient waterbed with you?" Aunt Doozie was laughing.

"No." Toni smiled. "I'm donating it to a shop that sells stuff from the Sixties and Seventies. They were thrilled."

"So you're getting a new bedroom set?"

"Yes and I'm so excited. They're delivering it on Tuesday. We got it from Bedrooms Galore, and it was quite a deal. I'm off work until Wednesday, so I can have everything ready in the new place." Toni spent ten minutes describing all the new furniture they purchased.

"Oh, I can't wait to see everything," Aunt Doozie said. "Give me your new address again so I can send a card, okay?"

Toni rattled off the new address. They spoke for a few more minutes before disconnecting.

"She sounds really wonderful," Boggs said. "Will she be here for our party?"

"Yes. They're arriving the Saturday before. I can't wait for you to meet her."

It was almost seven o'clock when the gang showed up.

"The place looks great," Vicky quipped. "Who's your decorator?"

"Very funny, Vic," Boggs said. "Help me move some of these boxes against the wall so we have room."

Patty was looking at the huge cat condo. "Wow, Mr. Rupert.

This is really nice." She had to reach up to pet him on his perch.

"Boggs got that for him and his new brother," Toni said. "Here, let me show our new little boy." She opened her laptop and pulled up the page from Stray Rescue. "Here he is." She turned the computer so Patty could see.

"Oh, my God. He's adorable. Have you picked out a name for him yet?"

Boggs piped up. "Not yet. We'll wait until he's with us for a bit. See what name fits him. I'm leaning toward Dexter, though."

"Let me see," Vicky said.

Toni turned the computer again and Vicky nodded her approval. Even Johnnie took a quick look. Jessie agreed that he was the cutest cat she'd ever seen, with the exception of Mr. Rupert.

"I'm really looking forward to having him home," Toni said as she closed out the screen and shut the lid of her laptop.

The woman frowned when her screen went black. But at least she'd gotten to see Toni up close for a few minutes. She made herself a drink and sat back down at her desk. Carefully she stirred the Scotch three times with her left finger, tapped it twice on the rim and licked off the drops. She took her first sip of the fourth drink and sighed at the familiar burn of the alcohol down her throat. This was going to be perfect. She knew once she had Toni in her bed, life would never be the same. She wasn't sure how Jan was going to accomplish the task, but she was positive it would happen. She'd called her immediately after she heard that Toni was going to be off work until Wednesday. She also gave Jan the address of the new place and the name of the company delivering the furniture. Jan had seemed excited about the information and told her to be ready on Tuesday afternoon for her date.

She just *knew* that Toni was the source of everything that had gone wrong in her life over the last few months. And since everything began with Toni, everything would have to end with Toni. Once she'd had her way with her, her entire life would change. Everything would turn around and there would be no more mistakes. She ran her fingers through the right side of her hair five times, paused and did it three more times. That sealed the deal. As of Tuesday, her life would be perfect. She took another sip of her Famous Grouse and checked her stocks and bank balance.

Jan was on her second rum and Coke and watching *Cops* on television. She'd already contacted Mike Johnson and he was going to verify the names of the delivery guys for Bedrooms Galore. Once she had the names of these guys, she'd put her plan in action. It was pretty simple actually. She'd intercept the delivery truck with Billy Hagers. He was a guy from Little Rock who was driving up to Fairfield tonight. He'd also worked with her cousin and could be trusted. He was staying at the local no-tell motel, a place that never asked for identification. She would pick him up on Tuesday and together they would stop the delivery truck. She'd use her police badge, compliments of Detective Johnson, and inform the drivers that they were to stay at the motel until they picked them up again. She'd take their cell phones as a precaution. Each would be given a hundred dollars while the police made the delivery. At least that's what she would tell them. The plan was for Billy to kill the real drivers when they were finished and leave them in the back of the delivery truck. Billy would then drive back to Little Rock. It was perfect.

Sometime tomorrow, Jan would leave her throwaway car a block from Toni's new loft. Once they had everything under control on Tuesday, Billy would get the car so Jan could take Toni to her boss. Then Billy would drive the delivery truck to the motel.

The only thing left to do was to have Davey make a small batch of chloroform for her. She'd looked it up online and found

203

that it was relatively easy to make. He'd said he'd be happy to do it for her, so she would pick it up tomorrow night. By Tuesday night, this would all be over. Her boss would have had her fun and Toni would be out of the picture forever. Then things could finally get back to normal, and Jan was really looking forward to that.

Toni had passed out fresh beers for everyone as they gathered in the living room. It was a pretty small room to begin with, but with all the boxes stacked around, there was barely enough space. Toni, Boggs and Vicky were sitting on the couch. Johnnie was sitting on the desk chair that she'd pulled over and Jessie and Patty were sitting on the floor.

"Still no luck with Dead Granny's missing grandkid," Johnnie said. "The only information we have is that her name is Jan. They all claimed they didn't have a phone number for her and we pushed pretty hard. Either they're telling the truth or they're protecting her."

Vicky had her notebook in her lap. "Dead Granny's phone calls are still coming from Fairfield. A few to Little Rock and a couple to the boy who is probably selling drugs. There have also been quite a few to Mike Johnson. But that's all I've got on that." She flipped a few pages in her book. "What did you get on surveillance?" she asked Johnnie.

"First is Judge Crayton," Johnnie said. "She went home after Pridefest and stayed there. A woman came over a little while later and remained there for about an hour. The tags came back to Janelle Conway. She's forty-two years old. Her occupation is listed as writer, but for no particular company or anything. Maybe freelance. Her IRS records show she makes about sixteen thousand a year."

"Jan could be short for Janelle," Toni said. "Maybe that's it. And Judge Crayton did have really dry and chapped hands."

"Oh, but there's more," Johnnie said. "Nothing is ever as easy as we'd like. Doris Jackson is next. She stopped at Gertrude's Garage on her way home from Pridefest. About an hour later her assistant manager came over and, get this, her name is Janet Folger. According to the agents watching the residence, this woman is a rough-looking character."

"Great," Toni said. "Another possible Jan. And Doris was the one who made the lemonade."

"True," Johnnie said, "but it gets better. Karen Young stopped at a liquor store on her way home. About two hours later, a woman came over and stayed for less than an hour. The car she was driving was registered to George Franklin. He's eighty-two years old. The agents called me immediately and I called Captain Billings. He arranged to have the car stopped when she left. He had some officer he really trusted stop her and give her a warning about her brake lights. Her identification came back as Janice West, age forty-five. Her occupation is handywoman. She works for herself and, according to her IRS records, she makes about twenty thousand a year. She lives a few houses down from old Mr. Franklin. So that leaves us with three suspects who all have contact with a woman who could be referred to as Jan."

"So now what do we do?" Toni asked.

"We keep watching," Vicky said. "And Jessie is going back to the bars tonight. Maybe we'll get lucky and catch the dealer."

"Tomorrow we close on the house at nine thirty," Boggs said. "And the movers are supposed to be at each of our places at ten thirty and the furniture delivered between noon and five. Let's figure out who will be where."

"I'm going to take Mr. Rupert over to my parents' house before we close, so he'll be okay during the move. I'll pick him up after the deliveries are done," Toni said.

"I'll stay with you at your place," Vicky said, "then go over to the new place with you. I've got my phone in case something comes up at work. I already checked with Captain Billings."

"Patty and I can go to the new place first," Johnnie said. She looked at Patty, who nodded in agreement. "We'll do a sweep to check for bugs, then wait for the furniture in case it comes before you guys get there. You just need to tell us where to have the movers put stuff."

"That sounds good," Boggs said. "Why don't you come with us to the closing so we can give you the keys, okay?"

"Perfect." Johnnie was stuffing her things in her messenger bag.

"Don't you have to be at work, Patty?" Toni didn't want her to get in trouble.

"I fixed that for her," Vicky replied. "Captain Billings has her marked out for court all day."

With all the details in place, they all chatted for a while, debating who could be behind all this. Each suspect had possibilities, but by the time they left, Judge Crayton was number one on their list.

Chapter 25

By the time Toni pulled in the parking lot at the title company, Boggs was already there, waiting for her with a check from her bank. Toni had taken Mr. Rupert to her parents' house, telling him she'd be back in time for dinner.

"Did you get Mr. Rupert settled in?"

"Oh, yeah. I showed him where his litter box and food were, and he was off exploring. With all the stuff in their house, he'll be busy all day. He's going to be pooped by the time we bring him to his new place."

"Are you ready to buy our new place?" Boggs asked.

"Absolutely." She kissed Boggs on the cheek and they went inside.

It only took about thirty minutes to complete the deal. Boggs gave them a cashier's check for the total amount and they both signed several documents. Aunt Francie hugged them and handed them two sets of keys.

"I'll be over later this afternoon with your housewarming gift," she said.

"Oh, you don't have to do that Aunt Francie," Boggs said. "Please come over, but don't bring us anything, okay?"

Aunt Francie just grinned and hugged them both again. "See you later."

When they went out to the parking lot, Johnnie and Patty were standing beside Johnnie's car. Boggs tossed a set of keys to Johnnie.

"The alarm is set," Boggs said as she dug through the paperwork, looking for the security code information. She found it and showed it to Johnnie.

"Nice system," Johnnie said. She repeated the code out loud once, then handed the paperwork back to Boggs. "Got it. We'll see you in a little while." She put out her cigarette and they got into Johnnie's car and left.

"I can't believe it's ours," Toni said, hugging Boggs. "This is a dream come true." She glanced at her watch. "I guess we better get going. I'll see you soon."

When Toni arrived at her townhouse, she was relieved to see Vicky's car already in the parking lot. Vicky was sitting at her front door with two lattés. She handed one to Toni. "Happy moving day!"

"You're a gift," Toni said, taking a sip. "Thank you."

Once inside, Toni punched in the code. Even though this had been her home for a couple years, everything seemed foreign to her. Just the thought that someone had been listening to her in her own home gave her the creeps and she shuddered.

"Don't worry, sweetie," Vicky said. "Everything is about done. We just have to watch the movers haul stuff." She picked up an empty box. "Let's finish packing up your bathroom stuff and clothes. We've got about forty-five minutes before they get here."

Toni hesitated. She didn't want to go upstairs.

"We'll just work quickly and we won't talk, okay?" Vicky put her arm around her. "It'll be fine. I'm with you. We should be able to knock this out in twenty minutes."

Toni took a deep breath and nodded. They went upstairs and didn't say a word until the last item was safely in a box. Vicky smiled and motioned for Toni to follow her back downstairs.

"Done. That wasn't too bad," Vicky said. "I've got a huge cooler on wheels in my car. I'll go get it and we'll pack the stuff in the fridge, okay?"

Toni touched her gun that was hidden under her T-shirt. "Sure. I'll start on the food from the cabinets while you're getting the cooler." She watched Vicky close the door and Toni quickly reset the alarm. Even though she was armed and Vicky would return in a couple minutes, she was still a little nervous. *Don't be ridiculous. She'll be back in a minute and you've got a gun.* Still, she stood by the door and continued to look out the peephole until she saw her returning. She opened the door and let her in. As if sensing her fear Vicky hugged her quickly before wheeling the large cooler into the kitchen.

They had just finished packing up everything in the kitchen when the doorbell rang. Toni froze and Vicky checked the peephole. "It's the movers." She let them in and asked for their identification. She'd gotten the names of the drivers and made sure they both had valid IDs. Satisfied that they were indeed who they said they were, Vicky showed them the furniture they needed to move. "The waterbed is to be delivered to a store over on Grand Avenue, so you might want to load that first and you can dump it off after you've moved the other stuff into the new place." The movers agreed and headed straight for the bedroom.

"Now what do we do?" Toni asked. "I've never had movers before."

"This is the hardest part," Vicky said. "We just sit here and watch." She plopped down on the couch. "That is, until they move this sofa, then we'll have to stand."

Toni joined her on the couch. "Want a soda from the cooler?" They'd long finished their lattés and she was parched.

"Nah, I think I'm okay for now," Vicky said. "Once they've loaded everything, I'll stop and get lunch for all of us. How does that sound?"

"Wonderful. And thanks, hon, for everything you've done for me. I really appreciate it."

"Oh, sweetie. No problem. You're one of my favorite people." Vicky laughed. "Anyway, it's totally selfish on my part. I'm anxious to get to your new place and try out the hot tub."

Toni rolled her eyes and got herself a soda. They chatted while the movers carried boxes and furniture. They finished in less than two hours. Toni walked through the townhouse, making sure that they hadn't forgotten anything.

Vicky wheeled the cooler to the front door. "I'm going to stop at Subs R Us. Is there anything else in here we need to move?"

"Nope, that's it. I paid the management fifty dollars to have the place cleaned, so I don't have to do anything else. Johnnie said she'd come in sometime this week and remove the security system and the bug up in my bedroom." She set the alarm and they left.

By five o'clock Toni and Boggs were alone in their new home. Aunt Francie had dropped off a bottle of Asti Spumante and a bouquet of flowers. The movers had transferred their furniture from the trucks to the new loft and the new furniture, except for the bedroom set, had arrived. Toni's old sectional couch was perfect downstairs in the game room. Boggs's bed was set up in one of the guest rooms on the second floor. The only thing in the master bedroom was the mattress on the floor and a few boxes. Most of the boxes full of clothing were stacked in the walk-in closet. Since they couldn't find their new sheets for the king-size mattress, they decided to make up Boggs's full-size bed for the night.

Toni was in the kitchen, attempting to organize, and Boggs was upstairs in the study setting up her computer system. When the doorbell rang, Toni jumped. She looked at the monitor on the countertop and saw her dad holding a cat carrier.

"Hi, Dad. Come on in."

Her father stepped inside and set the carrier down. Toni opened the carrier door and Mr. Rupert came bounding out, then stopped. Apparently he noticed that this wasn't his old house.

"Over here, buddy," Toni said as she walked into the nook off the kitchen. "Here are your new facilities." She pointed to his litter box, which he immediately examined and used. "And here is your food dish and water bowl," she said as she came back into the kitchen. Again he inspected both, then rubbed against her leg. "I think he's pleased," she said. "Do you want a tour, Dad?"

"No, your mother would kill me. My instructions were to drop off Mr. Rupert and come home immediately. I think she would have preferred if I hadn't come inside. We'll come over as soon as you're settled. We're both so happy for you." He grinned. "I should go, unless there's something I can help with?" He sounded hopeful.

"No, Dad. I think we've got everything covered. As soon as we've unpacked, I'll call you, okay?"

He gave her a quick hug.

"Thanks for watching Mr. Rupert."

"Always a pleasure. He's quite a charmer," her dad said as he left.

Toni reset the alarm and headed up to the study, calling Mr. Rupert to follow. "Look who came home."

Boggs crawled out from underneath the desk and petted the huge cat. "Hey, bud, did you see your fishtank in the living room? I set it up for you already. I even put an ottoman in front for you."

Mr. Rupert licked her hand in response.

"Where do you think we should put his condo?" Boggs asked. "I mean, I told them to put it in here, but I'm not sure where the best place would be."

"I think in here would be good if we put it by the window. That way the boys can look out."

"I don't like the idea of you staying home alone for the bedroom delivery tomorrow. I'm going to call Sam and have him do the interviews for me."

"No, hon. There's no need for you to stay home with me. I'm sure I'll be fine. We've got the cameras out front and Vicky already contacted the store and checked out the delivery people. They'll show up in a truck with Bedrooms Galore painted on the side. No worries. It should only take them a few minutes to bring in the stuff. Then I'll spend the rest of the day fixing up our bed, or at least attempt to find our bedding. It's got to be in one of these boxes."

"I just don't feel good about this," Boggs said.

"Oh, I'll be fine. Anyway, that witness isn't comfortable talking to anyone but you—isn't that what you told me last week? And Elizabeth's trial starts Wednesday. If I were her, I'd want it to be you who talked to my witness. Really, hon, it'll be fine. Vicky checked out the delivery people and I've got a gun. You come home when you can and then we'll go pick up our new little guy, okay?"

"Why don't you call me when the delivery people arrive and then again when they leave. How's that sound? I'd feel a little better."

Toni was touched by Boggs's concern and she hugged her tightly. "That sounds perfect. Now, what would you like for dinner tomorrow? I'll fix us something really good."

Boggs kissed her on the cheek. "Surprise me. How about having a glass of Asti to celebrate now?"

"You're a mind reader," Toni said. "Let's sit in our new living room."

As they drank the wine, they discussed where they would hang different artwork and possibly adding some more lighting. They talked about the upcoming party and things they'd need before then. They talked about anything except the crazy woman who was after Toni and she was grateful for that. No matter what they discussed, that fear still loomed in the back of her mind. She couldn't shake the feeling that even though they'd moved into a place with an elaborate security system, she still wasn't safe.

When they finally crawled into bed that night, Toni pushed those thoughts to the back of her mind. She tried to lose herself in the feel of Boggs's skin next to hers and the softness of her lips. She almost succeeded.

Chapter 26

Boggs left for the office at eight o'clock Tuesday morning. Toni kissed her good-bye and reset the alarm. The delivery people wouldn't be there for another two hours so she made herself a cup of coffee and sat at the kitchen counter. She made a list of all the things she needed to do. By the time she'd finished her coffee, the legal pad was full. She took a quick shower and began working. Once the bathrooms were finished, she started on the kitchen. She decided that she needed to wait until the furniture was delivered to start in the bedroom. She was just about finished putting all the kitchen items away when the doorbell rang.

She checked the monitor on the kitchen counter and saw it was a young guy in a baseball cap. She switched to a different camera and saw the delivery truck parked on the street with the store logo on the side. She quickly called Boggs and told her the furniture had arrived, then opened the front door.

"Delivery for Boggsworth-Barston," the young guy said. He was holding a clipboard.

"That's us. It goes up to the second floor."

"Okay." He went back to the truck and Toni noticed a woman standing near the back of the truck, also wearing a baseball cap pulled low.

She watched the two take the first dresser off the truck and carry it effortlessly into the house and up the stairs. She kept her distance, always aware of her gun tucked safely beneath her T-shirt. They went out again and came back with the second low dresser. Next came the headboard, then the footboard. She relaxed a bit. *I'm safe.* This was their new furniture, she told herself. The last item was the bedframe. Both of them went down the stairs and stood in the kitchen.

"Aren't you going to put the bed together?" Toni asked.

Concentrating on his clipboard, the young man simply shrugged.

Something wasn't right. But they'd delivered the furniture, so it was probably okay. She tried to push the feeling of dread from her mind. Why did he keep staring at his clipboard? Was she supposed to tip?

The arm around her waist startled her, but it was the hand over her nose and mouth that made her panic. She tried desperately to free herself, but the woman was too strong. Something smelled sweet. *Oh, my God. They're going to rape me.* She instantly felt lightheaded and fifteen seconds later everything went black.

"Billy, go get my car," Jan said as she tossed the keys to him. Toni had collapsed on the floor and she left her there. She noticed the gun and holster in Toni's waistband and pulled it off, placing it on her own belt. She pulled her shirt out to cover it. *Nice bonus.* She looked at Billy, who was still standing there staring at Toni. "Bring the car out front. There's no one around.

Then come inside and help me carry her."

Billy did as he was told and he returned five minutes later. The two of them carried Toni to the car and dumped her in the backseat. "How long will she be out?"

"She should start to come around in about ten minutes," Jan said as she got in the driver's seat. "Get the truck and take care of those delivery guys. I'll call you later on tonight, okay?"

"Sure, Jan. Are you sure you want those guys dead?" Billy was shifting back and forth outside her car door.

"Yes, damn it. Don't be such a pussy." She handed him fifty bucks. "Go get some beer after you're done. Now, get going." She started the car and left him standing in the middle of the street.

Jan got to her boss's house in ten minutes.

Toni became aware of her surroundings while in the backseat of a car. She knew she was in danger and she was sure the driver could hear her heart pounding. *Stay calm. Think.* She was pretty sure that this woman would drug her again. They'd tried twice before and each time they'd given her the date rape drug. Odds were, they'd try it again. She just had to figure out how not to ingest it. Before she could figure anything out though, the car stopped and the back door opened.

"Time to wake up, Toni," the driver said to her.

Toni decided that she needed to be compliant, but slow and clumsy. That should buy her some time, she thought. And Boggs should be worried by now. She never called her back to say the delivery people had finished.

Toni was led inside a house and up a flight of stairs. She purposely stumbled several times. The driver took her inside a study and shoved her down in a club chair. Toni casually scanned the room, looking for clues. Everything was neatly in its place. It had to belong to the obsessive-compulsive woman. *Maybe I can use her illness to my advantage.*

"Drink this," the driver told her. "It will counteract the knock-out drug." She handed her a small bottle of water.

Toni stared at the bottle. The seal had been broken, and she bet this had the drug in it. She looked up. "What did you say?"

"I said for you to drink the water. It will help you."

Toni noticed the wet bar on the side of the room. There were four glass tumblers on the counter. She stood up. "Thank you. Water sounds good." She headed toward the bar. "Is it okay if I pour it into a glass?"

"Sure. Whatever." The driver was standing by the door, probably to keep her from leaving or waiting for someone. Or both.

Toni kept her back to the woman and picked up the tumbler. She poured the entire bottle down the sink while holding the tumbler in her left hand. She made a show of pretending to drink from the glass, knowing she couldn't be seen. She put the tumbler in the sink. "Now what?"

"Just sit down and wait," the driver said as she looked at her watch.

She's timing me. Toni struggled to remember what it said on the Internet. Fifteen to twenty minutes to take effect. She looked at her own watch and noted the time. *This isn't the driver's room. It belongs to her boss. She's waiting for her boss.* Now was her chance. Toni began roaming around the room. The driver looked at her but stayed at her post by the door.

Every item in the room was carefully placed. The blotter, pencil cup, legal pad of paper—all were arranged symmetrically. She moved the items an inch or two. Then she returned to the bar and moved the remaining tumblers and reversed the bottles of liquor. She went to the bookshelf and pulled a few books out several inches. She nudged one of the club chairs slightly to the left. She didn't think she could do much more. She knew if she tried to run, the driver would stop her. And she couldn't use the phone. Even if she could dial Boggs quickly, she had no idea where she was. Her only hope was to distract the boss by moving things around. And time. She prayed that she had time on her hands. She looked at her watch again. By now she should start feeling a little drunk. And hopefully Boggs should be looking for her. *Please let her find me.*

Forty-five minutes had passed since she'd talked to Toni. This was way too long. She called the house. No answer. She tried Toni's cell phone. Voice mail. Boggs called her boss, Sam, and asked him to take over her interviews, and he agreed. Then she called Vicky and Johnnie as she sped home. *Please let her be okay. Damn it.* She should have stayed home with her. What was she thinking in going to work?

She pulled up in front of their loft in less than ten minutes. She ran to the door and fumbled with her keys. She was yelling for Toni as she opened the door. No answer. She ran from room to room. The furniture was in their bedroom, but it wasn't assembled. She ran back down to the kitchen and saw Mr. Rupert sitting on the counter. He was meowing loudly. "Where is she, buddy?"

He continued to meow as she ran downstairs to check the game room and laundry room. Nothing. She ran back upstairs and stood in the kitchen. Her hands were shaking and she jumped when the doorbell rang. She glanced at the monitor and saw both Johnnie and Vicky. She let them in.

"I should have been here," Boggs yelled as she paced. "Damn it. They got her."

"Let's look at the security tapes," Johnnie suggested and headed upstairs. The main system was in the study. Vicky and Boggs followed her. "What time was it when you talked to Toni?"

"It was a few minutes after ten," Boggs said. "She told me that the delivery people had come. If we don't find her in time, they might . . . they might do something." Her voice was shaky. *This is all my fault.*

Johnnie rewound the tape back to about nine forty-five and began playing the footage from one of the outside cameras. "There." She pointed to the screen. "The delivery truck. Is that the place where you bought the stuff?"

Boggs leaned in. "Yeah, that's the right place."

"It looks like a young guy and a woman," Johnnie said.

"Wait a minute," Vicky said, leaning closer. "There were supposed to be two guys. Not a guy and a girl."

"Let's keep watching," Johnnie said and they stared in silence as the man and woman carried in the furniture.

"Looks like that's all the stuff," Boggs said. A few minutes later on the tape the man left by the front door and went down the street on foot. "What the hell?" He appeared a few minutes later in a car and went back inside the house.

Boggs watched in horror as they carried Toni's lifeless body to the car and literally dumped her in the backseat. The woman then drove away and the man got back into the delivery truck.

Boggs felt sick, knowing that they could be hurting Toni at this very minute. "Do you still have surveillance on the three suspects?" she asked.

"No. We only did that Saturday night." Johnnie opened her phone and dialed. "But I'm putting them back on."

Vicky pulled out her own phone. "I'm going to check and see if Judge Crayton is at work." She called Anne Mulhoney, gave her the update and closed her phone. "She'll call me back as soon as she checks."

Boggs was pacing in the study. "We've got to do something. We can't just sit here. Every minute we waste is a minute they have with Toni." Her stomach was turning and she wondered if she was going to throw up.

"We can't do anything until we know where she is," Vicky

said.

The doorbell rang and Johnnie looked at the monitor. "It's Jessie and Patty."

Grateful they were able to come during the middle of a workday, Boggs let them in and they went back up to the study. Johnnie was looking at the footage again. "I can't make out the license plate, but it looks like an old Honda Civic to me."

Vicky's phone rang. "It's Anne." She listened for a couple minutes, cussed a few times then closed her phone. "Anne says that Judge Crayton left early this morning. Told her clerk there was an emergency at home. Something about a sick dog. Shit. Sick dog my ass. I bet she's got Toni there."

Boggs was already heading out of the study when Vicky stopped her. "You can't just drive over there and break in. We've got to have a plan."

"And we need to check on the others," Patty said. "Just in case. I'm going to call Gertrude's Garage and see if Doris is there and her assistant manager." She opened Toni's laptop and Googled the number. Everyone stood silent as Patty made the call. Minutes later she disconnected, shaking her head. "Neither of them is there." She tried Karen Young's home and listened to the message before closing her phone. "The message says that she's out of town until Friday."

"Boggs and I will head to Judge Crayton's place first," Vicky said. "Patty, you, Johnnie and Jessie go over to Doris Jackson's house. As soon as you know anything, call us, okay?"

Everyone agreed and took off. Boggs rode with Vicky and they sped through the streets, pulling up in front of Judge Crayton's house in less than ten minutes.

"We can't just break down the door, Boggs. Let me do the talking, okay?"

Vicky rang the bell and was greeted by a woman dressed in black slacks and a white sweater. "Yes? Can I help you?"

Vicky flashed her badge. "We'd like to speak with Judge

Crayton for a moment."

The woman seemed a little nervous. "She's not up to visitors right now. I'm sorry."

Boggs took a step forward, determined to get inside. "It's really important. And you are?"

"My name is Janelle Conway. I'm the judge's assistant."

"We really need to see her," Vicky said. "It won't take more than a couple minutes."

She hesitated again, then nodded. "Just a minute," Janelle said. "Please wait here." She closed the door.

"We'll wait five minutes, then I'm going in," Boggs said quietly, her anxiety growing.

They didn't have to wait that long. Janelle opened the door less than two minutes later. "The judge agreed to see you." She showed them inside and up to the second floor to the judge's study. Boggs went inside first, with Vicky on her heels.

Boggs looked around the room, searching for any telltale sign of Toni. The study was warm and inviting. Judge Crayton was sitting in a large leather club chair near a fireplace. Her eyes were red and puffy and she was clutching a tissue.

"I apologize, ladies," the judge said. "I've had a very trying day. My dog Buster died this morning." She blew her nose. "I'm sure many people would think it's silly for a grown woman to cry over an animal, but he was my boy." She blew her nose again. "What can I do for you?"

Boggs whispered in Vicky's ear, "She's not here. I can feel it."

Vicky nodded. "I agree," she murmured back. "She isn't the one." She turned to Judge Crayton. "I apologize that we interrupted you, judge. One of our assistant prosecuting attorneys was kidnapped this morning. You met her, Toni Barston."

"Oh, my goodness," the judge said. "Do you know who did it?" She paused a moment then smiled. "Oh, I see. You suspected me. May I ask why?"

Vicky smiled back. "We have several clues, but nothing solid.

We do know that the main suspect has an assistant named Jan."

Judge Crayton laughed. "Well, I certainly fit the bill then. Janelle has been my assistant for many years. She's more like a daughter to me. She's helping me write my memoirs. But please feel free to search my home. If you have a consent form I'd gladly sign it for you."

"I don't think that's necessary, judge, but I really appreciate your cooperation," Vicky said. "And I'm very sorry for your loss."

"Thank you very much." The judge looked at Boggs. "Is Toni your girl?"

"Yes, ma'am."

"Is there anything I can do for you?"

"I don't think so, but thank you," Boggs said.

"Do you need a search warrant?"

"I don't think we have enough for that," Vicky said.

"If you think you do, call me and I'll authorize one over the phone." The judge got a business card from her desk and wrote her phone number on the back. She handed the card to Vicky. "Now get going and find that girl. And please let me know when you locate her. In the meantime, I'll say a prayer for her."

They thanked the judge and left. Vicky flipped open her phone and called Johnnie. After several minutes she disconnected. "Johnnie and Patty are sitting in front of Doris's house. Jessie has searched the property and there's nothing unusual. No one answers the door, no car in the garage.

Boggs thought for a moment. "Have them go to her assistant manager's house. Maybe they're there."

Vicky agreed and relayed the information to Johnnie.

Boggs was tapping her fingers on the dashboard. "I think we should check out Karen Taylor's place."

"Even though her message said that she was out of town until Friday?"

"Yeah. Just in case, you know?" Boggs was feeling sick. She

knew it was her fault that Toni was in this predicament. If she'd just stayed home today, this never would have happened. She had to find Toni.

Toni looked at her watch and noted that the drug should have taken effect by now. She realized that the crazy woman would be appearing at any moment. She was sitting in a club chair on the opposite side of the desk. The driver was still at her post by the door. Toni began humming a tune, trying to pretend she was under the influence. *How am I going to pull this off? She should be here any minute.* Hopefully the driver would leave then. She heard footsteps in the hallway and then the driver said something Toni couldn't make out. Her heart was pounding so loudly in her ears that she was sure everyone in the neighborhood could hear. *God, please let this work.* She wanted to draw this out as long as possible until Boggs could get to her.

Someone walked into the room and Toni heard the study door shut. She was almost afraid to turn around, so instead she pulled her legs up on the chair and began singing a Christmas song. *Star of wonder, star of light.* She felt the woman behind her and the hair stood up on the back of her neck. *Please, God, don't let her touch me.* She smelled the strong scent of musk cologne. As soon as she felt the hand on her skin, she jerked around and grinned like an idiot. "Hi," she sang out in her best fake drunk voice.

She was stunned when she realized who it was. *I'll be damned.*

"Can I have more water?" Toni asked, desperate to get away from her.

"Sure. Let me get it for you." She went to the bar and froze. Deliberately she moved the heavy glass tumblers to their rightful place, then opened the mini fridge under the bar and took out a bottle of water. She must have noticed that the liquor bottles were switched, because Toni could see her hands begin to shake as she switched them back.

"You've got a really petty study," Toni said, giggling. "I mean pretty." She laughed harder this time. "Have you read all those books?" She pointed to the bookcase.

There was a marked change in the woman's face when she saw the books out of place. She thrust the bottle of water at Toni and nearly ran to the bookcase. This time Toni laughed for real, mostly out of nervousness and fear. While the woman's back was turned, Toni moved the end table in front of her and put her feet on it.

"Sit down and tell me about yourself," Toni said. She cracked the seal on the bottle of water and drank some. "I love your desk. Where did you get it? Did you have it made?"

The woman sat down at her desk. She smiled at Toni and it seemed as though she was about to speak when she saw the items on her desk had been moved. Toni studied her reaction. She couldn't push her too far, lest she might go totally psychotic and then no telling what would happen. *Be careful.* God, where the hell was Boggs?

The items were quickly restored to their proper places on the desk, and the stress was kicking in. The woman began running her fingers through the right side of her hair several times.

Destressing behavior, Toni assumed. *I've got her going now.* The things on the bar were placed just so. She bet if she made her a drink, she'd have a certain way to do it. *But she wants me, so she'll let me do it for her.*

"Let me make you a drink and we can get to know each other better," Toni suggested. She got up and went to the bar. "What would you like?" She stared into the woman's eyes and saw the conflict. *I'm right,* she thought.

After a moment, a weak smile appeared. "Yes, I'd love a drink. But I'll make it." She started to get up.

"Oh, no. I'm right here. Let me do it for you." Toni giggled and tried to smile as demurely as possible. "What's your poison?"

"I'll have Famous Grouse with three ice cubes, please. Fill it a half inch from the top." Her voice sounded a little shaky.

Toni purposely put four ice cubes in the drink, figuring if she asked for three, it was probably a compulsion. Then she filled it, stopping a full inch from the top, and set in on the coaster. As an afterthought, she moved the tumbler off center. *This is perfect. Her obsession with me is in direct conflict with her compulsions.*

The woman stared at the drink but didn't budge.

"Go ahead," Toni urged. "Take a sip and see if I made it right." She grinned at her and leaned over the desk. "It was so nice of you to have me over."

The woman stirred the Scotch with her left index finger. She made three slow circles and then tapped her finger on the rim. She licked the liquid from her finger and then took a small sip of the drink. Her hand was shaking as she set the glass tumbler on the center of the heavy coaster. Next she ran her fingers through the right side of her hair five times, paused, and then did it three more times.

Toni plopped back down in the leather club chair and put her feet on the table, which elicited a cringe from her keeper. "So, what's your favorite show on TV? I just love *Who's Line Is It Anyway?* Have you ever seen that?"

"I, um, don't think so." She got up from her desk and sat next to Toni in the other club chair. She put her hand on Toni's knee.

Toni tried not to jerk her leg away, but it was nearly impossible. She remembered she was supposed to be under the influence. If she didn't act the part, that assistant would be back in there on the double. She didn't think she'd survive that. She had to think fast. She had to change this woman's focus. She stared at the hand and her body reacted on its own. She flinched. *Shit.* She jumped up and went to the bar. "Can I have a drink?" *She looks confused. I think she's on to me. Shit.* "Maybe after a drink we could dance or something."

The woman seemed to relax just a bit. "I'll fix another one for both of us," she said. "You just sit back down. What would you like?"

Toni skipped back to the far chair, sat and pulled her legs up, wrapping her arms around them. *Damn.* She wished she had her gun. The driver must have taken it. "Um, what kind of alcohol do you have over there?"

"I've got Famous Grouse, rum, whiskey and vodka."

"Do you have any wine?"

The woman opened the small fridge. "I've got some red wine. Would you like that?"

"Sure. That sounds good to me." She watched as the woman located a wineglass, washed it, dried it and repeated the routine. She filled the glass almost to the top, then made herself another drink. Exacting in the amount of Famous Grouse she poured into her glass. She handed Toni the wine and set her glass on the end table. She watched the woman sit, then repeat her stirring routine before actually taking a long drink. Toni took the smallest sip possible, but continued to hold her glass. If nothing else, she could always throw the wineglass at her.

The woman set her drink back on the end table and smiled. "Why don't you sit here," she said, patting her lap.

Crap. If I'd actually taken that drug, I'd do whatever she asked me. She decided to play coy, not knowing what reaction she'd get. The obsessions were severe—there was no question about that. "Oh, I can't do that," she said, giggling. "I'm too big. I'd break your legs."

The woman frowned and took two large gulps of her Scotch, almost emptying the glass. "I don't think so. Come, sit here." She patted her lap again. Her expression was stern and it was clear she was running out of patience.

Think, damn it. She knew she was supposed to be compliant. If she resisted she knew the driver would be called back in. *She's used to having her way.* She searched the room for a way out. There was only the door to the hallway and another door that looked like a bathroom. Maybe she could stall for time in there? She glanced at the full glass of wine in her hand and smiled. "Okay, if you're sure I won't hurt you." She jumped up from her chair and promptly spilled the entire glass of wine on herself. "Oh, no!" She started to giggle. "I'm so sorry." She headed for the bathroom. "I'll just rinse this off real quick so I don't get you all red."

The woman got up and followed her. Toni tried to close the door but the woman put her foot in the way. "I'll be right here. Hurry up."

This wasn't good, she told herself. She's getting impatient and she's doing that hair thing again. She didn't know how much longer she could stall her. After soaking a hand towel with cold water, she made a show of trying to blot her T-shirt and shorts.

"Just take them off," the woman barked. "Put them in the sink." Her foot remained just over the threshold and she pushed the door open wider. She glanced at her watch and again ran her fingers through her hair, her hand shaking.

Toni knew she was running out of time. If she pushed her too much further she was liable to break. That could be good or bad. *Shit.* "Can I have some more wine? I promise to drink it this time." If she could at least shut the door, she figured she'd be safe until she broke it down or the driver shot a bullet through it.

The woman hesitated, obviously torn between taking what she wanted and granting Toni's request. The former won out and she came all the way into the bathroom, blocking Toni's exit. "I said for you to take those things off." There was no compassion in her voice.

Well, the ruse was over. Toni continued to blot her wine-stained shirt. "I think I'll leave them on, thank you."

The woman's expression went from disbelief to confusion to anger. Her jaw muscles became taut and her eyes narrowed. "I said take them off," she hissed. "Now." She took a step closer.

Toni scanned the room for any kind of weapon, but there was

nothing but a towel and a bottle of antibacterial soap. The woman was larger than her, but she had age and determination on her side. She needed to get out of this small bathroom. At least in the study there were things she could use. She pushed past her and went back into the study. The woman followed and went straight to her desk and sat down. When Toni turned to look at her, she was facing the barrel of a .38.

"Now sit down, Toni."

Toni did as she was told. "You don't need that," she said as calmly as she could. "Tell me what's going on. You wanted me here for some reason, right?"

The woman nodded but didn't lower the gun.

"So you had your assistant bring me. What's her name?" *Just keep her talking*, she told herself. *Pretend you're doing therapy. Change her focus.*

"Her name is Jan. I told her to bring you to me and she did." She ran her fingers through the right side of her hair five times, paused and did it three more times. The gun was steady in her left hand.

"Has Jan worked for you for a long time?"

Another nod.

"And has she *always* done what you asked her to do?"

Toni noticed the woman's gaze went up for just a moment. *She's trying to remember. This could be my way of causing doubt.*

"Yes. I think so." Her voice was quiet, barely a whisper.

"But things have been going wrong lately, haven't they?"

"And it's because of you." The gun rose a bit higher to accentuate her point.

"Are you sure?" Toni kept her voice level and warm. She couldn't afford to push her completely over the edge. She just needed to create some doubt.

"Yeah, I'm sure. It's because of you that Judge Smith and Butch were killed."

"And I'm sure that hurt your business, but I didn't do that. Is that what Jan told you? It was a sick young woman that did that."

Play your cards right. "And Jan and Detective Johnson could have found replacements for you immediately."

"They did. Well, it took a while." She lowered her gun slightly.

"I wonder why. There are several judges and attorneys who would have jumped at the chance to work for you."

"They wanted to be sure." She looked up again, her demeanor suddenly calmer.

She's trying to remember the conversations. I need to add more doubt. "And why didn't you ask me?"

"Because Mike said you wouldn't." She sounded confident.

"But he never asked me," Toni said. "I can barely live on my salary as it is. I'd have gladly worked for you." She paused to let that sink in a bit. "I wonder why he didn't approach me. Do you think he and Jan had some deal on the side?"

The woman shifted in her chair. She ran her fingers through her hair five times, then three more. Her hands were shaking again and she glanced over at the bar.

"Let me make you a drink so you can think better," Toni offered, noting a twinge of reluctance cross the woman's face. "I'll make it exactly right this time." She put three ice cubes in the tumbler and added Famous Grouse to the correct level. She carried it to the desk and set it directly in the center of the coaster before returning to her chair.

Shifting the gun to her right hand, she stirred the liquid three times, tapped her finger on the rim twice and licked the drops of Scotch. She then took a long swallow before putting the gun back in her left hand.

"Better?"

The woman nodded.

"Are you sure that maybe Jan isn't the cause of your troubles?" Toni asked softly. "She left me in your study for at least fifteen minutes, allowing me to move things around. She knew that would bother you, but she watched me do it. Why would she do that to you?"

"But you're the one who did that, not her," she argued. "It was you."

"Yes," Toni admitted. "But I didn't know it would bother you. I was just looking at all the beautiful things that you own. Jan knew it would bother you. She had to know. She's worked for you a long time, right?"

"Yes, she has, and she's very loyal." She picked up her cell phone and hit one button. "I need you in here. Bring the drug." She closed her phone and smiled at Toni.

Oh, my God. They were going to drug her again. And this time she was trapped. She wrapped her arms tightly around her legs in an attempt to protect herself.

The driver appeared a moment later with a small vial in her hand.

"It didn't work," the woman explained. "Do it again."

The driver grinned at Toni and she felt sick with fear. If she fought back, she knew they'd kill her.

Toni met the driver's glare and she knew she was done for. What choice did she have? She figured her only chance of survival was the passage of time. Time for Boggs to find her. The drug would take at least fifteen minutes to kick in, or would it? She noticed the driver was filling a syringe from the vial. She cringed and closed her eyes. She could feel Jan walk toward her but she kept her eyes tightly closed. In less than thirty seconds she felt the stab of the needle. *It's done. Now all I can do is pray.*

"If she gives you any problems, just yell. I'll be downstairs." Jan left and Toni noticed it was her gun and holster on the woman's waistband. *That bitch.*

She turned her attention to the gun still leveled at her. For the first time, she noticed the laptop. One window was open on the screen. She leaned a little closer. *What the hell?* That was their study, she realized. In their new place! *Holy shit.* That's how she'd been tracked. She felt violated. Toni closed her eyes and wrapped her arms around her legs again. She was going to be raped, she thought, shuddering. And when it was over, she'd be handed back to the driver, that Jan woman. And God only knew what torture Jan would inflict. *God, please help me.* She was going to die. Jan was going to kill her. She opened her eyes and glanced at her watch. *Only got ten more minutes.* She felt sick. Her mouth was dry and she felt a lone tear roll down her cheek. *I love you, Boggs. I love you, Mr. Rupert.*

Boggs watched Vicky dig through her backpack for Karen's address before she started driving. She was frantic. "Can't this thing go any faster? We've lost too much time." *Maybe it's already too late.*

"I'm driving as fast as I can without killing us," Vicky said.

As they turned onto the street, Boggs yelled for her to stop.

"What?" Vicky screamed as she slammed on the brakes and pulled over to the curb.

"Look," Boggs said, pointing ahead. "There's the car. The old Honda Civic. That's the one they took Toni in." She opened the door to get out. She had to get to Toni.

"Wait a minute," Vicky said, grabbing her arm. "Let me call Johnnie and Patty." As she quickly filled them in, Boggs started to get out of the car again. "Hold on a sec. I'm calling the judge." She quickly dialed the number and told Judge Crayton that they'd spotted the kidnapper's car. She thanked her and closed her phone. "We now have a search warrant. Johnnie and Patty are on their way, but—"

Boggs didn't wait for her to finish her sentence. She was already out the door with her gun drawn, running down the sidewalk toward the house. Vicky caught up with her at the driveway.

"Wait here and watch the front door," Vicky said. "I'm going to circle around the back so we know all the exits, okay?"

Boggs was crouched down by a bush. "Go," she whispered.

She spotted Vicky on the other side of the house two minutes later, giving her the go-ahead sign. They both approached the front door.

"This door is too sturdy for us to break down," Boggs said. "I say we ring the bell and see what happens." And she'd shoot whoever got in her way. She rang the bell and put her ear to the door. "I hear movement." She and Vicky stood on either side of the door and waited. Nothing. Boggs rang the bell again. *Answer the damn door. I know she's in there.*

Toni heard the sound of the doorbell, but it didn't make sense. Her entire body felt fuzzy. *Did I drink too much?* She looked at the woman sitting at the desk and noticed that her entire body had stiffened at the sound. Why was she pointing a gun at her? she wondered. *Where am I?*

The door to the study opened just a crack. "We've got company," Jan said. "Stay in here." The door closed quietly.

"What's going on?" Toni asked.

The woman put down her gun and went to Toni. She offered her hand and led Toni over to the couch on the far side of the room. Toni felt confused but went willingly. The woman sat next to her and put her arm around her. Then she kissed Toni's neck. *This feels wrong but I don't know why.* Toni scooted away and looked at the woman. "Karen? What's going on?"

The sound of a single gunshot made both of them jump.

"Someone's coming," Boggs whispered, hearing footsteps from behind the heavy door. They both had their weapons down by their legs. "I know she's in there. I can feel it."

"Who is it?" a voice called from inside.

"Police," Vicky said. "We've got a gas leak down the block and we're evacuating. We need all occupants to leave immediately."

"I'll stay," the voice answered.

"I'm sorry but the order is mandatory," Vicky said.

The door opened slightly and Boggs moved forward. She saw the flash and was blasted backward, a searing pain shooting through her shoulder. Vicky got to the door too late. It had already been slammed shut. Boggs grabbed her shoulder. "Shit. The bitch shot me."

Vicky pulled her away from the front door, flipped open her phone and called for help. She yanked off Boggs's outer shirt and tied it around the wound, leaving Boggs in only a tank top. Her shoulder was throbbing.

"I'm fine," Boggs said. "We've got to get in there."

Just then Johnnie's car pulled up. Jessie disappeared around back. Johnnie and Patty ran quickly up to the front. Vicky filled them in. A radio crackled and Johnnie pulled her walkie from her pocket.

"The back door isn't secure," Jessie said. "We can get in."

Boggs attempted to get up. She had to get to Toni.

"Forget it," Vicky said. "You and Patty stay here and watch the front door. We'll hit the back."

Johnnie handed her radio to Boggs before they ran around back.

The door to the study opened again and Jan ran in, slamming the door behind her. "Cops are here. And all because of this bitch." She spat the last words out. "And you haven't even done anything with her." Jan crossed the room and yanked Toni's T-shirt, ripping it down the front.

Karen pushed her away. "Get your filthy hands off her. She's mine."

Jan glared at her. "We need to get out of here. I've already shot one cop."

"But I'm not ready," Karen said quietly. She stroked Toni's arm.

Toni blinked several times. None of this was making sense. Did that woman say she just shot someone? *God, I feel sick.*

"We don't have time for this crap," Jan said. "We've got to go now before the place is littered with cops."

"And whose fault is that?" Karen asked, her tone cold. "If you'd done as you were instructed the first time, we wouldn't be in this mess."

"If *you* weren't so fucking obsessed with this bitch, we wouldn't be in this situation. You and your damn rituals." Jan was screaming now. "That ridiculous hair thing and refusing to drink your Scotch unless you've got three fucking ice cubes and you've stirred it just right." She laughed. "You're fucking nuts." She turned toward Toni and raised her gun. Toni's gun. "And you're just a pain in the ass. I should have taken care of you the first time."

The door to the study crashed open at the same time a gunshot rang out. Toni felt a burning sensation in her left shoulder. The pain coupled with her nausea caused her to double over, just as another shot was fired. Karen leaned over Toni in what seemed like an odd attempt to protect her.

Vicky's gun was pointed at Karen as she kicked the weapon away from Jan's body. "Get away from her," she snarled at Karen.

Karen scooted away. Johnnie also had her gun trained on Karen, and Vicky rushed to Toni's side. Jessie threw Karen to the floor and handcuffed her.

Johnnie was standing over Jan's body. "Looks pretty dead," she said to Vicky. "Nice shot."

Toni could hear sirens approaching. "Where's Boggs? What happened?"

"She and Patty are out front," Vicky answered.

Boggs appeared a moment later. "Babe, are you okay? Did they hurt you?" She stared at her torn T-shirt and the blood.

Toni reached up and touched her arm. "I'm okay, I think."

By now several officers had come into the room and Karen had been led away. Jan's body remained on the floor. An EMT tried to look at Boggs's shoulder but she directed him to Toni. "And she was given that date rape drug, I'm sure of it," she told him.

"It's not bad," the EMT said as he bandaged Toni's shoulder. "You need to be looked at."

Boggs wasn't changing her mind. "As soon as you've taken care of her."

Toni moaned and threw up in the trash can.

"Can't you help her?" Boggs was now sitting next to Toni on the couch.

"The more she throws up the better," he said. He nodded to his partner, who'd just brought in the gurney. "We'll start an IV on the way to the hospital."

"I'm riding with you," Boggs said.

Vicky ended a call to Captain Billings. "He's got a warrant out for Detective Johnson now," she explained. "But I don't understand how these creeps knew that the furniture would arrive today at ten."

Johnnie was standing behind the desk, looking at Karen's computer screen. "Hey, look at this."

"They were watching us," Toni said. Her head was spinning and she thought for sure she was going to lose her breakfast. She needed to lie down.

Vicky looked at the laptop. "That's their study," she said. "What the hell?"

"Shit," Johnnie said. "Toni's place was never bugged. It was the damn laptop. That's how they knew what was going on."

Vicky, Patty and Jessie stared at the screen. "But how in the hell did they do that?" Jessie asked.

"Must be the webcam," Johnnie said. "Damn. That's pretty slick."

Webcam, Toni thought. The damned webcam. *Shit.*

"Pretty freaky," Vicky said. "I don't think I'll ever use my webcam again."

Finally the EMT had Toni on the gurney, and she closed her eyes, the voices around her fading. She couldn't believe she'd survived this ordeal.

Chapter 27

It was nearly five o'clock when Vicky and Patty brought Toni and Boggs home from the hospital. They'd been sewn up, bandaged and given prescriptions for painkillers. Toni was still woozy but was grateful she and Boggs had only received flesh wounds.

"I guess our work is done," Vicky said as she put on the last pillowcase. She and Patty had stayed long enough to help them assemble their bed and put the sheets on. "I suppose we won't know who all is involved in this crap until the tech guys finish with Karen's computer."

"What about the guy who helped Jan? The other delivery guy?" Toni asked, nursing a bottle of lemon water. They'd hydrated her at the hospital, but she was still thirsty.

"Oh, I forgot to tell you. Captain Billings called while you were in the hospital. They found him, the truck and the two regular delivery guys at a crappy motel on the edge of town.

Apparently they were all in a room drinking beer. The guy—I think his name is Billy something—told the cops that Jan told him to kill the guys, but he couldn't. He thought they were too nice, so he bought beer instead. Those two delivery guys are damn lucky they were dealing with Billy instead of Jan."

"But how did Jan and Karen know about the delivery?" Toni asked. She had only a vague memory of something about her laptop.

Vicky filled them in about the webcam.

Toni was shocked. "I can't believe they tapped into my webcam," she said. "That's so creepy. To think that someone could watch everything you do in your own house." She shuddered. "And they did watch."

"I know," Vicky said. "Makes me think twice about having one. Are you guys okay being alone? Do you want us to stay?"

"We're good now," Toni said, looking at Boggs, then smiling at Vicky and Patty. "But thanks."

"Okay. Oh, yeah. Mike Johnson is apparently cooperating. He's blaming everything on Jan and Karen. I'm sure he's looking at a boatload of time." She smiled. "Okay, guys. We're out of here. Hey, you're not going to work tomorrow, are you?"

"We decided to take vacation days the rest of the week," Boggs said. "I had to beg Toni, but after we called Anne from the hospital, she insisted. Said we needed time to settle in and stuff."

Toni nodded. "Yeah, I think it will be good for both of us. We need some time to heal and I want to unpack."

"If there's anything you need, please call, okay?" Patty hugged them both.

After Vicky and Patty had left, Toni turned to Boggs. "I don't remember everything that happened." She was sitting on the couch in the living room with her knees drawn up and her arms draped loosely around them. Her shoulder was still so sore. "Was I . . . did they, um, hurt me?" Her voice was barely above a whisper.

Boggs scooted closer to her and put her hand on her knee. "No, babe. The doc said they didn't hurt you."

"Are you sure?" She couldn't allow herself to believe it until Boggs told her again.

"Positive, babe. Your shirt was ripped, but that's all."

Relief washed through her and she crawled into Boggs's arms, careful of both of their injuries. "Thank God. I was so scared, but I was more afraid of what I wouldn't remember."

"I know, babe. But you're safe now. And everything is okay." She kissed her gently.

Toni looked at the new cat carrier sitting on the floor. "Are you feeling up to getting our new kitten? I hate to think that he has to stay any longer than necessary."

"I'm good." Boggs was grinning. "Let's go."

They arrived at Stray Rescue a little before six thirty and were greeted again by Harriet.

"Oh, my goodness! What happened to you two?"

"A little work-related mishap," Boggs explained. "But luckily we're both right-handed."

"So, you're ready to take your little gray guy home?" she asked.

Toni held up the carrier and grinned.

"Come on back." Harriet led them back to the cat room and took the tiny kitten from his cage.

Toni and Boggs each held him for a moment then put him in his carrier. "Thank you so much for taking care of him, Harriet," Toni said. "We'll give him a good home."

"I know you will," Harriet said. "And if you decide you want another, just let us know. Or maybe even a dog?"

"We will," Boggs said.

When they arrived home, Toni set the carrier down in the mudroom off the kitchen. The little guy poked his head out and trotted over to the litter box. Toni had scooped out the box before they left. The little guy hopped in and rolled around on his back, kicking litter everywhere. Then he used the box and hopped back out.

Toni laughed. "Well, that was unique." She showed him where the food and water bowls were in the kitchen. He took a quick drink, then rubbed against Boggs's leg.

"Time for him to meet his big brother," Toni said, calling out for Mr. Rupert.

He appeared a moment later and stopped ten feet short of the little gray ball of fluff and stared. The tiny kitten was batting a piece of cat food across the kitchen floor. It stopped in front of Mr. Rupert's paw. The kitten ran straight for the food and skidded to a stop just inches from Mr. Rupert. He looked up and squeaked. Mr. Rupert thomped him on the head with his huge paw. The little guy had a shocked expression on his face and he cocked his head to the side, then lifted his own paw in the air. Mr. Rupert meowed loudly, then wrapped his big arm around the boy and licked his head before strolling away. The tiny cat trotted off behind him.

"I think they'll be okay," Toni said. "Mr. Rupert let him know he's the boss." She watched Mr. Rupert hop up on the ottoman and stare at his fishtank. The little guy climbed up the ottoman and sat beside him.

"We need to think of a name," Boggs said. "He's such a little tough guy." She grabbed one of the toys, a long stick with a feather attached to one end, and went into the living room. Toni followed and they sat on their new sofa.

"Hey, little toughie," Boggs said, wiggling the stick. "Come here, buddy."

The little gray cat tumbled off the ottoman and jumped for the feather. Toni smiled while the woman she loved played with the newest member of their family and she and Mr. Rupert watched. The kitten jumped and crashed into furniture but kept coming back.

"I think he is a tough guy," Toni said. "Maybe we should call him Mr. Tuffy."

"Hmm. Maybe."

After about ten minutes of playing the little tough guy crawled into Boggs's lap and promptly fell asleep. Boggs petted him for just a couple minutes before she too fell fast asleep.

Chapter 28

Two weeks had gone by and they'd finally settled in. Toni's stitches had been removed from both her forehead and her shoulder. They'd unpacked everything and shopped for a few new items. There was a brand new flat-screen television hanging over the fireplace and one in the game room downstairs. The fridge was stocked with beer, wine and burgers waiting to be grilled. Several salads were already made and the counter was full of bowls containing several different kinds of chips and dips. They'd borrowed Vicky's huge cooler, which stood full of ice and soda on the deck. The Fourth of July party was about to begin.

Vicky was the first to arrive with her date, Dr. Claire Henson. Next came Jessie and Helen, followed by Johnnie and Patty. Anne Mulhoney and her husband, Bill, arrived with Sam Clark and his wife, Betty. Aunt Francie came with her new beau, Howard, and Toni's parents arrived with Aunt Doozie and Uncle

Tom at the same time. Judge Crayton knocked on the door carrying a huge bottle of wine. Harriet from Stray Rescue arrived with cat toys.

While Boggs manned the gas grill on the deck, Toni gave several tours of their new home. Each of the guests was more enthusiastic than the last, and she felt so proud. And of course everyone raved about Mr. Rupert's new cat. The weather was unusually cool for July, and people mingled on the deck, in the living room and the kitchen. At nine o'clock, everyone refilled their drinks and climbed to the third floor and out on the rooftop deck. Toni had taken up several pillows earlier in the day and placed them around the bench seats that encircled the railing. The group settled themselves in to wait for the city fireworks to begin. Fifteen minutes later they were rewarded with a spectacular view.

By ten o'clock, Toni and Boggs were saying good-bye to everyone at the front door. When the last person left, Toni closed the door and wrapped her arms around Boggs.

"That was the best party I've ever been to," she whispered. "And it's because it was our first party together in our brand new home." She kissed Boggs tenderly. "Why don't you make sure everything's locked up, then come up to the bedroom. I've got something I want to show you."

Boggs raised her eyebrows. "What?"

"Just go ahead and you'll see. Give me five minutes, okay?"

Boggs nodded and Toni ran up to the second-floor master suite. She lit several candles and turned down the bed. She took off all her clothes and slipped on an old denim workshirt. She buttoned only a couple of the buttons and rolled up the sleeves partway. It covered just enough. She started the water in the tub and added lots of bubble bath. When she heard Boggs coming up the stairs, she leaned against the door to the bathroom. As Boggs entered the room, Toni thought she heard her gasp.

"Hi, hon. I thought I'd treat you to a bath and a massage."

Boggs had stopped in midstep. "Holy shit." Her mouth was open.

"Let me help you out of those things," Toni said as she moved closer. She grabbed Boggs's hand and led her into the bathroom. She turned off the water and sat Boggs down on the tub ledge. After removing her shoes, she pulled her T-shirt over her head, then leaned down to kiss her neck. Toni knew her breasts were now at eye level and she caught Boggs's hand before it reached her. "Not yet." She unhooked Boggs's bra and pulled her to her feet. Boggs tried unsuccessfully several times to touch her, but Toni kept her at bay while removing her shorts.

"Now climb on in."

Boggs did as she was told and sank into the fragrant bubbles. She stared up as Toni slowly unbuttoned her shirt and let it slip to the floor. She climbed in and positioned herself behind Boggs, her legs straddling her. She wrapped her arms around Boggs's waist and pulled her close, kissing her neck. Using a giant sea sponge, she squeezed warm water on her shoulders and neck. Only a small scar remained in her shoulder from the flesh wound.

"This is heaven on earth," Boggs whispered. "What's the special occasion?"

"I just wanted to show you how much I love you and how grateful I am to have you in my life," Toni said as she continued to use the sponge. "I want every day to be a celebration."

Boggs turned around and took the sponge from Toni. "And I want us to share everything, even this." She held up the soapy sponge, then began caressing Toni's skin. After five minutes, Boggs set the sponge on the ledge. "Now, we can either sit in here until our skin wrinkles and the water gets cold, or we can dry off and continue this in our king-size bed. You choose."

Toni pulled the drain and stood up, grabbing a fluffy bath sheet from the towel rack. She stepped on the bath mat and wrapped the towel around her. "I don't know about you, but I'm not wasting any time drying off."

Boggs grabbed another bath sheet and stepped out. She dabbed at the clinging bubbles then pulled Toni into the bedroom.

As Toni fell back into the huge bed, she felt as though she was living a dream. For the first time in her life she felt safe, happy and loved. And the feel of Boggs's skin against her own made her entire body tingle with desire. What started off as a slow and lingering kiss ended up being a wild night of lovemaking. When they finally stopped two hours later, Toni was on cloud nine. Boggs ran downstairs for a couple bottles of water and when she returned her spot was taken by Mr. Rupert and Little Tuffy.

"I guess you'll have to squeeze in on my side," Toni said, chuckling. "Good thing we got a king-size."

Boggs slid in next to Toni and put her arm around her. "Now this is what I call heaven. You, me and our boys."

Toni fell asleep knowing that her life was complete. At least for now.

Publications from
BELLA BOOKS, INC.
The best in contemporary lesbian fiction

P.O. Box 10543, Tallahassee, FL 32302
Phone: 800-729-4992
www.bellabooks.com

WITHOUT WARNING: Book one in the Shaken series by KG MacGregor. *Without Warning* is the story of their courageous journey through adversity, and their promise of steadfast love. 978-1-59493-120-8 $13.95

THE CANDIDATE by Tracey Richardson. Presidential candidate Jane Kincaid had always expected the road to the White House would exact a high personal toll. She just never knew how high until forced to choose between her heart and her political destiny. 978-1-59493-133-8 $13.95

TALL IN THE SADDLE by Karin Kallmaker, Barbara Johnson, Therese Szymanski and Julia Watts. The playful quartet that penned the acclaimed *Once Upon A Dyke* and *Stake Through the Heart* are back are now turning to the Wild (and Very Hot) West to bring you another collection of erotically charged, action-packed, tales. 978-1-59493-106-2 $15.95

IN THE NAME OF THE FATHER by Gerri Hill. In this highly anticipated sequel to *Hunter's Way*, Dallas homicide detectives Tori Hunter and Samantha Kennedy investigate the murder of a Catholic priest who is found naked and strangled to death. 978-1-59493-108-6 $13.95

IT'S ALL SMOKE AND MIRRORS: *The First Chronicles of Shawn Donnelly* by Therese Szymanski. Join Therese Szymanski as she takes a walk on the sillier side of the gritty crime scene detective novel and introduces readers to her newest alternate personality— Shawn Donnelly. 978-1-59493-117-8 $13.95

THE ROAD HOME by Frankie J. Jones. As Lynn finds herself in one adventure after another, she discovers that true wealth may have very little to do with money after all. 978-1-59493-110-9 $13.95

IN DEEP WATERS: CRUISING THE SEAS by Karin Kallmaker and Radclyffe. Book passage on a deliciously sensual Mediterranean cruise with tour guides Radclyffe and Karin Kallmaker. 978-1-59493-111-6 $15.95

ALL THAT GLITTERS by Peggy J. Herring. Life is good for retired Army Colonel Marcel Robicheaux. Marcel is unprepared for the turn her life will take. She soon finds herself in the pursuit of a lifetime—searching for her missing mother and lover. 978-1-59493-107-9 $13.95

OUT OF LOVE by KG MacGregor. For Carmen Delallo and Judith O'Shea, falling in love proves to be the easy part. 978-1-59493-105-5 $13.95

BORDERLINE by Terri Breneman. Assistant Prosecuting Attorney Toni Barston returns in the sequel to *Anticipation*. 978-1-59493-99-7 $13.95

PAST REMEMBERING by Lyn Denison. What would it take to melt Peri's cool exterior? Any involvement on Asha's part would be simply asking for trouble and heartache . . . wouldn't it? 978-1-59493-103-1 $13.95

ASPEN'S EMBERS by Diane Tremain Braund. Will Aspen choose the woman she loves . . . or the forest she hopes to preserve . . . 978-1-59493-102-4 $14.95

THE COTTAGE by Gerri Hill. *The Cottage* is the heartbreaking story of two women who meet by chance . . . or did they? A love so destined it couldn't be denied . . . stolen moments to be cherished forever. 978-1-59493-096-6 $13.95

FANTASY: Untrue Stories of Lesbian Passion edited by Barbara Johnson and Therese Szymanski. Lie back and let Bella's bad girls take you on an erotic journey through the greatest bedtime stories never told. 978-1-59493-101-7 $15.95

SISTERS' FLIGHT by Jeanne G'Fellers. *Sisters' Flight* is the highly anticipated sequel to *No Sister of Mine* and *Sister Lost, Sister Found*. 978-1-59493-116-1 $13.95

BRAGGIN' RIGHTS by Kenna White. Taylor Fleming is a thirty-six-year-old Texas rancher who covets her independence. She finds her cowgirl independence tested by neighboring rancher Jen Holland. 978-1-59493-095-9 $13.95

BRILLIANT by Ann Roberts. Respected sociology professor, Diane Cole finds her views on love challenged by her own heart, as she fights the attraction she feels for a woman half her age. 978-1-59493-115-4 $13.95

THE EDUCATION OF ELLIE by Jackie Calhoun. When Ellie sees her childhood friend for the first time in thirty years she is tempted to resume their long lost friendship. But with the years come a lot of baggage and the two women struggle with who they are now while fighting the painful memories of their first parting. Will they be able to move past their history to start again? 978-1-59493-092-8 $13.95

DATE NIGHT CLUB by Saxon Bennett. *Date Night Club* is a dark romantic comedy about the pitfalls of dating in your thirties . . . 978-1-59493-094-2 $13.95

PLEASE FORGIVE ME by Megan Carter. Laurel Becker is on the verge of losing the two most important things in her life—her current lover, Elaine Alexander, and the Lavender Page bookstore. Will Elaine and Laurel manage to work through their misunderstandings and rebuild their life together? 978-1-59493-091-1 $13.95

WHISKEY AND OAK LEAVES by Jaime Clevenger. Meg meets June, a single woman running a horse ranch in the California Sierra foothills. The two become quick friends and it isn't long before Meg is looking for more than just a friendship. But June has no interest in developing a deeper relationship with Meg. She is, after all, not the least bit interested in women . . . or is she? Neither of these two women is prepared for what lies ahead . . . 978-1-59493-093-5 $13.95

SUMTER POINT by KG MacGregor. As Audie surrenders her heart to Beth, she begins to distance herself from the reckless habits of her youth. Just as they're ready to meet in the middle, their future is thrown into doubt by a duty Beth can't ignore. It all comes to a head on the river at Sumter Point. 978-1-59493-089-8 $13.95

THE TARGET by Gerri Hill. Sara Michaels is the daughter of a prominent senator who has been receiving death threats against his family. In an effort to protect Sara, the FBI recruits homicide detective Jaime Hutchinson to secretly provide the protection they are so certain Sara will need. Will Sara finally figure out who is behind the death threats? And will Jaime realize the truth—and be able to save Sara before it's too late?

978-1-59493-082-9 $13.95

REALITY BYTES by Jane Frances. In this sequel to *Reunion*, follow the lives of four friends in a romantic tale that spans the globe and proves that you can cross the whole of cyberspace only to find love a few suburbs away . . .   978-1-59493-079-9 $13.95

MURDER CAME SECOND by Jessica Thomas. Broadway's bad-boy genius, Paul Carlucci, has chosen *Hamlet* for his latest production and, to the delight of some and despair of others, he has selected Provincetown's amphitheatre for his opening gala. But Alex Peres realizes the wrong people are falling down, and the moaning is all too realistic. Someone must not be shooting blanks . . .   978-1-59493-081-2 $13.95

SKIN DEEP by Kenna White. Jordan Griffin has been given a new assignment: Track down and interview one-time nationally renowned broadcast journalist Reece McAllister. Much to her surprise, Jordan comes away with far more than just a story . . .

978-1-59493-78-2 $13.95

FINDERS KEEPERS by Karin Kallmaker. *Finders Keepers*, the quest for the perfect mate in the 21st century, joins Karin Kallmaker's *Just Like That* and her other incomparable novels about lesbian love, lust and laughter.   1-59493-072-4 $13.95

OUT OF THE FIRE by Beth Moore. Author Ann Covington feels at the top of the world when told her book is being made into a movie. Then in walks Casey Duncan the actress who is playing the lead in her movie. Will Casey turn Ann's world upside down?

1-59493-088-0 $13.95

STAKE THROUGH THE HEART: NEW EXPLOITS OF TWILIGHT LESBIANS by Karin Kallmaker, Julia Watts, Barbara Johnson and Therese Szymanski. The playful quartet that penned the acclaimed *Once Upon A Dyke* are dimming the lights for journeys into worlds of breathless seduction.   1-59493-071-6 $15.95

THE HOUSE ON SANDSTONE by KG MacGregor. Carly Griffin returns home to Leland and finds that her old high school friend Justine is awakening more than just old memories.   1-59493-076-7 $13.95

WILD NIGHTS: MOSTLY TRUE STORIES OF WOMEN LOVING WOMEN edited by Therese Szymanski. 264 pp. 23 new stories from today's hottest erotic writers are sure to give you your wildest night ever!   1-59493-069-4 $15.95

COYOTE SKY by Gerri Hill. 248 pp. Sheriff Lee Foxx is trying to cope with the realization that she has fallen in love for the first time. And fallen for author Kate Winters, who is technically unavailable. Will Lee fight to keep Kate in Coyote?

1-59493-065-1 $13.95

VOICES OF THE HEART by Frankie J. Jones. 264 pp. A series of events force Erin to swear off love as she tries to break away from the woman of her dreams. Will Erin ever find the key to her future happiness?   1-59493-068-6 $13.95

SHELTER FROM THE STORM by Peggy J. Herring. 296 pp. A story about family and getting reacquainted with one's past that shows that sometimes you don't appreciate what you have until you almost lose it.   1-59493-064-3 $13.95